CRY FOR PEACE

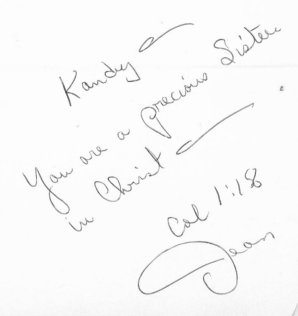

Kandy —

You are a precious Sister
in Christ —

Col 1:18

Joan

CRY FOR PEACE

Jean Springer

Dedicated to
my husband and daughters
for their patient and encouraging
support

Table of Contents

Chapter 1 9
Chapter 2 18
Chapter 3 26
Chapter 4 41
Chapter 5 51
Chapter 6 66
Chapter 7 84
Chapter 8 93
Chapter 9 101
Chapter 10 111
Chapter 11 127
Chapter 12 134
Chapter 13 139
Chapter 14 146
Chapter 15 158
Chapter 16 169
Chapter 17 179
Chapter 18 185
Chapter 19 192

Chapter 1

It had been a long, difficult day at the nursery and Leigh Gordon sighed wearily as she locked her office door in the educational wing of her father's church and turned toward the corridor. An intermittent July rain had turned the hot day into a heavy, muggy one which made the children restless and difficult to handle.

She met her next-door neighbor and co-teacher, Dorothy Perry, shepherding two lively little black-haired girls from her classroom.

"Ready to go home, Dorothy?" They usually waited for Thad, Leigh's older brother, to walk them home, even though they lived just down the alley from the church. It was unwise to be alone on the streets now, even in the daylight hours.

"No, the Blakes have invited me to supper, but I won't be long."

The two girls ran down the hall to wave to departing friends and Dorothy called after them. "Girls, wait for me at the door. Your father should be here any minute."

She was a perky, optimistic brunette, a little shorter in height than Leigh, who was tall and slim and sometimes envied by others because of lustrous brown eyes setting off long dark lashes and a flawless complexion. But her face now showed great weariness; Dorothy could see dark circles under her eyes.

"You look exhausted, Leigh."

"Oh, I'm just concerned. This constant warfare is making the children emotional wrecks, and I feel so helpless.''

"I know. Tempers are sharp, tears flow easily, and . . .''

"And,'' Leigh cut in angrily, "they're afraid—all the time! I wish Mom and Dad were here. I could use some guidance about now.''

"Well, cheer up. You'll see them tomorrow. You did get a travelling permit, didn't you?''

"Yes, Thad and I both did, for one week. He has a friend who makes regular truck deliveries near the conference grounds and has agreed to let us ride with him. We'll leave early tomorrow morning.''

"Well, I'll stop in when Mr. Blake brings me home, and we can go over any last minute things I need to know about the nursery. O.K.?''

"Fine. I'll try to be in a more productive mood by then.'' Leigh waved to the little girls and turned to lock the outside door just as Dorothy left with the last group of parents and children.

The enclosed courtyard, now empty of children, seemed ominously quiet, but perhaps it was merely an invention of a weary mind. The increasing problems she faced as director of the nursery seemed insurmountable.

Moving slowly up to the heavy metal gate, which looked so out of place in the lovely old stone wall, Leigh wondered what was keeping Thad.

What happened next was like something out of an old gangster movie, for her touch on the gate to push it open seemed to trigger several events at once.

The sound of running feet pounded down the alley toward her and a voice shouted, "There he is!''

A machine gun exploded; a man moaned softly, appeared for an instant in the slightly opened gateway, and then fell, sprawling almost at her feet.

Leigh stood horrified, unable to take her eyes off the still form in front of her, hearing his pursuers advance down the alley in a jeep. With a great effort she slowly pulled the gate shut and stood there, unable to move, terrified by what she had just seen and by the thought of what might soon happen.

The injured man was dressed in work clothes and probably part of the forbidden Citizens Militia. The pursuers were soldiers, and if they found her standing there — well, they were part of an army of amoral, depraved and unpredictable men. It was all too easy to imagine what they might do, for she had heard of other young women being raped and murdered. Nothing like this had happened to her before. All she knew of the past year of civil war in America had been through quiet talks in the secure company of friends and relatives, or radio and television announcements.

She stood there trembling. *Oh, Lord, please, don't let them look in here! Please, please!* She felt as though she screamed the plea aloud.

"Do you want us to search the area, Sergeant?"

Leigh stepped back away from the gate at the soldier's question, called so nearby. She searched frantically for a hiding place, but there was nothing except an empty barrel which stood on the opposite side of the playground. She doubled her fist against her mouth, knowing that if the gate opened and a soldier walked through, she wouldn't be able to stop her screams.

The next few seconds seemed like an eternity, as she waited for a reply. She sank weakly against the wall when it came.

"No, don't bother. Leave him where he is, and let's get back. The general is due any minute."

The jeep reversed with a loud grinding sound, quickly backed down the alley, and roared away into the quiet evening. Even then Leigh did not move. She was trying to summon up enough courage to step out into the alley where the man still lay on the ground. And it was possible that a soldier had been left there, waiting to trap anyone who came to help.

Swallowing hard, she put out a hand to push at the gate, but it began to open slowly. Squeezing back against the wall, she caught her breath, her eyes wide with terror.

"Leigh, are you there?"

"Oh, Thad! I thought you were a soldier."

"No, I was coming to get you when I saw what was happening and ducked back into our garage. I'm surprised they didn't search the alley."

"I heard the officer in charge say," Leigh's voice trembled with the emotion of her sudden deliverance, "that . . . that some general was coming and they needed to get back to their post. Do . . . do you know him?"

Thad turned to look into the alley. He put an arm around Leigh's trembling shoulders and gave her a squeeze. "No, I don't think so."

"Is . . . is he dead?"

"He must be, with all those bullets in him." Thad spoke in helpless anger as he moved back into the alley.

Leigh followed reluctantly and watched as he knelt to touch the man's wrist and neck for a pulse. He shook his head and spoke while searching for an identification card.

"We've got to get him out of sight before a patrol comes along." He looked up for help just as two neighbor men came quietly out of their homes.

"Dead?" One of the men asked.

Thad nodded his head. "Yes. Can we use your shed? We must get him out of sight."

The neighbor agreed readily and Thad turned to Leigh. "Here, Leigh, take his I.D. card to Tom. He can call the relatives."

Leigh took the card in her hand but felt shackled to the lifeless form as the men lifted it from the pavement. A dark red spot on the pavement caught her attention.

"Leigh?" Thad's quiet tone snapped through her thoughts.

"Yes, I'm going, Thad."

That evening, Thad and Leigh sat at the supper table in their dimly lit kitchen with their Uncle Paul and his son, Tom, discussing the murder.

Paul Maers, their mother's older brother, and his son had been living with them ever since Aunt Miriam's death in the year of the nation's bicentennial celebration. Leigh was especially grateful to have the two other men in the house now that her parents were away. Her uncle had the same stable, unexcitable temperament as her mother, and was a great encouragement to everyone.

Thad was getting angry. "The dead man's family—what will they do now?"

Uncle Paul spoke calmly, as was his usual manner, his white hair gleaming in the light. "His wife told me they have relatives in Lock Haven. They plan to go there."

"The country is being torn apart! Riots, strikes, arrests of innocent people, murders! Why?!" Thad glared at his cousin, demanding an answer.

"It was coming a long time ago, Thad," Tom answered quietly. "We are only getting from the hand of God what we deserve."

Thad threw his fork down on the table. "Stop hiding behind God, Cousin. The unrest of the 1970's and the increasing disenchantment with the government in the following years led to one emergency after another. Finally, an unsolvable energy crisis crashed down upon us."

"Yes, because no one believed it could happen in America," Leigh interjected.

"Well," Thad went on, "it was the opportunity for a new political faction to take charge, and they did. The Peoples Party bombed and destroyed the city of Washington in one day, and set up their new government here in Harrisburg." He always tried to lay the blame on the politics of America, instead of on its moral and spiritual life.

Uncle Paul lifted his empty cup and looked imploringly at Leigh. "It has just been a year since then, and every day the New Democracy has grown stronger."

Leigh reached for the coffee pot, waiting for Thad's next statement, for she knew he wasn't finished venting his anger.

"Of course it grows stronger! Our former national leaders are either dead or imprisoned, all political organizations have been suspended, our freedoms have been restricted, and how many times have we had martial law in the last few months!"

"What do you think is the answer, Thad?" His cousin questioned him placidly. "The Citizens Militia?"

"I don't know," Thad replied irritably. "It is a small unorganized protest against the government. It needs strong leadership to be successful."

"Tom," Leigh protested, "don't encourage him. You know our parents don't want him joining the militia."

Tom grinned, telling her with a look that he did not have anything like that in mind. "How is your Dad, Leigh?"

"Well, we have only heard once since they went out to the cottage. Mom wrote that he seemed a little more rested."

"But it is still quite serious, isn't it?"

"Yes, the doctor said either two months' rest, or," she paused, frowning, "or we could not expect him to live out the year."

Uncle Paul reached over to pat her hand. "He will feel better after he has been away from all his responsibilities for awhile, Leigh. You'll see. He is a conscientious pastor; every man's burden is his, and these months have been most difficult for him."

A knock on the side door which led directly into the kitchen stopped the talk around the table. It was not the loud, pounding kind used by the soldiers at night, but Leigh could feel everyone tense a little. Everyone but Uncle Paul; he never got excited, it seemed.

Thad pushed back his chair, took three quick steps to the door and opened it cautiously. "Dorothy, come on in."

"Thanks, Thad," Dorothy said as she entered the kitchen and greeted the others. "Hi, everyone. Supper over?" She sank down in the chair Uncle Paul held for her, and looking unusually sober, said, "Guess what I just heard from Mr. Blake?"

Tom laughed. "His daughters are getting married tomorrow and will not be in your class anymore."

"No, silly," she replied, snapping a finger on his arm. "The government has ordered all the city's grocery stores closed for one week."

Thad pushed back his chair in disgust and said, "What now!"

Uncle Paul merely sat waiting for the rest of the story. Tom looked down at his plate and said nothing, but his expression was not one of surprise. Leigh suddenly wondered if he already knew the story Dorothy was about to tell.

"Why?" Thad asked.

"Well, it is in retaliation to the latest militia attack. They bombed two troop trains that were leaving the city, supposedly going into the mountains for a raid on the local militia headquarters."

Uncle Paul looked at his son questioningly. Tom was a train engineer and it was quite likely he had seen this latest sabotage taking place. "Did he say when it happened, Dorothy?"

"This afternoon, about 1 o'clock, I think."

Tom looked up to see his father's gaze and answered his unspoken question. "I was on a run to Scranton this afternoon."

"That isn't all," Dorothy continued. "There was a riot at one of the stores in an attempt to keep it open, and three women were . . . trampled to death."

At this bit of information, Thad exploded. He stood up and began pacing around the kitchen. "Why must the innocent always suffer?" He continued pacing, the others silently watching, waiting for him to expend his anger.

"Well, they do, don't they?" he asked accusingly. "What about the two children from the nursery. They stood in paralyzed disbelief while soldiers shot their father for refusing them entrance into his home. And . . . and what about Glenn Thompson from church, now a widower with three small children because his wife happened to step off the curb just as a military convoy sped around the street corner."

"Thad, please," Dorothy implored, reaching out to take his hand as he passed her. "Please, sit down." She was the only one who had any influence on Thad when he was angry, the only one who could calm him down. And the others watched to see if she would be successful again.

He stopped, looked down at her hand holding his and took a deep breath. The sigh that came from him then was one of total frustration and pain.

"We are all upset about this, Thad," Uncle Paul reminded him softly.

Thad smiled ruefully, "And getting angry does not help, does it?"

"Leigh, I'll help you do dishes and we can talk about the nursery, if you want." Dorothy smiled up at Thad, then gave his cousin a significant look that said he should do something.

Tom stood up and stretched himself lazily. "Come on, men, let's go into the living room and see what we can get on the news before the electricity goes off." He threw a loving arm around his father's shoulders as they left the room.

Later that night, Leigh stood alone in her bedroom at the back of the house. She had observed, while waiting for the soldiers to discover her standing in the school playground, that she was as cowardly as she had always suspected. She had frozen with fear, with not the least bit of concern for the man who had been shot.

She shook her head, tears of frustration coursing down her cheeks. This was America, the land of the free! She recalled as a child hearing people say such terrible things would never happen in America.

But they were.

She leaned against the desk, too frustrated and sick at heart to think of preparations for the next day's trip to see her parents.

That same evening, in a government building in Philadelphia, someone else stood leaning against a desk, feeling the same depths of frustration.

His emotion came from the decoded letter he held; its message brought concern but not surprise. He had been expecting just such a document for weeks now, but the first time in his life he found it difficult to make a decision.

Pushing his tall, muscular body away from the desk, he

moved toward the empty fireplace. It would be unusual to have a fire in August, but he could use his moving out of the office as an excuse. These days no one left any papers behind which might be altered and used by an adversary. So, he would burn many of them.

He lit a match and held the letter to the flame, then tossing it on the grate, watched until it was nothing but ashes.

The letter had been a request to consider an official position, but there was really no decision to make, he thought with irony. Months of training and preparation had led to this moment and he should have felt triumphant.

Instead, the victory had a bitter taste, and he felt the need to confer once more with his associate before making a formal reply.

He turned to a metal file in the corner, opened the top drawer and pulled out several files no longer needed. Striding quickly to the fireplace, he put them in the flame, his blond hair shining as he leaned over to add fuel to the fire. He returned to the cabinet for more files, flicking on the air conditioner to cool the room.

When he had enough ashes to eliminate suspicion, he picked up a briefcase from a small table beside the door, laid it on his desk and clicked it open. The small gold letters above the handle glittered for a moment in the firelight: *Steve Houston, Aide to the President.*

Opening a desk drawer, he proceeded to remove the items he would need: two black note books, a tape recorder, some official-looking papers, a handful of pens, and several books on army procedures. That should look innocuous enough, he thought.

He pushed a buzzer on the desk and in a moment a slightly built, dark-haired army private opened the door, saluted and stepped inside.

"Sir?" His voice cracked. Private Findley cleared his throat, wishing fervently that his nervousness of his superior would not always reveal itself so quickly.

"Private, I am leaving this evening for an inspection tour of these towns." Steve Houston handed him a list. "I expect to be out of the city for several days, but will call you if necessary."

"Yes, Sir. Anything special you want me to do while you are away, Sir?" Private Findley took the list and stepped back away from the desk.

"No, just your usual job. You are dismissed."

"Yes, Sir. Good night, Sir." The private saluted smartly,

backed quickly out of the office, and sighed with relief that he had again retired from the lion's den without a scratch.

He would have been surprised had he seen the smile of amusement and softening expression on the lion at that moment. Steve Houston had played his part so well that none of his associates knew what he was really like.

Even those who had worked closely with him for the past year would have been surprised to know of the reasons that lay behind his new assignment.

Chapter 2

The trip out to the Bible conference grounds in the foothills of Pennsylvania, once just a quick two hour ride, had taken six hours because of the bombed portions of the highway.

The octagon-shaped cottage the Gordons rented each summer stood among oak trees up the hill overlooking the conference grounds, and from the steps where Leigh sat, she could hear someone playing the piano in the auditorium. The instrument was out of tune, and the pianist not too accomplished, but the familiar hymn being played brought much comfort.

As she listened, she traced the driveway on the hill below with her eyes. Beginning at the entranceway it penciled a straight line up through tall evergreen trees to make a complete circle around the large old-fashioned hotel which housed offices as well as guest rooms. To the left of the hotel, the drive curved around several small buildings used for study areas; to the right, it passed a long, low building which provided extra space for youth camps. Behind the hotel, and on a higher level, the road coiled around the large brick auditorium, a dining hall to the left and the maintenance building to the right. Between these the road continued up the hill to come to a dead end beside their cottage.

Leigh turned to look at the cottage. It was small but beautifully built in maplewood, which was shining now in the late afternoon sun. Folding doors opened two sides of the living room and Leigh smiled as she thought of the evenings spent there. When the doors were pushed open, the room seemed to become part of the forest surrounding the cottage.

Just then Thad came through the doors and sank down on the steps beside her. "Good morning," he mumbled. He ran his hand through hair yet uncombed and touched a whiskered chin.

"Well, when did your day start?" Leigh laughed. "It's afternoon already and I have even been down for an hour of Bible study."

"H'm," he grunted, grinning sheepishly. "I guess I did sleep in a bit; but I have been visiting with Dad for awhile. I saw you go down to the hotel this morning."

"Yes, I had a little visit with Mrs. Miles, and then had lunch in the dining hall so I could see everyone. This is our fourth day here and I have been hiding most of the time."

He nodded knowingly. "And how many people did you counsel today?" She always seemed to draw confidences from others, people responding to her loving, caring nature almost before they realized it.

"Oh," she replied nonchalantly, shrugging her shoulders, "Mrs. Miles did say she was concerned about her husband's workload. It seems that he is not only director of the grounds, but has become involved in what amounts to state-wide refugee work among the Christians."

"I'm sure that is needed now. Mom was telling me that the staff has developed three or four garden plots back among the hills. They not only use the produce for the dining hall, but give it to the needy."

"I know," she replied with a twinkle in her eye.

"And you have volunteered to help!"

"Well, not exactly. Mrs. Miles did ask if I would go with a group of teens tomorrow."

"Might have known."

"Well, Thad, shouldn't we help?"

"I promised Mom that I would stay with Dad tomorrow while she goes in to the village with some of the ladies."

"Good, then I will go with the teens."

Thad's hand shot out to ruffle her hair, then he stood up. "That's fine. I had better go in and shave. I hear Mom in the kitchen working on supper."

Leigh started to get up. "Oh, I'll go help."

"No, just sit here and enjoy yourself. I'll help her tonight."

Alone, she stared out over the grounds below, thinking of her brother. They looked enough alike to be twins, but were totally different spiritually. He was a fun-loving but headstrong young man, and was surely headed for trouble. He would not accept what was happening in America and was outspoken in his criticism of the new government. If only he knew Christ as his Saviour, if only he had a spiritual perspective about life perhaps he could then escape the grim future she felt sure was ahead of him.

Suddenly she stood up. Perhaps a walk along the trail overlooking the cliff would help shake off her pensiveness. It was a favorite spot, and she had spent many hours along that trail. She waved to her mother through the kitchen window and started toward the path.

But the sound of a car coming up the drive brought her to a startled halt. Staring at the low-slung sports model as it came into view, she wondered what that car was doing here. How had the owner gotten an official permit to own a car and to buy gasoline? And why would anyone with such obvious government sanction be visiting a black-listed Bible conference grounds. The average American citizen, especially Christians, found it almost impossible to own cars and Leigh wondered who the driver might be. She thought of the ancient, rusted-out van owned by the conference. No one would ever want to confiscate it, because it seemed to run on chewing gum and prayers; gas was still obtainable for it because of the charity work done by the conference association.

"I'm sorry, have I done something wrong?" A deep, quiet voice tinged with amusement spoke nearby.

Leigh flushed and looked up at the man standing before her. She did not come even to his shoulders and felt like a small child caught in a misdemeanor.

"Oh, no," she replied solemnly, "but it has been a long time since I have seen anything like that." She nodded toward the car. "Are . . . are you looking for someone? The offices are in the hotel," she added, pointing downhill.

"No. I've been told the trail up here has an excellent view from the cliffs." Clear blue eyes twinkled as he studied her. "I thought I would find out. I was under the impression it was a public trail, but . . ." He waited, one hand on the car door.

"It is public, and it is beautiful." She hesitated and then surprised herself by adding, "I'll . . . show you the way if you like. I am just going for a walk myself." Something inside her was held suspended as she waited for his response, and she was appalled at her boldness. In the city she would never dream of speaking to a stranger who might be a member of the secret police, or someone ready to strong-arm a woman off to the local army barracks to provide sexual entertainment for the soldiers.

She opened her mouth, ready to excuse herself and to give him directions, when he spoke, intercepting her intentions.

"Thanks, if it wouldn't trouble you. I would appreciate it."

Without a word, Leigh shrugged her shoulders and turned toward the path to the back of the cottage. Well, Thad would tell her that she was being impulsive again.

It was only a few minutes' walk to the cliffs and neither spoke as they followed the trail. Leigh's misgivings seemed to be dispelled by the peace and quietness of the woods, and the stranger made no attempt to speak.

The path dipped slightly around a large boulder and opened upon a long rocky ledge just at the cliff's edge. In the distance, the hills were greenly carpeted with trees. Here and there a tan ribbon road could be seen, and several white farm houses peeked through the greenery.

Distant hills were turning a dull grey through a summer haze, and little black puffs of smoke followed a train as it wound around the hills, on its way into the city. The faint rumble of its wheels, in a steady slow clickity-clack, was carried across the air to where they were.

Leigh stopped just beyond the boulder, meaning to turn and leave. "I like it here," she said hesitantly. "It has always been my special place."

He nodded his understanding and thrust his hands into the pockets of his slacks as he walked over to the edge.

"Do you come here often?" he asked as he scanned the hills before turning toward her again.

"To the conference or the cliffs?"

"Both." His smile brought that sparkle again to his eyes and unnerved her slightly. A nod of his head and a hand motioning toward a backless old stone bench, invited her to stay.

Not really knowing why she obeyed, Leigh moved toward the seat. "My family usually rents the cottage for a week or so each summer. Have you . . . ever been here?'' Leigh faltered, still reluctant to prolong the conversation.

"No, this is my first visit." He spoke evenly, keeping his voice soft, for he was aware of her hesitancy, and he wasn't ready for her to leave. "Do you come often to the cliffs?"

"Every day we are here." Motioning to the rocks behind her, she said, "Even in the rain I can come and sit under there." She was curious about the man before her and thought that if he could ask questions, so could she. "Are you from the East?"

"No, the Midwest, but I've been . . ." He hesitated slightly and then continued, ". . . in the area for awhile."

Behind him the sky glowed with vibrant paint-brush colors as the sun began to set, and Leigh glanced at the horizon. "Oh," she whispered, unaware that nature's beauty was bringing a soft glow to her face and catching his attention, "look at that gorgeous sky."

"Yes, it is beautiful," he replied, searching her face thoroughly, and then turning to see the sunset.

They fell silent again, each suddenly content to enjoy the scenery and the quietness around them. For Leigh, the beauty chased away the ugliness of the city world and the menacing life under the New Democracy. She felt clean and at rest, and looked toward the man standing against the rail, wanting to share those good feelings.

But he seemed to have forgotten her presence. He reached out for the railing that guarded the edge of the cliff and clenched it until his knuckles were white. A look of intense suffering crossed his strong face and Leigh realized he was living through some difficult torment. His whole body, strong and muscular though it was, seemed to bend under a heavy load.

Why wasn't she afraid of him, she wondered. And why would she like so much to help. She did not even know his name, had never seen him before today. Yet, she sensed there was something good in him—something in his face, his actions. While she was ready to admit that he was a handsome man, there was something deeper that was appealing to her.

Her curiosity was aroused as she sat watching him. He was not dressed like the average American who could not afford more than worn, outdated styles or the cheaper clothing which was a product of a broken national economy. He could be connected with the new government and as an official have access to the very best. Perhaps he was one of the many businessmen who supported the new party strictly for financial gain. She could not quite make up her mind where he fit.

His blond hair, height, and good looks would set him apart in any group. But there was something else—a military bearing? Yes, that was it.

Instinctively she knew that in any situation he would prove to be the commanding authority. And those eyes that had only been soft blue in friendliness toward her could, she was sure, turn cold and penetrating when opposed. He seemed an enigma that she could not fathom, and he was having more of an effect upon her than she liked.

It was true that in the present national struggle, the church was driven to deeper commitment in caring among believers. No one could afford to be an island unto himself now. But Leigh did not know if he were a follower of Christ, as his presence at the conference grounds might indicate. Perhaps he was a government spy bent upon destroying the conference grounds and everyone there.

And so she waited and watched, unwilling to move for fear she might trigger some anger or hostility in him.

Then his expression changed. His face, turned slightly toward her, revealed a determination struggling to override his torment. He did not look at peace, but rather as though he had come to terms with some adversary.

Realizing that she was surely intruding Leigh felt a compulsion to leave. She stood up quietly, and just as she turned toward the path, he spoke.

"Please, don't go."

Startled, she swung around to face him. He had not moved nor turned around. Had he sensed her feelings and actions?

"I apologize for being such a terrible tourist." His voice, strong with emotion, broke slightly in his effort to lighten the moment.

"I think I am the one who should apologize," Leigh responded. "We should never have to bear the scrutiny of others when we are involved in private soul battles."

He turned quickly then, aware that she had seen and understood. Looking at her for a long moment, he smiled slightly. "I can't thank you properly for understanding. I don't even know your name." He waited, wondering if he would get an answer, for her reluctance was as heavy as a winter wrap.

"Leigh Gordon," she said slowly, still held by his look.

He moved as though to come nearer but stopped. "Thanks, Leigh, for bringing me here and sharing the beauty and my - my preoccupation." And then he added, "My friends call me Steve, Steve Houston."

Under his intense gaze Leigh faltered and looked away, unwilling to allow him to look into her eyes any longer. The strain he had been under intensified the feeling between them. They were both aware of it.

But Leigh drew back. "I must get home. It's time for supper." She turned toward the path.

"Must you?" When she did not respond, he said, "I would like to stay a little longer."

He did not move again but was still watching, willing her to remain. Leigh felt it and was confused. Her emotions were pulled in every direction, for she was by nature a comforter. Part of her wanted to stay, to supply his need for companionship; but another equally strong emotion made her keenly reluctant to face any kind of relationship with this man. Her dark troubled eyes looked quickly to his once more.

"Good-bye, Steve Houston," she murmured, her face a mirror of consternation.

"Good-bye, Leigh." His response was low, but had a definite captivating effect upon her emotions and she rebelled at responding to a stranger like that. Frowning, she turned quickly and walked back up to the path, past the boulder, and without a backward glance, was gone.

Steve did not move, but stood looking at the now empty pathway. A smile softened the suffering on his face, and then he turned toward the hills. I must remember, he thought with satisfaction, to express my appreciation to my host for insisting we meet here. Otherwise, I might never have met the one women in the world I could love.

It was an easy task to bring her image to mind, for he had been well trained to remember even the smallest detail. The pale yellow dress, cut in a simple style, had only accentuated the dark hair that fell softly about her face. High cheek bones gave her an innocent, child-like quality; and her brown eyes, so large and full of emotion, had shared much more information than she realized.

He was accustomed to appraising people quickly; it was a part of his job as well as a necessary element for his survival. And he knew that her beauty was not like that cultivated today by those women who were the exclusive property of government officials, women who used their bodies and physical beauty to get what they wanted. Nor was she hard and ruthless like so many of the women of the Peoples Army, whose short haircuts and severe black uniforms set them apart from others.

He was thirty years old, and guessed that she was five or six years younger, and judging from her actions, unmarried. In spite of the fact that marriage was an old-fashioned institution today, he knew she would be one of that minority who still held to its importance. And he had no doubt that she would disapprove of the free-love society being adopted by the new government.

She was different. She had an inner strength and beauty that he had not seen since his mother died.

A gratefulness flooded over him as he realized that during the dark days ahead he would have the comfort of her in his mind and heart, even though she might never be his.

His past training in the old Central Intelligence Agency and his involvement in every avenue of military service would surely lead him into grim circumstances where she would not fit. But he could wish that she would, for he was suddenly overwhelmed with the desire to have her with him for the rest of his life.

It was later, while the Gordon family sat at their evening meal, with one small oil lamp casting its light from the center of the table, that Leigh heard the car move down the driveway, and looking up, saw Thad watching her intently.

She knew he was about to question her, wanting to know who the stranger was and what brought him to the cottage. And for some unaccountable reason she did not want to discuss the subject.

"Oh, I forgot to put the fruit on the table," she said quickly, and glancing at her brother, fled the room.

Chapter 3

The next morning Leigh was awakened by the sound of a hard rain hammering on the roof top and swishing down through the oak trees. It produced a cozy, lazy feeling.

For a moment, she could imagine being a teen again, with no concern other than a picnic at the waterfalls, or a hike with her parents, or a day with camp friends. And there had been some special life-molding decisions made during past vacations here, like the time she had pledged to live for Christ, so that her goals and ambitions would be ones that would honor Him.

One of her aims was to work with children, to be a positive, good influence in their lives; and after college training she became the nursery director at her father's church. And with that thought her feeling of euphoria was gone.

She thought of the problems facing her at the school: increased governmental controls, the difficulties of finding food, and especially the civil war's impact upon the children. She loved them and wanted to insulate them in a happy and safe atmosphere. But it was not possible in the present climate of war and hurt and fears and pain.

Sighing, she reached for her Bible lying on the bedside table and began to read from her favorite Scriptures, the book of Psalms. How she loved the beauty of the words, the powerful flow of emotions, the declarations of God's might and majesty, and the simplicity of the writer's dependence upon God Himself: "My help comes from the Lord."

After breakfast she found Thad reading in the living room, his face showing the intense concentration he always had while studying.

He looked up when she dropped a pair of hiking shoes on the floor beside his chair. "Well, what construction job are you on today?"

She sank down in a chair next to him and began pulling on a shoe. "I'm going to work in the gardens. Remember?"

"But you look so elegant, my dear, all dressed up for a worker's style show."

Crossing her legs, Leigh put on the second shoe and yanked the strings tightly. "My jeans and shirt are years old," she replied, wrinkling her nose, "so you needn't tease."

"You don't sound too excited about your venture."

"I am reluctant only because this is our last day here, and I want to be with Mom and Dad all I can," she replied, sighing as she pulled her hair back from her face.

Walking into the kitchen to prepare her lunch and fill a water flask, she called over her shoulder, "Sounds like the rain has stopped. Too bad you can't come, Thad. As a high school teacher, you would make a very efficient chaperone."

Thad settled deeper into his chair, put his feet up on a footstool, and sighed in his comfort. "Not me, thanks. School sessions start soon enough. Besides, Dad and I plan to do a little walking later on."

"Such dedication. You look as though you could not get out of that chair, let alone go for a walk." Leigh got out two slices of bread and reached into the cupboard for the jam. It came to her mind that having Thad along might settle the strange, nagging feeling she had about the day's activity, but it was also important for him to stay with Dad.

"I'll just wait here to nurse you back to health," he said, grinning at her. "Meantime, I am going to take a nap while Dad is resting." He yawned, closed his eyes and squirmed deeper into his chair.

Leigh packed her lunch in a brown shoulder bag, picked up a battered old cowboy hat Thad used to wear, and left the cottage by the front door. Starting down the pathway she could see about twenty teens standing outside of the maintenance building, and their laughter and bantering charged the air. Nearing the end of the path she searched the group for her companion chaperone, for Rev. Miles had not mentioned who it might be.

"I hope you are looking for me," a deep voice behind her said. Startled, Leigh wheeled around to see Steve Houston sitting on a bench sheltered from the walkway by some tall evergreen bushes. "Oh, I didn't see you there. You gave me a fright!" Once again she felt her emotions being stirred by this stranger as he walked toward her, and she resented the fact that she found him more interesting than anyone she had ever known. She hardly knew the man!

There was not a lazy move in his stride as he came toward her, and she sensed again that unleashed power that hinted at unquestionable authority lying just below the surface.

"I . . . I was looking for the other chaperone," she said, eyeing his green slacks and shirt, which looked too much like work clothes to suit her suddenly disturbed spirit. Taking a deep breath she tried to hide her agitation.

"You've found him," he said with quiet satisfaction at her surprise.

Leigh turned hastily toward the teens, wary of being too near him, and was startled to hear two of the boys greet Steve by name; but there was no time to ask how they knew him because the group was eager to go and quickly surged around the tall, blond man.

"Quiet, please." Steve did not raise his voice, but he had everyone's attention. "Most of you have been out to the gardens, but I want to remind you of a couple of things. Several people have gotten lost on this trail before, so let's be careful. There was also a teen gang in this area recently who burned down a farmhouse and left the owner severely beaten. You know the consequences of being captured by any such groups. Let's stick together and have a good time. Any questions?"

"Yes, Sir," one of the boys spoke up. "Will we split up in groups to work the gardens?"

"No. It is a two-hour walk there. We will work the one furthest away and then stop at the second one on our way back here. A group going out tomorrow will take care of the other two plots." He smiled and then picked up a cloth sack and several garden tools stacked outside the building. "Let's go."

Leigh felt that she was watching a military operation. It was uncanny that Steve's action should bring that to her mind, but the teens' response as they picked up the remaining tools and sacks confirmed what she felt. While they were in good spirits, they were not wasting time and seemed ready to obey him instantly.

Two girls from the Harrisburg church fell in step with her, and as they chatted together she watched several of the boys in animated conversation with Steve before they were even off the conference grounds.

After they had been on the trail about thirty minutes one of the girls giggled and whispered, "I think he likes you, Leigh."

"Who does, Ann?" Leigh spoke as nonchalantly as her quickening pulse would allow, scolding herself mentally for such an empty-headed response.

"Steve, the other guide."

"What on earth makes you think that?"

I've been watching him—he's so handsome, and every chance he gets, he looks back at you." Her sigh was a dreamy one and Leigh had to smile at her.

"He is only looking back to check on the group, and we happen to be near the end of the line." Leigh sought for a reasonable explanation to keep her own mind from playing foolish tricks, and it did not help to admit that those sky-blue eyes made her knees weak. This was ridiculous. She had never acted so silly over any man and was determined not to allow Steve Houston, whoever he might be, to affect her like this!

The trail wound its way around the base of a smaller hill and then went up the side of the next one, cutting its way through a forest of trees, over fallen logs, and around thick laurel bushes and large slabs of rocks. Above them, the brilliant blue sky was trimmed with an occasional whipped cream cloud. It was just the sort of day that Leigh enjoyed, even though the trail was still wet and slippery from the morning rain.

The laughter and talk was muted by the density of the woods. Two older boys had taken positions at the end of the line, but there was a continual shuffling back and forth as the others stopped to talk with a friend or watch an interesting animal. This gave Leigh opportunity to meet a number of them and she was encouraged by their eagerness to share their thoughts and especially to talk of what God was doing in their lives.

Even Ann's giggly spirit disappeared as she shared what was happening in her family. "Dad hasn't had a paycheck all summer because people just don't have money for home repairs; but he has an opportunity now to work for the army, building barracks. If he turns it down, I'm afraid he can get into real trouble. So, we are praying that the Lord will work out the circumstances as He wants.''

Keith, a curly-headed, smiling teaser, got serious long enough to share his situation with Leigh. "My Dad has been dead for three years now, and Mom tries to keep a sewing shop open, even though she has a bad heart. She can't get any medication because all that is available is on the black market and unaffordable. Most of the time she can hardly walk when she finishes the day. I try not to worry, because the Lord has promised that He won't give us anything we can't handle; but I sure wish I could get a good job so she wouldn't have to work so hard.''

All the while Leigh was keenly aware of the man leading the group and began pondering the emotions she had seen already in him: strength that could override torment, tenderness checking authority, a commanding leadership held back in easy rapport with teens. She caught glimpses of him when the trail straightened and it was evident that he was in complete control of the hike. Stopping once to encourage two wanderers back on the trail, he waited for Leigh to reach his side.

"Holding up all right?" His eyes watched the teens ahead, but his interest was focused sharply on Leigh.

"Yes, thanks. I enjoy walking this trail, probably because I am such a coward and I feel sheltered against the world here.''

She spoke quietly, yet wondering what made her confess such a thing to a stranger, and he leaned closer to hear. Glancing up, she found herself looking straight into his eyes as she had recently done at the cliffs, and the group sounds faded away for a moment.

"You have much more strength than you are aware of, Leigh," he said encouragingly. "I wish we could talk more about that, but we both have a job to do. Perhaps later?''

Leigh nodded and smiled slightly. "Perhaps," she said, stepping back on the trail and finding herself next to Ann again.

"Oh, I wish he would look at me like that," the young girl moaned.

"Hush, young lady! Your imagination is behaving like a runaway train." Leigh laughed at Ann's mournful expression, but wondered if anyone else had noticed Steve's interest.

Coming around the side of a hill twenty minutes later, Leigh was surprised to see a small garden, about a half acre in size covering the lower section of the hill. There was an old shed in among the trees on the right, and it was there the teens left their lunches and several large water containers.

Steve directed the work quickly and efficiently. "Girls, take a row and begin weeding. You fellows can start hoeing from the other end. We won't need to haul water from the river because of the rain this morning, so just leave the plastic buckets at the shed."

Leigh began working on a row of carrots, pulling up weeds from the earth softened by rain. The sun felt good on her back and she was glad for the battered cowboy hat that shaded her eyes.

When half of the weeding was completed, Steve directed part of the group to begin filling the sacks with produce. They pulled up carrots and onions, picked three rows of green beans, and dug up two rows of potatoes. Leigh worked on a row of onions, pinching off the tops. As she finished the last one, she looked up to see Steve pause in his work, and check the hills about them. Perhaps he was thinking of the gang that had been so cruel to a helpless farmer. She knew he felt responsible for the teens, but she wondered what opinion he had concerning the New Democracy and the disruption of normal life. Did he support the Citizens Militia or the secret police. She wished she knew.

After an hour's work they stopped to have lunch, washing their hands in a bucket of water brought from the river at the bottom of the hill, and sat under the shade of the trees bordering the garden. Leigh sat down beside Ann, spread her lunch out on a napkin, and watched while two of the boys began distributing food packed by the conference cook. There were boiled potatoes, fresh carrots, cauliflower, and slices of homemade bread. One of the boys then gave thanks to God for the food before them, and they began to eat.

"Man," one boy remarked as he stared at a boiled potato in his hand, "I can remember when we could buy potato chips and dips, and all sorts of cookies . . ."

Like shots from a gun, others spoke up.

"Yeah, and soft drinks . . ."

". . . and pizza . . ."

". . . and nuts . . ."

". . . and fresh fruit and chocolate candy bars."

"That is true," Steve interrupted mildly, "but have any of you been in a food riot, or has anyone in your families starved to death?"

"Right," a red-headed young man commented, "we have many blessings. Most of us live in rural areas where we can still grow a lot of our own food."

"The Lord never fails," added a tall, lanky boy with thick glasses and a shock of brown hair falling over his forehead. "My Dad lost his job as a television studio manager because he witnessed to a co-worker about Christ. But he found a janitor's job, and his pay just meets our needs. We really prayed about that situation, and the Lord helped us."

They all shared then of the ways in which God had been working in their lives. As Leigh listened, she was impressed that these were teens who, through the seriousness of the times, were maturing quickly. They knew what it was to ask God for material provisions, for physical safety, for comfort in the death of a parent, and to see God enable them to be bold Christians.

They continued to talk as they packed up to leave. Steve instructed them not to leave even a scrap of paper. "We don't want anyone else to know we were here."

They finished picking what food they wanted from the garden and then started back on the trail.

All this time, Leigh was as aware of Steve's presence as one would be aware of a tiger prowling around the perimeter of one's lawn. Even while her thoughts were elsewhere it seemed as though he waited to fill her mind with his presence, his magnetism. She wondered about his spiritual life. He did not enter into the conversations about the Lord, but neither did he discourage the teens as they shared and encouraged each other.

"He reminds me of a military guard," Ann whispered as they walked the trail together.

"Yes," Leigh agreed, "he does act that way now."

"I watched him while we were at the garden, Leigh, and he was continually checking everything out, even while he worked. He would look out over the hills, and nothing seemed to escape his notice. Look, I wonder what is wrong?"

Ann nodded toward Steve who had stopped the group at the edge of a clearing and was looking intently out to their left.

As Leigh drew nearer, she glanced past him, trying to see what had his attention. "Anything wrong, Steve?"

"There is something going on at that farmhouse," he replied, pointing toward the next hill.

"Yes, I see what you mean." Leigh stared at the farm and several possible situations tumbled about in her mind, none of them pleasant. "It looks like an army patrol is there. Do you think they have seen us?"

"They seem too intent on their own situation, but I am going to get our group away from this side of the hill, just in case. We need to get back into the woods."

"Is there anything you want me to do?" Leigh spoke with far more calmness than she felt.

He turned and smiled. "Just what you have been doing all along, Leigh. We will be fine," he added reassuringly. Then he turned to speak to the teens who stood waiting for instructions. "Let's make a trail through those trees," he said, pointing to the woods further up the hillside. "It will be much slower, but I want all of us out of sight."

The teens regrouped under the trees, taking care to stand out of view, but still watching the scene across the narrow valley. Steve was helping Leigh over some rocks to join the group when the sound of an army jeep driving into the farmyard caught their attention, and they turned to watch.

A group of soldiers jumped out and joined the several already surrounding the family. One of them, probably an officer, stood talking loudly, his actions quite menacing. They could hear his voice but his words were indistinguishable.

Leigh was afraid for the unfortunate family. "Steve, can't you do something?"

He stood with feet wide apart, fists on his hips, looking like some modern-day avenging angel, his eyes blazing with anger. He shook his head and started to speak, but his words were cut off by a piercing scream.

Leigh whirled around in time to see the officer strike the woman with his fist, sending her sprawling to the ground.

He waved his hand and two soldiers grabbed the farmer, dragging him over against a tree where he was securely tied.

Leigh could hear the children crying as they huddled close to the mother and that must have irritated the officer. He whipped out a pistol and threatened her, perhaps demanding that she silence the children.

Then, while the horrified group of teens watched, he turned quickly toward the farmer, raised his gun, and shot the man.

There were stunned gasps from the group on the hillside as they saw him slump forward, and Leigh cried out softly, "Oh, no!" She turned to put a hand out toward Steve, her legs suddenly too weak to hold her up.

"Let's get out of here," Steve ordered tersely. His movements were quick and almost rough as he helped Leigh through the underbrush and away from the ugly scene they had just witnessed.

But they had only gone a few yards when gun shots rang out again from across the hillside, and it stopped everyone as quickly as a parade command might. All eyes were upon Steve, waiting, wondering, pleading for some miracle that would remedy the hideous spectacle across the way.

"Wait here," Steve commanded reluctantly. As he turned away, he glanced at Leigh, his expression telling her that he knew what he would find.

She watched him go straight down the hillside instead of following their trail, stepping lightly over rocks she had just clambered over with difficulty, and catching hold of a tree branch to stop his slide down a short but steep incline. He made it look so easy, but for a moment she thought he might go over the edge. He moved slowly around a screen of rocks and stood looking at a scene beyond her view.

His expression was impassive as he made his way swiftly back up the slope to the silent, somber group. He had to be in superb condition; his breathing wasn't changed in the least.

"They've shot the entire family," he said grimly, looking at Leigh. "The soldiers are rounding up the cows from a lot behind the barn."

His eyes moved over the group, acknowledging what they were feeling, and he silently allowed them a few seconds to absorb the significance of what he had said. They stood motionless, stunned by his words, and he knew that while they had not been close enough to see the fear and desperation on the faces of the doomed family, they felt as though they had been physically linked to each life.

Then to forestall any foolish reactions from the anger forming in some of the young people, he began issuing terse orders, his voice low, but clipped and commanding.

"Pick up your things," he said, motioning to the sacks of

food and tools lying on the ground.

"Mike, lead the way. Every man walk beside one of the girls. Keith, you and Mark walk at the rear of the line. I don't want any more noise than necessary. We want to get to the other side of this hill as quickly as possible."

Walking forward to the front of the line he smiled reassuringly at each teen. "Let's not get excited, but let's get out of here."

Thirty minutes later when they reached the second garden, Steve stationed the boys out among the trees encircling the open area, telling them to signal if they saw anything unusual. He then put the girls to work picking the produce needed to fill the remaining sacks. They were not going to take the time to do any weeding.

While Leigh worked with the girls, she heard Steve in conversation with Mike son of the maintenance manager and an expert of the trails in that area.

"Mike, does our trail get anywhere near the road that leads up to that farm?"

"Yes, about forty-five minutes from here."

"How close do we get to the road?"

"About a quarter of a mile."

"I didn't notice that on the way up here." Steve sounded irritated at his failure.

"No, Sir. The road isn't visible, but sounds carry up the hillside. If there is a jeep moving on that road, we can hear it from the trail."

Leigh marveled at the calmness about her. No one seemed afraid, but she was gritting her teeth, trying to swallow the panic she felt. The teens were subdued and solemn, thinking of the family, and perhaps wondering when that might happen to their loved ones. Leigh saw several of the girls wiping away tears as they reached down to pick the fresh vegetables, and she wished with all her heart that she could keep such slaughter from their experiences.

They were on the trail about forty minutes when Steve suddenly stopped and held up his hand. Every teen was immediately stilled, waiting, listening. Leigh strained to hear any sound that might mean danger, and her heart began to pound as she feared the unknown before them.

Then they heard it.

Loud voices and swift movements were coming toward them

through the woods. Leigh tensed and began praying silently for the Lord's help.

Steve whispered some instructions to Mike, who started down the line, directing every boy to find protective covering for one of the girls and to stay with her. Soon only Steve could be seen on the trail and he was moving forward for surveillance.

Leigh hid quickly in a large clump of thick bushes, and since her view was completely obstructed unless she parted the branches, she felt fairly secure.

She heard a girl's voice whispering. "Lord, help Steve now . . . we trust you, Father, to protect us."

Suddenly there was a thunderous bellowing noise just down the trail and Leigh peeked out cautiously in time to see four men in black uniform chasing a cow through the trees.

The soldiers were so intent on catching the frightened cow that they were completely unaware of all the people in hiding along the trail. All that could be heard was the bellowing, the pounding of feet on the ground, and the men cursing the evasive animal.

Then without warning, the cow swerved off the path toward Leigh's hiding place, hit the bush with such a smack that it sent her crashing to the ground, and then stood absolutely still, heaving deep breaths and undoubtedly eyeing her pursuers warily.

A horrifying thought flashed through Leigh's mind as she lay tangled in the bushes, afraid to pull away from the branches that were sticking her painfully. If that animal did not move there would be four soldiers discovering her presence in a matter of seconds!

Without warning a man's arm encircled her waist. Her hand flew to her mouth to stifle a gasp. Then another hand holding a sharp stick shot out through the bushes toward the cow.

The hapless animal bellowed a deafening protest at being struck and thundered off back down the trail, scattering startled soldiers in all directions.

One of them shouted, "Get that dumb cow or the lieutenant will string us up by our thumbs!" And off they went in wild pursuit.

No one moved until the sounds had faded away completely. And it was only then that Leigh realized that she was still being held tightly. She knew without looking who it was that held her so securely against his shoulder.

She turned slightly to face him. "How did you get back here without being seen? How did you find me?"

Steve laughed softly. "It was easy. Those soldiers can't even catch a cow, much less find us."

There was safety in being held so closely, Leigh thought, and something with which she should not become accustomed. His expression told her he might take advantage of his embrace to kiss her. When he didn't, she wondered if she felt relieved or disappointed.

He looked at her scratched and bruised hands as he helped her out of the tangled bushes. "Are you hurt anywhere else?"

"I don't think so." Leigh glanced down at her clothes and her laugh was a bit shaky. "Not even a rip in these old jeans."

Then her dark eyes widened as the full impact of their escape hit her. "Oh, my word, Steve, that was close. Thank you!"

She began to shake uncontrollably as she realized what might have taken place, and Steve put his arm around her waist and led her toward a large rock. "Just think what could have happened to these kids!"

"But it didn't. Now sit down and let's take a look at your injuries."

As she gingerly sank down on the rock, the teens began emerging from their hiding places and Steve instructed one of the girls to clean Leigh's hands. "Mike, come with me, and let's see if the trail is clear."

Leaving his water flask and a clean handkerchief for Leigh to use, he turned and moved down the trail in soft, leopard-like strides, Mike following just as silently behind him.

While they waited, several prayed spontaneously, thanking God for their deliverance. Everyone knew their lives had been in grave danger, especially since they had just seen an entire family wiped out by the officer in charge of the cow-chasing soldiers.

Steve and Mike were soon back with good news.

"The trail is clear. We can leave. We've just a couple of miles to go."

It seemed like a long two miles before they finally arrived back on the conference grounds where the teens put away tools and deposited the fresh vegetables in the dining hall. Calling their thanks to Steve and Leigh, they were soon dispersed.

"How do your hands feel now, Leigh?"

She held them up for inspection. "Stiff, but useable, I think."

"I'm glad. It could have been worse if the cow had decided to sit on you."

She laughed and said, "I would prefer to forget the whole incident," adding soberly, "especially the part about that family. We can't do anything about it, can we?"

"No, not now. But I do promise to ask someone in town to check on the farm."

"Good." She stopped to look up at him, wanting to ask if he would come up the hill to meet her family. "Steve, would you like to meet . . . what's wrong?"

His face had become granite hard, his eyes cold blue. He looked extremely displeased and she wondered what she had done. Then, following his stare, Leigh turned to see a man leaning against the maintenance building, watching them.

"I can't walk up the hill with you, Leigh—I would like to meet your parents, but it seems I have an unexpected, and undesirable guest." His voice hardened as he glanced at the man now moving slowly toward them.

"Who is he?" Leigh did not like the shifty, mocking manner the man displayed, and could not understand what he and Steve would have in common.

"You might say that he is a business acquaintance." There was a softening in his expression as he saw her puzzled look. "There always seems to be some interruption to our talks. Perhaps I will see you later tonight."

She smiled, a little perplexed, and said, "I'll be in a meeting in the auditorium tonight. Thanks again for your help this afternoon." She turned to take the path up the hill, still disturbed by the strange guest waiting to talk with Steve.

He watched until she had neared the top of the path, intentionally ignoring the man nearing his side; then he turned to stare at him. He kept his voice mild and expressionless, hiding his violent dislike.

"Well, Barnes, I thought I told you to wait in town. What are you doing here?"

"I just got curious," Barnes slurred, "wonderin' what a religious place was like." He laughed condescendingly, and tucking his thumbs in his belt, he rocked back on his heels. "Pretty lady there, the one you were talkin' with." His eyes were watchful, his manner more than curious.

"Let me get something straight right now, Barnes. You've just been assigned as my aide, but if you find it difficult to obey orders, then I feel sure we can find a place for you somewhere else. The army always needs good foot soldiers." Steve turned to walk down to the hotel, leaving Barnes to scurry a bit to catch up with him.

His aide was taken back with Steve's authority and his face showed surprise. "Yes, Sir," he mumbled defensively, "I didn't mean nothin', Sir."

Steve was unimpressed with this instant humbleness and pressed his message further. "Then get back to town and wait until I have finished my business here. It's impossible to do any investigation with a stranger roaming the grounds, and I intend to find out a few important facts before I leave here. You don't have anyone's permission to obstruct my work."

"Yes, Sir. I'll go now, Sir."

"Do that. And remember, this is my last warning!"

The revolutionary party was too interlaced with spy investigating spy that Steve knew he could never trust this aide and planned right from the beginning of this assignment to be extremely careful with him.

Barnes began to raise his hand but was stopped by a sharp "Don't salute me! You've forgotten that order as well!"

"Sorry, Sir. I'll go now." The aide's voice was full of submission, but Steve was not fooled, and he did not miss Barne's final, significant glance up the hill as he turned away.

Steve watched him move slowly away, walking with his own peculiar strut to a car waiting halfway down the drive. After the car pulled out of the front entrance, he turned in disgust and went to his room on the second floor of the hotel. Staring out the window, he thought of the report he had received on his new aide.

"Barnes, John T.; born, Hartford, Connecticut; now forty-five years old. Spent fifteen years in the army. Lost his sergeant stripes three times due to insubordination. Army reports read like a criminal record. Barnes had a vicious animal streak in him. Somehow got into the FBI, but was never successful, never commended for his service. Actually dismissed because of some bungled job that had cost the government a lot of hush-money. All reports mentioned his greed for power at any cost."

He would be the perfect type to be attached to Steve's new

assignment, the exact type to spy and to alter events to suit his private ambitions. But that was his flaw—he was so ambitious that it left him unwise and even stupid in some judgments.

The next few months would be taxing and dangerous. But if Steve were to accomplish what had been discussed, it was unavoidable.

Chapter 4

That evening was the last night Thad and Leigh would be at the conference. They both had to return the next day to their teaching positions in Harrisburg, Thad at the high school and Leigh at the nursery.

It was unusual for Thad to attend the meetings since he took spiritual things so lightly; but Leigh was sure he was there tonight to please his parents, for he loved them dearly. And apart from not responding to Christ as they had longed for, he had never given them any trouble. It was his strong will that distressed Leigh now. He hated the New Democracy and freely voiced his displeasure. No matter what happened, he was unwilling to admit that man's sin caused man's difficulties and problems.

The circular auditorium had only one electric light, which was situated over the long wooden pulpit on the platform. The energy crisis had only become worse in the last several years, and every building, public or private, felt the consequences. Electricity was a very precious item, not to be used recklessly. Leigh wondered how much suffering there would be the next winter because of insufficient heating.

"I'll bet the conference grounds will soon lose its permit to use the little bit of electricity it gets now," Thad said, plugging into her thoughts as he so often did.

"No one minds, Thad. It's a small sacrifice considering what we may have to give up soon." How much easier it was, she thought, to surrender the use of electricity rather than one's freedom of worship or life itself.

There was not enough light to use hymnals, but the congregation sang from memory many old familiar songs that brought encouragement and comfort to every heart. Even Thad seemed to enjoy them. He wasn't singing, but his foot kept time to the music.

The Gordon family sat together on the left side of the auditorium, Thad with his parents on one side and Leigh on the other. She leaned over to smile at her Dad. This was the first evening he was allowed out of the cottage, and he looked very pleased about it.

People of all ages crowded the room, although attending such meetings was ridiculed, particularly by the press. And once the New Democracy had full control of the nation, it would put even more demands upon the young people to curtail their attendance.

Just as Rev. Miles opened his Bible and began reading from the book of Daniel, Leigh saw someone enter the door across the room and take a seat against the wall. It was her trail companion of the day, and his presence made her realize that she had been looking for him all evening. She forced her attention back to Rev. Miles, who was now talking about the Scripture they had just read.

"My dear friends, these are indeed troubled times. And this evening we need to hear God's message through the experience and words of Daniel. The pressures to conform to the king's court were as great then as the ones facing us today. How was Daniel to keep his balance in the midst of a totally heathen environment? Some of us here tonight have already grappled with that question, have already been through similar times. Others of us will yet go through these trials. . ."

Again Leigh's eyes shifted back across the room. It was easy to find him, for his blond hair set him apart from those seated nearby. His face was turned toward the speaker and Leigh thought again of his inner battle of the previous afternoon.

Was he still struggling? What could the problem be? Would he find some help and strength from the message tonight, or was he there to condemn it? Fleetingly, she prayed that God would help him in whatever way was needed.

Thad stirred, restless and uncomfortable on the wooden bench, and it brought a guilty flush to Leigh's cheeks; her eyes darted quickly back to the speaker. His words flowed back into her thoughts.

"Daniel's entire life was a vital testimony of the living God. He was pressed in on all sides, with no way out. Only then could God perform miracles before the unbelieving; only then would they recognize God's power.

"Here was a man who made a decision and then would not be moved from it. There were threats of punishment and almost sure death in the den of lions. But he never wavered."

Thad felt Leigh's hand involuntarily grasp his arm, and, following her gaze across the room, was surprised to see Houston still around. In spite of the dimness of the room, Thad could see the grave expression on his handsome face, and he felt a mounting frustration.

He had seen his sister deeply concerned over friends, taking their worries as her own, consumed with sympathy over their burdens. But this was something new in her life; he just knew it! He had such an affinity with her that he knew she was going to suffer if this relationship blossomed.

Suppose the man were a spy? Informers of all shades and kinds were as abundant as the colored leaves in the fall. There was no telling what misery he might bring into Leigh's life.

Well, no man was going to hurt his sister while he was around. He would do all he could to block this association. Reaching over to squeeze Leigh's hand, he sighed inwardly, wishing the meeting were over so that he might begin formulating his plans. Turning his attention back to the sermon, he listened just long enough to determine how near it was to completion.

"God made no promises of ease," Rev. Miles was saying, "or wealth or influence to Daniel; nor does He for us today. But Daniel willingly submitted to God's plan for his life—not knowing if it would bring life and prosperity, or torture and death. He was a willing instrument in God's hands. Are you a willing instrument? Am I? No matter what price we may have to pay?"

Rev. Miles paused, letting his question sink into the minds of those present. No one stirred, for every person was fully aware of what the cost might be.

"Let me remind you of a joyous truth. The record of the life of Daniel reveals to us what true dedication means, and more importantly, what the living God will do through those who are totally committed to Him. There can be no other way for us!''

He paused again, and then concluded, ''Rather than having a closing hymn of praise tonight, I am going to ask that we spend time in silent prayer. Those who wish to participate may remain in the auditorium.''

At his words most of the congregation followed his example and knelt to pray. Leigh did not look across at Steve, for she was afraid to know what his response was. She knew her parents were kneeling, and as Thad stood to go, she reached out to grasp his hand, her eyes pleading with him to stay.

Shaking his head, he leaned over to whisper, ''I'll wait for you outside.'' Pulling his hand free, he walked hurriedly out into the night.

Leigh had much to pray about: her parents' health and safety, the nursery school, Thad's need of Christ, her own fears of being persecuted, and Steve.

She wanted to find peace about what was ahead but all her life had struggled with her fears. And now a new concern faced her as well. What kind of relationship was she to have with Steve Houston? She was honest enough to admit to the Lord that she had more than a passing interest, and that she was sure Steve did not intend to drop the matter. She could only commit to God the conflicting emotions in her heart and ask that He work out His will in her life.

When she got to her feet there were few left in the room, and walking down the aisle, she was dismayed to find no peace in her heart. Just as she neared the door there came flowing into her troubled mind the words of Scripture: ''Fret not thyself because of evildoers . . . fret not . . . fret not . . . fret not.'' It came again and again as she walked out into the summer night.

Glancing around, she tried to find Thad in the darkness outside of the auditorium. Then she heard him calling, ''Leigh, over here.'' He was standing beside a wooden bench, looking up into the sky. ''Isn't it a beautiful night. Just look at that moon.''

Leigh sensed the strain in his voice and realized he was attempting to maintain their normal relationship. Even though she had never pressured him, he was aware of how much she longed for him to become a Christian. Yet he had never expressed any need for Christ.

''It ought to be a full moon by tomorrow night, Leigh. Are

you ready to go up the hill?''

But she did not answer, for just as he spoke, a figure emerged from the shadows of a nearby tree and walked toward them. Instinctively, she drew nearer her brother as they waited, but as the man came closer, his blond hair gleamed in the moonlight, and Leigh relaxed immediately.

"Leigh, may I speak to you alone?'' Steve stood before her, waiting for an answer.

Thad took her arm protectively and scowlingly shook his head, but Steve ignored his presence, and Leigh had eyes only for the man before her.

"I'll be fine, Thad. Would you wait here for me?''

He released her arm reluctantly and growled, "I won't be far away.'' He watched Steve take her by the arm and walk back under the tree, and he muttered to himself, "He sure likes the shadows.'' He dropped down on the bench, folded his arms across his chest, and stared into the darkness under the tree.

"I . . . I saw you in the meeting,'' Leigh said shyly, aware of Steve's firm grasp of her arm, and wondering what was so important that he had to speak to her immediately. "I thought you might have already left the grounds.''

Reaching for her other hand and holding them both in his strong grip, he said, "No, I'll be leaving later tonight. But I had to see you.''

"Me?'' Leigh groaned inwardly. Why did she have to sound so inane? She should have had some more intelligent response than that.

It did not seem to matter what she did, for Steve looked extremely purposeful. He released her hand to put an arm around her waist, pulling her into the light of the moon.

"Is there any special man in your life?''

She did not even pretend to misunderstand. "No,'' she answered with a shake of her head.

"I don't have much time for polite conversation, Leigh. And I don't know how much time we will ever have together. But I must tell you . . .'' He paused, searching her face intently, perhaps wondering how much he ought to say.

"I must tell you,'' he continued, underscoring his words, "I care, very deeply, for you.''

Stunned at this abrupt declaration, she looked up, staring into his face, probing for the truth. "Steve, you . . . you don't know me! We've only just . . ."

He interrupted her stuttering speech with a finger laid to her lips and said with a smile, "I know how I feel. My life sometimes depends upon my quick judgments and I've never been wrong."

Somehow, she knew this was not an idle boast, but a true statement spoken in matter-of-fact terms.

"But . . . but . . . how can I care for . . . ," she stopped, then said in a rush of words, "for someone I've only been with twice?"

His hand gently pulled her chin up, forcing her face into the moonlight. "You do. I see it in your eyes."

She could not hide her face from his penetrating search, but said nothing. She was attracted to him, yes, but this was one time she was not behaving impulsively.

"I wish there were time to let our relationship develop in a normal way, Leigh, but these are not normal times. The future is too uncertain, life far too fragile. I may never see you again."

"Then why . . ."

"I need you," he said fervently.

She tried to pull out of his embrace, instantly suspicious.

"I don't mean physically. I need your trust," he said, emphasizing the word. "No matter what happens, I need your faith in me."

So urgent was his need for her sympathy and affection that he was unaware of kissing her lightly on the forehead. His voice was insistent.

"I must know you will."

She opened her mouth to question him again, but her words were stilled by the pleading look he gave her.

"Leigh?"

"I . . . I want to trust you, Steve. But I don't know you. I don't know anything about you. Can't you tell me what's wrong?"

He shook his head. "I'm going to be involved in something important, and dangerous; I'm not asking for your pity. And I realize it is absurd for a stranger to ask this of you, but in the few hours we've been together, I've come to know you quite well."

"Yes," she cut in sharply, "I feel as though you've put a computer to my mind and understand me completely."

He laughed. "Yes, I know a lot of things about you. You are a warm, sensitive person. You are full of compassion and ready to give of yourself to anyone in need. You underestimate your courage, your inner spirit, and your beauty. You worry about the nursery children, your fears, and your family. And I love you.''

"You what?" Leigh needed to sit down and recover from the shock of his statement, but the figure of a man passed them in the darkness, and as Steve glanced up, he said reluctantly, "I must go. Trust me, Leigh, please.''

She felt his lips brush hers and knew he had released her from his tight hold, but that was all. She stood rooted to the spot, trembling in the flood of emotions washing over her. She was puzzled by his talk of trust, and a bit angry that he could declare his love in one second and then leave her in the next. She found it hard to sort through the experience.

"Hey, Sis, snap out of it." She stared at Thad until his next words penetrated her daze. "Did you see where he went? Looks like he had a secret meeting.''

"Why?"

"Someone drove off in his car with him. I'd sure like to know who it is," he said angrily. He looked closely at his sister. She was totally bemused and he felt sorry for her.

"Come on," he said, putting an arm around her shoulders. "Let's go home.''

She nodded mutely and let him lead her up the path toward their dimly-lit cottage. Her mother must be waiting up for them, she thought. She never likes to leave the oil lamp burning unattended.

"What did he want, Leigh?''

"He said that . . . that . . .'' She spread her hands in a helpless gesture, unwilling to complete the sentence.

Trying to sort out her feelings as she walked slowly up the hill, she wondered if she cared for Steve as much as he thought she did. He was definitely a man who knew what he wanted. But why could he not tell her what lay behind his need for trust. And why was he asking this of her? He had declared his love, but how could he be so sure? And most importantly, was he committed to living for Christ?

She stopped short and said with dismay, "Thad, I don't know anything about him but his name!''

"Well, don't worry, honey. You've probably seen the last of

him, anyway."

The look she gave him then was one of total disbelief, and he knew she was right. That man would be around again, and it was not going to be a happy experience for Leigh. He grew angry thinking about it.

Just as Thad had surmised, Steve was in a secret meeting.

The two men made every effort not to be seen together on the conference grounds, so there would be no association between them; it was only by chance that Thad had seen them in the car together. They could be thankful for the darkness that hid the identity of Steve's companion.

They rode silently for a few minutes, Steve guiding the car down to the front entrance and pulling out onto the highway where they headed east for a mile and then pulled into an isolated rest area. He pulled the car behind the building to a row of thick evergreens and cut the lights. They watched the road for any unwanted company, prepared to speed out onto the highway if necessary.

"When did you get the news?" his rider asked.

"It came in a coded letter the first of the week," Steve answered. "We have waited for this opportunity for a long time, and I'm not reluctant to take it, but I have wondered how successful we will be."

"But think what it will do for our cause," his companion argued.

"I don't know. I've wondered about that. With the wrong people in charge, it may not help us a bit."

"That's why it is vital that you take the assignment. When you have your mind made up, very few people have the courage to oppose you. You aren't going to give up, Steve, before you have even begun? I can't believe that of you."

"No, I'm not."

"Good. When will the President announce your appointment?"

"I'm not sure. He doesn't even know I have been informed."

"Will you return to Philadelphia?"

"Yes, for a day or two. But I had to see you before I got too involved. I want to be sure you understand the problems involved. The President could change his mind on a whim at any time and appoint someone else. He has done that before. He could also give me some other position, and that would place some of our men in jeopardy."

"There isn't a man in our group who isn't prepared for that."

"Yes, I realize that," Steve said. "Are they also aware of how zealous the President is for detailed agency reports? And if there is the slightest question, someone could be imprisoned. He has thrown several of his closest comrades in jail just for that reason."

"I know," replied the man seated next to him. "If your reports are not thorough, he will be the first one to get suspicious."

"Right, and I won't have any of our people on my personal staff for quite awhile, in order not to arouse suspicion. My new aide will watch every move I make, and if there is just one person showing the slightest interest in me, he will pounce on that."

"That will put you in isolation, Steve."

"It won't be unusual. I've worked that way most of my life."

"Tell me about your new aide."

Steve grunted in disgust. "He is the most depraved, mean-spirited, vicious man I've ever met. He will do anything to get the power he wants. And since he is highly unpredictable, he is dangerous. I will need to keep a constant watch on him."

"Why?"

"He wants my job," Steve answered. "And in the climate we're living in today, he is the kind that could get it. I expect that one of the first things he will do is to try digging up my past, hoping to get some blackmail material."

"That will be difficult," Steve's companion said. "We've had your name erased from all the computer files in the country. No school records, no superfluous information that might be useful to our opponents. All they can find is your birth certificate and your army records."

"But," Steve cut in, "if anyone wants information badly enough, he can interrogate co-workers, acquaintances, neighbors, whomever. It would take time, but he could do it."

"Perhaps by that time, your job will be finished. Tell me," the man said, changing the subject, "how did you get along with the teens yesterday? Any problems?"

"None. They responded as you thought they would, in spite of seeing a man killed by an army patrol." And Steve went on to relate the full story of all that had taken place on the hike.

"What did you think of Leigh Gordon?"

Steve's hands tightened on the steering wheel. He would not share his feelings about her, even with the man who was one of the closest comrades he had.

"Very helpful," he said, and then said, "We need a new code. I don't want to use the old one at all." And they spent a full thirty minutes working out a new plan.

"I'll have our men in Harrisburg available for any job you need, Steve. They use the code name "Concord." You can get in contact with the local leader by calling this restaurant. He owns it." He handed a business card to Steve. "I suggest you memorize the number and destroy the card."

At last, their discussion ended; they drove back to the conference grounds, each man silent in the face of what they were to begin.

Steve was guiding the car into the front entranceway when his rider said, "Let me out here, Steve. I'll wait a few minutes and then walk up through the trees to our cottage."

"Right." Steve stopped the car, turned off the lights, and pulled two train passes from his pocket and handed them to his companion.

"Would you get these to Thad and Leigh Gordon for tomorrow? I don't want them to know where they came from."

"Yes, certainly. Offers of rides and passes are sometimes left at the office by the militia. I'll have someone else deliver them tonight, so I won't have to answer any questions."

Steve thanked him and added a reminder. "We'll use our new code, even through the restaurant owner. The less he knows of my job, the safer it will be." Then he added gravely, "Well, having decided upon this course, we can only hope it doesn't fail."

With a nod of agreement, the man stepped from the car and turned to say good-bye.

Steve raised his hand and smiled. "Good night, Pastor Miles. Do be careful!"

Chapter 5

Public transportation was reduced to a bankrupt shadow of its former standards, and could now advertise danger on its list of dubious benefits. Major highways, scarred by the militia's struggle against the Peoples Army, and filled with bomb craters and ambushed wreckages, were nearly inoperative. Non-party members had only hazardous choices of travel: they could take a dangerous truck ride, obtain a spot on a freight car, or endure a bicycle trip. They seldom got passes for a train seat.

So far in the civil war, passenger trains had been left unharmed. The two permits for Leigh and Thad not only simplified, but also lessened, the difficulties of the return trip to the capital. However, Thad's gratitude would have been tempered with great restraint had he identified the anonymous donor.

Bending his head toward Leigh, he whispered, "The old grey coach isn't what it used to be."

She smiled apprehensively and glanced up from her book. "Shh, someone might hear you."

"Hardly, with those party songs blaring forth like that. I'd like to rip that speaker right off the wall!"

Leigh nodded in agreement. "I know. One minute of that is enough to blot out all the quietness I've stored up the last week."

She sighed as she watched a cleaning woman working her way down the aisle. Whisk broom and dust rags looked innocent enough in the hands of one dressed in the black uniform of the Peoples Army, but they both knew the woman's most important tools were her eyes and ears that picked up useful information for the party. The more important the information, the better her chances of advancement in the army.

The woman was short and a little on the chubby side, but her uniform was still about a size too large. She looked as though someone had tossed the outfit over her head, and it had fallen in layers around her body. Her straight brown hair was pulled back and tied at the neck with a black ribbon, and her army cap was jammed down tight over her forehead. It was obvious by her slow, quiet movements that she was listening to every scrap of conversation available.

She scrutinized the young couple. Most passengers were army personnel, government officials, important businessmen and those who were in support of the party. She was not sure where the young couple fit. An army man on leave? No, his haircut was not military length. A businessman? She hardly thought so by the look of his clothes which were neat and clean but definitely threadbare from age.

Glancing at the book on Leigh's lap she asked in feigned friendliness, "Oh, do you enjoy books on child training?"

Leigh smiled tensely and replied, "I work with children." Trying to block the flow of questions, she opened the book to continue reading. It was a blatant dismissal that failed.

Dark eyes glinted in anticipation of the information she might have shortly, and the woman probed further, her hands automatically dusting and redusting the worn leather seat opposite them. "My, how rewarding. Do you keep the children in your home?"

"No, I work at a nursery."

"Oh, that's nice. Do you have a large group of children?"

"No, just a few. It is a small school."

Leigh hoped this would satisfy the woman and the interrogation would cease, for she saw that Thad was restless and was afraid that in his growing irritation he would voice his true feelings. She wanted to protect the church-related facility as long as possible, and if Thad became angry the cleaning woman could have them arrested for disturbing the peace. Other complications might arise when it was discovered that Leigh worked in a Christian atmosphere. Some church schools had already been closed on the pretext that they had insufficient room, or the building was unsafe, or teachers unqualified. She had acquaintances who had disappeared completely after arrest, not to be heard from again.

Leigh could visualize the woman enlightening her superior, who would file a report which would be sent to the secret police in Harrisburg, and the nursery would be investigated. She did not wish to undergo that experience or be asked to submit to a loyalty oath to the New Democracy.

She knew that the secret police worked under the National Intelligence Organization, an octopus sweeping in and clutching, pulverizing and killing an increasing number of helpless people in its unavoidable tentacles. Leigh wanted no part of that!

Just as the woman began asking the location of the school, a voice came over the intercom, cutting sharply into the blaring music.

"Sgt. Martin, report to the office immediately!"

The guise of a friendly cleaning woman faded rapidly as uncontrollable fear swept over her face. The change was startlingly pathetic. She turned awkwardly in her haste and fell on a smartly dressed businessman, her cap sliding down further into her eyes.

"Watch what you're doing," he snarled.

"Oh, I'm sorry, Sir. Please excuse me. I'm sorry!" She turned and ran down the aisle, still apologizing, and rushed through the coach door.

"That's interesting," Thad muttered under his breath.

Leigh felt rather sorry for her. "It must be terrible working in such fear of your superiors."

Shortly after this episode two soldiers entered the coach for a routine check of passengers, and as they began asking for identification cards and permits, Leigh wished she could fade from view. She hated dealing with any part of the military. And there were thousands of men, who through desperation of survival or hardness of heart, had willingly put on the black uniform with its grey-colored insignia of a clenched fist on sleeve and cap.

The army was a fitting product of the past years, she thought, when the nation was fed a steady but revolting diet of the glories of crime, sadism, sexual perversion, and the supposed death of God—until human life itself was worthless and people were killed for the change in their pockets. Humans turned against humans, like a kingdom of animals where only the strongest and most cruel would survive. Most of the men in the army were like that, and she tensed every time one came near, apprehensive that he would become interested in her.

The soldiers accosted an elderly, well-dressed man whose identification card seemed unsatisfactory. They taunted and probed until he was openly fearful of their harassment. Then, tired of playing with him, one of the soldiers smirkingly tossed the cards down on his lap and moved on.

Leigh had worn her oldest jeans and an oversized, faded blue shirt with a bandana tied over her hair. She hoped the severe, insipid look she had created would cool anyone's interest.

As they neared her seat, Leigh kept her eyes on the pages of her book, posturing more self-control than she felt.

A hand came into view, the fingers snapped, waiting for her response. She hastily pulled the cards from her small shoulder purse, and without looking up, put them in the outstretched hand.

The soldier sorted through them, saw the train pass, and flipped them all back into her lap, not caring that they scattered and slid to the floor. After reviewing Thad's credentials, the two soldiers readjusted the rifles slung over their shoulders and moved on down the aisle and out the door.

Their presence brought to Leigh's mind all of the girls in the capital city, and probably in the nation, who had been taken by force to the army barracks and subjected to a night of horror as they were sexually abused, and then pushed out into the streets at dawn to make their own way home—if they survived. The underground newspaper sometimes reported the discovery of a woman's body left outside the barracks, a woman who had died either of physical abuse or shock. Some who lived were emotionally unable to cope with their experience and were now being cared for in mental hospitals. This was part of what was experienced in other countries, in other wars, but surely not in America!

These tragedies, of course, were never publicized by the official news media, but were instead, whispered here and there, or found in the illegal *Freedom News,* a clandestine, spasmodically published newspaper.

"Five years ago," Leigh murmured to her brother, "I never would have believed that our country would be in its present state. But I can still hear Dad saying that if spiritual revival doesn't come soon, America will be a place of incredible sorrow. He was right!"

Thad did not answer, but his face mirrored his thoughts—bitter ones of the revolution and conditions they faced. He could not accept these events as being from the hand of God for ultimate good. All his life he had heard his father preach about God, but why did not this God of the universe intervene in the affairs of man and set things right?

The train passed a small town gutted by the war. The depot was half destroyed by fire, the warehouses merely empty shells, the streets emanating a ghost-town atmosphere.

"What was in that small, insignificant town to cause such destruction?" he asked angrily. "That comes from the evils of greed and war, not the spiritual state of our nation."

Leigh's restraining hand on his kept him from saying more, but he sat staring out the window, his frustration a hard knot in his stomach.

He mentally numbered off the larger cities that were, for all practical purposes, wastelands. New York had been the first to succumb to economic hardships, then Atlanta, Chicago, Houston, and Los Angeles. It was unbelievable! Bankruptcy, food riots, gangs of people sweeping through city areas to claim what they needed to survive, and finally, the civil war.

And he grew furious each time he thought of the total destruction of the former capital city of America. The nation had been panic stricken when the news was flashed on television that Washington, D.C., was being blown up—building by building. It had been a strategic move by the new political party and brought the intended result—national paralysis, which gave them time to overthrow the existing power and set up a new government.

And while this New Democracy engaged in skirmishes with the Citizens Militia in order to seize total power, two foreign nations sat waiting to move in and take control as they had done in most of the world's nations.

The Citizens Militia, organized secretly all over the country, was outnumbered, without capable leadership, without weapons, and only seemed to be nipping at the toes of a massive bear. Thad wanted desperately to join, nearly doing so on several occasions, but he knew this would be an added burden to his parents.

But deep inside lay the knowledge that, sooner or later, it was inevitable that he would be compelled to take a stand.

He frowned, thinking of the next week of "training" for teachers before the school year opened. He would endure hours of boring political speeches, only because he wanted to remain a high school teacher. There was still time to reach some of those young minds with—with what, he wondered. He could not honestly say he thought God was the answer, for he did not believe that himself. What could he tell them? What reasons could he give for all the bloodshed, destruction, and war? There must be an answer somewhere. Mankind must be something more than chessmen on a board, manipulated by some unknown force; there must be more to life than pain and death.

Leigh interrupted his thoughts. "If there isn't any trouble on the lines, we ought to be home in about an hour."

They arrived at the sub-station in the late afternoon, and joining the many pedestrians leaving the building, walked the two miles home. The few who still owned vehicles found it extremely difficult to obtain a ration card. Consequently, most automobiles and trucks on the road were government owned. The TransBus Lines still ran their city routes, but schedules were cut to the bare minimum.

Black-uniformed soldiers were on the streets, and their presence created a heavy, oppressed atmosphere. Up and down the sidewalks they patrolled, stopping citizens, asking for I.D. cards, questioning activities, peering into packages, detaining— doing anything to manifest their importance and strength. The possibility of being picked up by soldiers or the secret police was always present, and Leigh sighed with relief when they were actually inside their home.

The Gordon house was situated in one of the older sections of the city, where the houses stood like red brick dominoes in a row, two-storied, narrow buildings with a garage on the side and fourteen feet of lawn on the other. Each one was exactly like dozens of others in that area and only the added touches of the occupants made any difference—a white fence, a small front area of rose bushes, brightly painted steps, a distinctive front door, or perhaps a shady oak tree.

Their house, in the middle of the block, had a white fence encircling a well-groomed lawn. A climbing yellow rose bush bloomed profusely in the corner.

Thad checked through the house, making certain everything

was in order and opening windows to let in the fresh air, while Leigh prepared supper. Home air conditioners were forbidden by the government due to the energy crunch, and the house was stale and stuffy.

Leigh put two place mats on the table which sat in the middle of the square kitchen, admitting as she did that she was already missing her parents. Everything around her was a reminder of their love-filled lives. Dad had built all of the cupboards, and Mother took great pride in the old-fashioned hutch he had refinished. In one cupboard, and lining several basement shelves, were rows of home-canned food Mother had prepared for the winter. It was difficult to get vegetables, but this summer several ex-parishioners, now living in the country, had come in the night, bringing food they wanted to share with the Gordons. Always an unselfish person, Mother Gordon had dispensed much of those canned goods to needy people in the church. Even now, Leigh did the same thing, often taking food to nursery families.

The kitchen was a comfortable room crowded with good memories, and Leigh tried to remember only those events while putting supper on the table. A jar of homemade vegetable soup from the basement, cheese and crackers, apples they had brought from the conference grounds, and some hot coffee, diluted to make the contents of the jar go further, completed their meal.

"How about this." Thad came into the room with a full-blossomed yellow rose he had just picked from the front lawn.

"Oh, Thad, how beautiful!" She breathed deeply the delicate fragrance and reached into a cupboard for a vase. "It will make our supper just elegant."

He reached out and tugged a curl of her dark hair. "Huh," he grunted, "you and your elegance."

But Leigh was not fooled by his gruffness, for he was as sensitive to beauty as she. Why else would he have thought of picking the flower.

"I'm ashamed," she confessed while filling the soup bowls, "but I find it impossible not to be nervous on the streets. I know I should trust the Lord, but my courage fails me so often. I'm glad the nursery is just down the alley."

Thad pulled out a chair as she poured the coffee and sat down.

"Leigh, if there were ever anyone whose life of trust in God could convince me to follow Him, it would be you. You shouldn't feel that way."

He bowed his head and listened as Leigh thanked the Lord for safety in travel and for the food before them, and asked for His future protection. He had heard a thousand such prayers in his lifetime and wondered if God heard those pleas and if He were really able to do anything about them.

As they began to eat, he said, "I hate to think of all those speeches this week. I've heard it all before and it's the same rot we get in the news every day—'glory to the revolutionaries'!" He raised his cup in mock salute.

"I sympathize, but I'm grateful I haven't had to endure it yet. The government seems content to send us books to read and forms to fill out." She took a bit of cheese and reached for the crackers. "I wonder how long it will be before we have soldiers guarding the halls and endless meetings."

"It's bound to come," Thad answered, helping himself to more soup.

"Hello, anybody home?" a voice called into the hallway as the front door closed.

"Uncle Paul," they both responded, grinning at one another as they anticipated his cheery disposition. Thad pulled out a chair as the older man walked briskly into the room, planted a kiss on Leigh's cheek, and sat down.

"How about some supper?" Leigh asked, offering him the cheese platter.

He ran his hand through snow-white hair and answered, "No, thanks, honey. I had something earlier. But I'd love a cup of coffee. I thought you would be here by now and was anxious to find out how your Dad is feeling."

"Dad looks more rested," Thad answered, "but it's going to be awhile, I'm afraid, before he has the doctor's consent to come home."

He looked very innocent as he changed the subject, but Leigh never got any answers from him about Tom's activities and she could not help but wonder if he were involved in the militia.

Leigh gathered up some of the dishes, put them in the sink with a little soap, and turned on the tap.

"I'm afraid Mom is more worried than she lets on," she said, rinsing some silverware in warm water and stacking it in the drainer.

"Well, we'll need to keep praying, won't we?" Uncle Paul took a sip of coffee, glancing at Leigh over the rim of his cup. "The church people need his counsel and spiritual strength. The two lay pastors, Kirby and Lantz, are filling in quite well, but it is always difficult when the senior pastor is gone."

"I don't know if anyone missed him like we do," Thad remarked soberly, surprising Leigh by his openness.

She turned from the sink, a dripping plate in her hand. "Uncle Paul, many of our people have found your counsel so helpful. I'm sure the Lord will use you a great deal while Dad is away."

"That may be," her uncle responded, "but, we'll just take one day at a time." He finished his drink, got up from the table, and put the cup into the dishwater. "Well, thanks for the coffee. I think I'll go to my room and read a little before retiring."

"You needn't hurry off, Uncle," Thad said with a flashing smile at Leigh. "Why don't you keep me company while Leigh works?"

"I don't think that is what she plans tonight," Uncle Paul laughed, noticing the expression on Leigh's face. "An old man like me needs plenty of rest; otherwise, I just might lose my janitorial work for sleeping on the job."

"I hardly think the school would fire you; you've been there too long." Thad smiled, thinking that it was good to have such a stable person around. Nothing ever seemed to upset his uncle.

"You never know," laughed the older man. He patted Leigh on the shoulder and smiled at them both. "Well, good-night. God keep you in His care."

After he left the room, Thad reached for a dish towel from the cupboard door rack. "Only Uncle Paul could talk so lightly about his job. He doesn't worry, even when hundreds of people are losing their jobs every day. Did you see the picture in the *Freedom News* that showed hundreds standing in bread lines? I saw a copy on Rev. Miles' desk the day I took some of Dad's study books to him. He didn't even seem bothered that I noticed it either."

"I shouldn't wonder. You don't exactly keep your opinion of the government to yourself."

Thad grinned. "No, I guess not. What position does Houston take? Did you discuss the government?" Thad shot her a quick glance to see how she reacted to his questions. She had not been willing yet to discuss the man, no matter how often he opened the subject.

"No," she replied slowly, "we didn't discuss it at all. But I do remember how angry he was when the patrol shot that family."

"Just because he doesn't approve of such cruelty doesn't mean he is not a member of the Peoples Party."

"No, it doesn't," Leigh admitted, "but he just didn't seem the type. I can't believe he would be a party member."

"Why—because you don't want him to be?"

Leigh was silent, pondering his question. It was something she had already asked herself many times in the past two days.

She was trying so hard to look at Steve Houston with a pragmatic mind, not wanting her heart to rule her head as it so often did. She was a tender-hearted, sometimes impulsive person. This time, in this situation, she wanted to use a level-headed approach. But, she admitted to herself, it was extremely difficult considering the compelling, powerful personality that had swept into her life like a whirlwind. And it did not help to remember the obviously romantic scene he had created the last night she saw him. Was the constraint she felt a warning sign from the Lord? Oh, what did she feel!

Thad waved his hand before her face. "Hey, where did you go? I've been waiting minutes for an answer."

She glanced at him soberly. "No, I don't want him to be involved with the government. Now, to change the subject, what do you plan to do for the rest of the evening?"

"I want to unpack and get some books ready for tomorrow," he answered, submitting to her wish to stop discussing Houston.

After the kitchen was cleaned up and all the dishes put away, Leigh wandered into the living room. She felt too unsettled to put her mind to mundane things like unpacking and preparing for the next day. Going straight to the small music case in one corner, she selected a classical record and put it on the stereo. The deep emotion and thunder of Rachmaninoff was her favorite music, but tonight she needed the soothing sounds of Brahms and several of her hymn albums. If she kept the lights off she would not use up too much electricity.

Sitting in the comfortable blue lounge chair beside the fireplace, she closed her eyes. A tiny breeze stirred through the room, coming from the opened window at the front of the room, and instantly she was walking through the woods with Steve. It was so vivid a picture that she was startled to realize it was just a flashing memory. Her thoughts went back to that first meeting and the subsequent events. All the questions came tumbling back into her mind; the more they came, the more confused she felt.

Not one word had Steve said about ever seeing her again, and for all she knew, he could be hundreds of miles from Pennsylvania by now. Yet, he had announced his love with total conviction, and she confessed it was an exciting thought. She sighed deeply, deciding the only sensible course of action was to put him completely out of her mind.

She was so immersed in her thoughts that she failed to hear her cousin enter the house and come into the living room. "I said, hi!" Tom repeated laughingly. "Glad you're back!" His face was full of laughter and teasing, but he drove a surprised gasp from Leigh.

"Oh, Tom, I . . . I was thinking." She rose from her chair and went to greet him with a quick hug. "How long have you been standing there?"

"Just long enough to be talking to myself," he teased, "and to hear a deep sigh from you." He sauntered over to an easy chair and slowly submerged his long, lanky body down into the comfort of the cushions.

"Ahhh, I like this chair."

He gave her a quizzical look. "You were deep in thought—the records are finished." He nodded toward the music case and saw Leigh's face turn pink.

"I guess I wasn't really listening."

Thankful for a chance to hide her embarrassment, she went quickly to the stereo, stopped the clicking needle and turned the records over. While she stood there she wondered why she should feel so flustered, and decided it was because her cousin was not only a terrible tease but seemed to have an uncanny ability to notice little things. He was aware of her emotions and was probably about to embark on a question and answer period to discover the cause of her discomfort. Trying to direct his attention elsewhere she asked about the Sunday afternoon Bible study, but he would not be distracted.

"My, my, you must have had a very interesting vacation," he said, watching her carefully.

Thad entered the room in time to hear his cousin's remark and stopped further enquiries by a slight shake of his head.

"Well, Tom, old buddy, did you manage to keep the nation's officials in line while we were away?"

Tom glanced at Leigh with raised eyebrows but directed his comment to Thad. "Indeed I did," he replied banteringly. "I've even ousted that old man who played at being the head of the secret service. We will soon have a new National Intelligence Director."

"No kidding. What happened?" Thad was eager for any information that would feed his smouldering rage. He hated the government, but seemed compelled to know all he could about its activities.

"Well, we heard on the news this morning that Major Fieldston was resigning because of ill health. But the underground news says that he was not doing his job, which is true, but at least he had not started any major campaign against the churches yet."

"Who's the new man?"

"No one knows yet. Supposed to be announced any day, I understand."

"And you haven't even had a hint?" Thad found that hard to believe, for Tom somehow always seemed to have inside information, which he declared came from friends.

"It seems to be the best guarded secret of the year."

"Well, I'm sure we'll have the good news soon enough," Thad said with heavy sarcasm.

Leigh walked to the front window and stared out, listening to the soft music and trying to ignore their discussion. The revolution frightened, disgusted, and saddened her. People dying, girls molested, prison terms, bombings—ah! When would it all end?

She admitted that she often wondered just what she would do if faced with physical danger. The fact that she had been desperate to escape the soldiers, not help the man shot in the alley, was surely proof of her timorous heart. She could quickly recreate in her mind the horrible panic that completely dominated her mind when she saw the farmer gunned down, and when she had heard the soldiers on the trail.

But what worried her, more than anything else, was that someday she might be so frightened that she would deny Christ; that thought saddened her deeply.

She wondered if a person's strength in persecution came from daily spiritual growth and the thousands of little opportunities of learning to trust God. Perhaps Christians refused many moments of growth God offered because they were too caught up with the world and its pleasures. She did not want to be obsessed with these thoughts, but why could she not have peace about it all?

The Psalmist wrote, "I sought the Lord . . . and He delivered me from all my fears." What Leigh wanted to know was just how that came about.

She would sometimes remember stories of those who had faced persecution victoriously and was afraid she had not been cast in the same mold. Pondering over their lives, she wondered if they were special people that God used. There were many promises from God's Word for help and protection, but suppose He had chosen her to suffer as others had. What then?

A group of soldiers passed by on the sidewalk like a symbol of her fear and she drew back, bumping into Thad who had come to close the window.

"Sorry," she murmured, not looking at him as he locked the window.

"It's all right. I don't want any of them knowing you live here either." Had she turned, she would have been shocked by the look of hatred flooding her brother's face as he stared out the window. When he was honest with himself, Thad admitted this hatred was growing, and in the long, dark hours of the night when he could not sleep, he wondered what would be its end.

"Leigh, Tom has already gone to his room. He said goodnight, but you didn't hear him."

She frowned, turned from the window and walked slowly across the room, intending to turn the stereo off and put the records away.

"I've already taken care of the music," Thad said softly, aware that she had been deep in thought for over twenty minutes. "Go on to bed; I'll check the house." He turned to pick up an oil lamp from the coffee table and waited for her at the door.

Leigh bid him good-night and moved toward her room, passing her father's small study, which separated her room at the back of the house from the living room. Thad's bedroom was directly across the hall from her. Uncle Paul and Tom occupied two rooms directly above their bedrooms, and she could hear her cousin's footsteps on the bare floor. He was pacing back and forth, but it registered only vaguely in her mind. How good the Lord was to give her three men in the house rather than leaving her to face life alone in an apartment as some of her friends did.

She was still uneasy and a little depressed with her earlier thoughts, and after preparing for bed, she took her Bible, pulled back the spread, and got into bed. The candle lamp on the bedstand was bright enough to allow her to read if she held the Bible nearer the light.

Several weeks previously she had determined to study all the Bible had to say about courage. The small notebook tucked in the back of her Bible revealed what she had learned.

Using one of her father's reference books she learned that the Hebrew word for courage meant "to fasten upon."

Leigh grimaced ruefully, for that was certainly the thing she needed to do—fasten herself upon God. As she meditated on the Scriptures, one verse caught her attention. It read, "The righteous cry and the Lord hears, and delivers them out of all their troubles."

And the words that God had spoken to Joshua hundreds of years before came so clearly to her mind: "Be strong and of a good courage . . ."

Her heart was full of thankfulness as she began to pray. How kind God is to speak tenderly His word of encouragement. She thanked Him for His presence, His care of her parents, His patience with Thad.

"Surround them with your love and keep them in the center of your perfect will. Open Thad's heart to love Christ."

Then she hesitated, wanting to pray about Steve. *"If this feeling of joy is from you, Oh Lord, I thank you. If not . . ."*

She could not think further, for never before had she felt so confused, so strangely moved, about someone else. It was a new thing in her life, and she was not at all sure it was right. She could only commit it entirely to God who knew that her heart's desire was to please Him.

Suddenly her thoughts were interrupted by a noise in the hallway outside her door. She could hear footsteps, but whoever it was went past the bedrooms toward the back door. Frowning, she blew out the candle and slipped quickly from bed. Hearing the back door open she pulled the window curtain back slightly to peer out into the darkness. All that could be seen was a shadowy figure disappearing around the side of the house.

She moved quietly out into the hallway and stood at Thad's door, listening for any sound of his presence. She thought she could hear him moving about, but just to satisfy her uneasiness, she tapped softly on the door, and when he stood before her, said, "I heard someone go out."

"Tom probably had to stretch his legs a little," he answered reassuringly, thinking that Tom exhibited some activities that were appropriately militia-like. "Don't worry; I'll listen for awhile. I'm sure he will be back soon."

As he walked her back to her room, he teasingly asked, "Shall I tuck you in bed?"

"No, but don't tease me. I just wanted to be sure you weren't going out somewhere."

"Not me, I'm too tired." He waited until she had lit the candle again, then said good-night and closed her door.

Later, as Leigh drifted off to sleep the words of Scripture returned, "be not afraid." Her dreams were a jumble of those words, hiking through the woods, secret meetings, and Steve.

Chapter 6

After breakfast the next morning Thad rode his bicycle three miles to the high school, grumbling about the speeches as he left. "If I didn't have to get up earlier, I think I'd become a janitor, too."

Taking the yellow rose for her desk, Leigh locked the back door of their home and started down the alley, passing four houses before coming to the back of the church property where she opened the gate and walked into the playground.

Several friends who were just leaving their children for the day called their greetings and asked about Pastor Gordon. Most of the parents were members of the church, but there were a few new faces, and Leigh wondered what connection they might have with the National Intelligence Organization. It was terrible how suspicious one became living in a world of war, but she knew how innocent children could be used, to spy and report what was taught, who worked there, and the names of the families involved. It always saddened her to hear the children talk so easily of the revolution and killings, and see them role-play these events.

Entering the building through the back door, she could hear the happy chatter of the children as they greeted one another and talked about yesterday's happenings and today's anticipations. It took her longer than usual to get to her office at the end of the hall. There were many little friends to greet after a week of vacation, and they all had something special they simply had to tell her that minute. They crowded around, interrupting each other in their excitement, tugging at her hand for her attention, pushing others aside to stand close. It was a time she loved almost more than any other in her life, to be with children, to share in their lives and to be a recipient of their love.

Little Mark Kelly, a chubby, blond, blue-eyed fellow, was one of her favorites. This morning his light hair and beautiful eyes brought someone much older and a great deal taller to mind. Because they had a special relationship, Mark was usually satisfied just standing with his small hand in hers, while others vied for her attention. But today his eyes sparkled as he motioned for her to lean over so that he might whisper in her ear.

"Are you coming to our room today?" he asked softly.

Leigh smiled understandingly down into his face, wanting to hug him tightly, but merely said, "I'll try my very best, Mark."

"O.K.," he returned with a satisfied smile, and releasing her hand, skipped off to his room. Leigh continued down the hall, unlocked the door of her office, and glanced around the room as she put the vase on her desk. There was a metal desk and chair, a three-drawer file in one corner, built-in book shelves lining one wall, and two easy chairs for visitors. It would have been a plain, uninspiring room, except for the added touches which brought warmth and color to the simple furnishings.

Rich brown-colored drapes accented the multi-shaded brown rug, and bright orange floor pillows in the corner were used by the children when they visited her office. Admittedly these things were used items given to the school, but they suited her room perfectly. There was a fall landscape over the bookcases, painted by one of the nursery parents, and a small bulletin board on the opposite wall was full of cheery pictures and notes from the children. It was a room she enjoyed.

Because the church was working on a tight budget, the school had no money for a secretary and most of the paperwork was her duty, in addition to her other responsibilities. There were daily conferences with teachers concerning the needs of the classroom. She also worked with parents, often helping those who could not afford the small student fee, accepting clothing which she gave to other students, or exchanging weekly hours of labor in the church or nursery in place of fees. She spent extra hours combing stores for vitamins and food for the nursery kitchen. The director's job was never boring, until it came to the government paperwork.

Sitting down, she turned the swivel chair around to look out the window on a corner of the play area that was visible and already filled with a group of children earnestly exercising.

She smiled as she watched and decided that the difficulties of running a nursery and living in a war-torn city were amply compensated by being involved in shaping a life for eternity with Christ. She prayed that the school would remain open and functioning independently of the government for a long, long time.

The morning passed quickly as she conferred with some of the teachers about the week she had been away and tried to tackle the mountain of papers waiting. She flipped through them and frowned. It would mean hours of evening work at home in order to complete it all in time.

Lunch hours were always spent with the children, because it was so important to be with them. But the daily schedule had been arranged to allow each teacher a half-hour free time in the morning and again in the afternoon. Leigh liked to go upstairs to the church sanctuary, away from the noise and bustle, to regroup herself spiritually and mentally. It was a cherished opportunity, being alone with God in that special place; glancing at her watch, she was amazed to see that it was already time for her break.

Leaving her office, she walked up the stairs, into the sanctuary, and recognized the young woman at the front. She walked softly down the aisle, over a worn, green carpet, knelt beside the figure at the altar, and laid a hand on the one resting on the rail.

"Leigh, I'm glad you're home," Dorothy said, a smile lighting her face but not camouflaging tears glistening in her eyes, which she tried to blink away as she hugged her friend.

"Anything wrong, Dot?"

"No, I've been praying for Thad." No further explanation was needed, for she had loved Thad almost all her life, and had always shared her thoughts with Leigh.

Together they prayed, kneeling in the silence, feeling God's peace and tender care. In a moment, Leigh spoke softly, her eyes seeking the stained glass cross above them. "We thank you, Father, for your promises. Help us to believe them today."

She searched her friend's face as they walked out the door and back down the hallway to the stairs leading to the nursery below. "Would you like some fruit juice before you go back to class?"

"I'm fine now, Leigh. Please don't worry." Then with a thin veil of cheerfulness in her voice, Dorothy asked about the week of vacation. "Did you have a good time?"

"Yes." There was something in Leigh's response, too calm, too rigid, and Dorothy turned to stare at her.

"Are your parents all right?"

"Yes."

"Did you have trouble traveling?"

"No."

"Thad didn't upset your parents, did he?"

"No, we had a beautiful time together."

"Well," Dorothy said decisively, "something happened!"

"Oh?"

"Come on, Leigh. I know you as well as I know myself. You're answering my questions like a naughty child caught by the teacher."

"Now stop jumping to conclusions," Leigh responded evasively. "I'd better get back to that pile of work. See you later."

Dorothy stood rooted to the floor in surprise as her friend abruptly turned toward her office. Leigh had never evaded her questions before. Something must have happened, and Dorothy's eyes brightened as she determined to find out what it was.

Leigh sat down at her desk, but did not touch any of the work before her. Her thoughts, instead, were on Dorothy.

She had come to live with her grandparents next door to the Gordon home the day her parents had died in an airplane crash, when she was four years old. And they had been inseparable friends for twenty years.

Together they had gone through that awesome first day of school, fearful of being separated but armed with a remedy should it happen. They had agonized over the prospect of being in different classes all through their years of study, until college days when they maturely deferred to a heartless computer placing them in divergent schedules.

They had giggled together over all the girlish secrets of dreams and boys and plans, had tried their first skates, lipsticks and new hair styles together. They had attended the same church, the same summer camps, the same college. And when the desire to give life and heart to God in total commitment came, that, too, was done together.

For as long as Leigh could remember, Dorothy had been attracted to Thad. In elementary school they had been a happy trio, and it was hero worship then. In high school she became shy in his presence, but chattered constantly to Leigh about him. In college days she was radiant whenever he was near, her effervescent spirit bubbling over.

Now that she was a nursery teacher and the days were dangerous ones, she still held firmly to the hope that he would one day receive God's eternal life, and perhaps, sometime, would return her love. She adored him, but knew she could never be more than a friend as long as they were separated by their differing relationships to God. She loved the Lord with all her heart; Thad rejected Him in every area of his life. She prayed daily on his behalf and once confided, "God has never given me any indication that my hope is false."

A short knock on the office door broke through Leigh's thoughts, and at her response, Marian Becket, one of the ladies of the church, opened the door and asked if Leigh could use her help.

She was a small, quiet, middle-aged woman, one of the most unassuming, humble women Leigh knew. Always ready to give voluntarily of her time, she was the kind of person who did far more for others than most people realized. Leigh enjoyed her presence, for she was a confident and cheerful Christian.

"Isn't it a bea-u-tiful day," she said, bubbling over with enthusiasm as she sat in the easy chair nearest the desk. Her husband had dropped her off while he went to work in a nearby drug store. "I'll stay the day, if I can be of help, Leigh."

"You are a godsend, Marian. Just look at this stack of papers I have to struggle through!"

So they began to work, each one taking a set of papers and sharing answers, because the forms were so similar. One had to be sent to the city education department, another to state offices in Philadelphia, and another to national offices in Pittsburg. One form asked for the names of every student, and Leigh sighed.

"I have to do this list so often, I'd love to mimeograph copies, but they aren't acceptable. I know this is about the tenth time I've filled out these same papers this year. I wonder what they do with all of them?"

"Perhaps," her helper said with a smile, "they are used for wallpaper."

"That would be more valuable than filling some forgotten file drawer," Leigh responded, shaking her head and picking up another set of papers.

"Marian, you live in the same apartment building as little Mark and his mother, don't you. How are they getting along?

"Struggling, like everyone else. They've lived here ever since Mark was born, but I've only seen his father two or three times. That *is* hard on them."

Leigh nodded. "He was a salesman for one of the steel companies until half the plant was shut down. I wonder what he's doing now."

"Mrs. Kelly told me that in the summer he was in the Midwest, following the wheat harvest. His father owns a small farm out there somewhere. This winter he has been traveling anywhere he could find work."

"Is he able to send money to them?"

"Yes, I think so. But it's a real shame. They miss him so much."

"I'm sure they do," Leigh sighed. "I get so irritated thinking about the problems they face. I know Mrs. Kelly has pernicious anemia; is she able to work at all now?"

"No, but Martin and I help out all we can."

Leigh stopped her work and thought for a moment. "I have extra canned goods stored in the nursery kitchen. Take some with you today. And the next time we get some vitamins, especially B-12's, I'll save some for her."

It was soon lunch time. Marian spent the rest of the afternoon working as an aide in several of the classrooms, and Leigh was able to finish all the reports by the end of the day.

Walking home that evening, Leigh invited Dorothy over for supper. I'm going to use up the last of mother's homemade noodles, to stretch a bit of canned meat we have. Bring something along if you want."

The three of them had a good time together over supper. Thad was at his best, reminiscing over humorous experiences from their childhood days, reminding them of the crazy things they had done together. And he was successful in helping the girls forget the present and relax a little.

"Do you remember the time we built the raft to take a trip down the river Tom Sawyer style?"

"Yes," laughed Dorothy, "and did we ever get into trouble. We got stuck on the sandbar down by the bridge."

"It's a good thing we did," Leigh added. "We would have been in real trouble if we'd gotten close to the rapids on that flimsy thing!"

"It wasn't flimsy!" Thad said indignantly.

"It was too," Leigh retorted. "We had two barrels from the gas station, a piece of plywood left over from somebody's building, and a rope that wasn't much bigger than my thumb."

"What I remember," Dorothy interjected, "is that we were properly punished for our adventure."

"Well, so much for rafts," Thad quipped with a grin. "I can't spend the entire evening entertaining you two."

Above the mocking groans of the two women, he said, "I've got a ten-page report to fill out before tomorrow morning, and I'd better get it done. If I wait too late, it's bound to put me to sleep before I'm half through. Enjoy yourselves."

"Over the dishes, I suppose. It's kind of you to run out when there is work to be done." Leigh taunted him in fun while Dorothy sat watching him with undisguised adoration in her eyes.

"Well, first things first, you know," he answered, and with an amused look at their faces, left the room.

As they put food away and washed the dishes, Dorothy questioned Leigh again about her vacation.

"Something happened while you were away, Leigh, and it's not like you to keep things from me. We've always shared everything. Aren't you going to tell me?"

Leigh scrubbed a pan lid until it was shining in the dim light, not quite knowing what she wanted to share.

"Dot, I want to talk about it, but I just don't know what my feelings are."

"You've told me that talking to someone else helps crystalize your thoughts," Dorothy prodded. She took the lid from Leigh's hand, rinsed it and then wiped it slowly, waiting for her to begin.

"You're right," Leigh said hesitantly. "I . . . I met a man . . ."

"Ahah," Dorothy interrupted. "I knew it! You had that funny look about you today."

"I did?" Leigh looked up in surprise. "What kind of look is that?"

"The kind you say I have when I look at Thad," Dorothy

murmured knowingly. "Come on—dishes are done. Let's go sit in the living room."

They sat together on the sofa; Leigh's legs curled up under her as she absentmindedly played with a pillow while explaining about the tall, blond man who had shared a sunset with her and then knocked her emotions about like a Ping-Pong ball.

"I've never met anyone like him, Dot. It's rather unexplainable, feeling so close to someone you hardly know."

"After a few minutes at the cliff?" Dorothy asked, astounded at her friend's impulsiveness. "Did you see him again?"

"Oh, yes, and what a day that was! We took a group of teens to work in the gardens back in the hills and saw an army patrol abuse a farming family." Then she went on to tell how the entire family had been killed, and the sobering yet amusing story of the same soldiers chasing a cow.

"How did he ever find you in those bushes, Leigh?"

"I asked him the same question, but didn't get much of an answer. He just laughed. It was odd, Dot, the way he kept reminding me of someone with a lot of military experience. He reacted that way during the entire day. And the teens responded to him like nothing I've seen before."

"He sounds terrific. What else happened?"

Leigh hesitated a long moment as her mind went back to the last time she saw Steve, standing in the shadows near the conference auditorium.

"Well, he . . . he said that he cared for me," she added slowly.

"Really! He sounds like a fast worker to me."

"No, it wasn't like that, Dot." Leigh tried to explain the conversation of that last night of his reasons for speaking so quickly and how extremely concerned he had been that she trust him.

"I really don't know what to make of it all," she said with a sigh.

"Is he a Christian?" The question brought a worried frown to Leigh's face, and she plucked at the fringed pillow in her lap.

"That's the problem; he never came right out and said so, but we didn't have much time for long talks. He was warm and gentle and . . . wholesome . . . and . . ." Leigh paused and shrugged her shoulders helplessly, "and there was just something good and strong about him." She found it difficult to put a definitive finger on what she wanted to express.

"How do you feel about him?" Dorothy asked.

"I don't know. I find myself thinking about him a great deal, and I've never felt like this before." She cupped her chin in her hand and stared across the room. "I just don't know if the Lord is leading in this."

"Well, don't worry about things before they happen. You do that, you know. I'm sure you've prayed about it, and the rest is up to the Lord."

"Well," Leigh said, affecting a nonchalant pose, "I'll probably never see him again."

They talked for a long while, until Thad came into the room moaning about their constant chatter. "How can you talk so much?"

"Do you have your report done already?" His sister looked up at him in surprise.

"Already! Do you realize it's been almost two hours? I'll never understand how women can talk so long without even realizing it. What on earth do you find to discuss so intently for so long?"

His puzzled frown made the girls burst into laughter, and they teased him about all the fun he missed while slaving away on his report.

He walked Dorothy to her door a few minutes later and asked, "Did Leigh mention her new friend to you?"

"Yes, why?"

"Oh, I was just wondering. I have an uneasy feeling about him, that's all."

"It isn't brotherly jealousy, is it, Thad?"

"Well," he smiled sweetly at her, "I do have to watch over my best girl friends."

"Oh?" For once in her lifetime her usually quick tongue was stilled. Dorothy wanted to pursue that statement, but was reluctant to press further. Suddenly overcome with the love she felt for this man, she searched his face sadly, reached up to touch his arm and said, "Let's allow the Lord to take care of it, Thad."

Her plea underscored more than Leigh's problem, and Thad knew it. He felt her loving concern, more than he ever had, and it touched something deep inside. But, unwilling to allow it to flower, he pursued the former subject with a stubborn spirit.

"I don't like him, Dot. And I'll do all I can to keep him away from her!"

"Don't do that, Thad." Dorothy's voice was soft but urgent.

"I know it will work out." She waited for a response that did not come, and knew it was time to close the subject. "Well, I'm sure Grandma is waiting for me. Good night, Thad."

He watched her disappear through the door, wondering why he had never noticed how beautiful she was. Her vivacious spirit and positive outlook on life made her more noticeable than his quiet, impulsive loving sister. Their differences complemented one another, and they made a good team.

He sighed as he retraced his steps to their kitchen door, unlocked it slowly, and let himself in. As he turned to bolt the door for the night, he admitted that he would never stand a chance with Dorothy, should he get to that point, until he had a change of heart about religion. And he was too honest to fake that change in order to marry her.

As if mocking his thoughts, there came the sounds of distant gun shots and moaning of sirens ripping the air. The nightly raids were beginning again, somewhere in the city, and he felt sorry for the victims caught in the turmoil.

It was an hour later, while Thad moved from room to room, securing the house for the night, that Dorothy cautiously opened her front door, and after checking both directions, walked quickly down the steps to perform an errand for Grandma Perry.

Mrs. Cummins, an eighty-six-year-old widow who lived two doors away, had called for help.

While attempting to move through her kitchen in the darkness, she had slipped and fallen, and unable to get up, had pulled the telephone to the floor and called the Perrys. Hurrying down the sidewalk, Dorothy admitted she should not go alone but hated to disturb anyone else for such a small thing. There had been no sign of anyone on the street when she left her house, and since it was such a short distance, she felt she would be safe.

She rescued Mrs. Cummins from the floor, made sure there were no injuries, and put the old lady to bed. She gave her an aspirin to help relieve possible pain from the fall, and sat beside her bed for about twenty minutes. Then, emphatically reassured by Mrs. Cummins that she would be perfectly fine, Dorothy started for home.

Outside on the sidewalk, she felt the darkness closing in and chided herself for not bringing a flashlight. The quietness was oppressive and unsettling; she quickened her steps, fighting an overwhelming urge to look back over her shoulder.

She passed the neighbor's driveway, stumbled over a slight rise in the sidewalk, and just as she neared the edge of her lawn heard a jeep roar around the corner and come to a screeching halt in front of her home.

Terror filled her mind and she made a wild dash for the safety of the front door, but halfway there was jerked backward by two chuckling, highly amused soldiers.

"Not so fast, my dear young thing," a hard voice whispered in her ear as a hand clamped down over her mouth.

She struggled furiously against the strong hands that pinned her arms down and steered her toward the street, but it was useless. Her attempts to get free were as successful as the struggle of a bird in a trap, and her mind was screaming in sickening revulsion.

Still unable to cry for help, she felt the soldiers lift her like so much baggage and push her roughly into the arms of someone in the back seat.

"Let's go!" commanded one man as he leaped into the jeep. The driver shoved the jeep into gear, slammed his foot down hard on the accelerator, and they sped away, a panic-stricken Dorothy catching a glimpse of the Gordon home as it flashed by.

She thought she saw a silhouette framed in the lighted front window, and it mocked her silently. Was Thad standing there, wondering what the soldiers were doing? She groaned aloud. He may never know he watched the jeep that carried her away to the army post and a night of unrelieved horror.

The soldier on her right threw a thick piece of cloth over her mouth, jerking her head back as he tied it in a knot.

"Be careful with her," a voice from the front seat warned, "we don't want her bruised—yet."

She continued to fight as they bound her wrists together, wanting to fling herself out of the jeep, letting its tires crush her to death rather than face the immediate future; but her captors weren't giving her the opportunity. *"Oh, Lord, help me!"*

They drove swiftly across town, purposely avoiding the busier streets since the authorities ignored their evil activity as long as the public did not actually see what happened.

All too soon the main gate of the military post loomed up before them. After stopping at the check point to allow the guard to wave them through, they moved slowly down the main road.

In the glaring perimeter lights of the post, Dorothy saw long rows of drab green barracks, and tensed at each building they came to, expecting momentarily to be dragged from the jeep. But they drove on, passing one unit after another, the men laughing at her mounting apprehension.

The soldier in the front passenger seat turned to look at her. "You're going to keep company with the brass tonight," he said spitefully, calling her the filthiest name he knew; she turned her head away, refusing to acknowledge his information.

The rows of ugly barracks gave way to a new residential section, and the jeep finally rolled to a stop in front of an apartment building marked "Officers Quarters." Dorothy felt her heart jerk once in silent protest, and she cringed inwardly as two of the soldiers pulled her from her place in the back seat and began marching her down the sidewalk, hardly giving her time to put one foot in front of the other. One of them pulled a key from his pocket, unlocked the front door, and shoving her inside, walked down a shadowy hallway until they arrived at an apartment near the back of the building. The door bell under the name plate reading "Colonel Montagano" was pushed, and a deep voice called out, "Come in."

Dorothy tried to resist the men, making one last effort to get away, but they held her firmly by the arms and pulled her through the opened door into the most richly furnished room she had seen in years. Even in her fear, it made an impact upon her senses.

She saw dark mahogany woodwork everywhere: the coffee table, the stereo and television unit, the edges of chairs and sofa, and the bar. Mirrored squares filling one wall reflected the shining brass light fixtures, especially an unusually shaped lamp hanging in one corner. The upholstery, the rugs, and the accent pieces were all in deep blue, and Dorothy knew she would hate that color for the rest of her life. It was a heavy, luxurious room calculated to being overwhelming.

She was unaware of the tall figure standing in an alcove to her right until both soldiers stiffened to a salute as he moved forward into the edge of her vision, his black eyes making a sweeping inspection of her as she stood, bound and trembling. Satisfied, he reached into his pocket, withdrew a roll of bills, and handed them to her abductors.

"She'll do very well," he said, a burning light growing in his eyes. "You're dismissed." He returned their departing salute, locked the door behind them, and moved leisurely forward to stand in front of Dorothy.

At her frantic glance at the door, he murmured, "It's locked and the back door is heavily bolted. You can't get out, and it is useless to scream, because no one will come to your rescue."

He reached out, his fingers running lightly over her cheek and she recoiled from his touch, her look of disgust only bringing a smile of satisfaction to his face. "I enjoy your contempt, but I"ll see that you don't carry it too far."

She closed her eyes against his eagerness and felt his hand on her arm, guiding her to the sofa. "Sit down," he commanded, reaching out to untie the gag. "I want to know if the sound of your voice is as pretty as you are."

Dorothy reluctantly sat down and when the cloth was removed, touched her mouth with hands still bound together. The gag had been too tight and left her mouth sore. Warily she waited for the Colonel's next move.

"What's your name?" he asked, turning toward the bar at the end of the room. When she refused to answer, he repeated his question, his voice sharp and his eyes narrowing as he looked at her across the small space of the room. In his black uniform, with black eyes and hair, he seemed a demon incarnate, and Dorothy shuddered.

"I asked your name!"

Still she said nothing.

The anger swirled up into his face as he took the space between with wide, quick steps. Reaching out, he grasped her by the shoulder and gave her a hard shake. "Don't give me any trouble! Answer me!"

"M-my n-name is Dot," she stuttered, realizing that a refusal to talk would only increase his wrath and perhaps spark something wild and unpredictable in him.

"That's better." Releasing his hold, he asked, "How old are you?"

"Twenty-four," she whispered. Then she began to speak aloud what had been a silent, fervent prayer during the entire last hour. With her eyes closed she pleaded, "Oh, Lord God, I need your help. Stop Satan's influence. Take away this evil spirit. Deliver me from . . ."

"Shut up," he growled, slapping her across the face. "Your prayers won't help! Perhaps," he said, his black eyes blazing, "perhaps you'd be wiser to pray to me. Yes, do that!" And he pulled her forward so that she fell on her knees before him. "Pray, Dot. Pray to me and not your God. I can hear you, and He can't!"

But she began to pray again, looking him straight in the eyes as he tilted her head back, and speaking again to the Lord God who was the only power in heaven and earth that could help her. Another slap across the face and a roar of "Shut up!" stilled her voice, but she continued to kneel, and the tears were spilling from her eyes and running down her cheeks. She saw a look of pure sadistic pleasure in his face as he watched her agony.

"You'll get no reprieve from me because of tears," he spit out, and releasing her, turned back to the bar.

She struggled up on the sofa, and sat staring at him, her mind unable to accept the fact that she was about to be physically assaulted. That happened to other women, not her!

The Colonel would have been a handsome man, she thought, but his satiated look advertised how he had gorged himself on every sin known to man, and it was an acute revulsion to her. Her heart fluttered and began to pound; she could feel it in her finger tips as a horrifying thought came seeping into her mind. If he were that depraved, there was no end to what he might do to her in the next few hours. She was shaking so hard she could do no more than turn to look wildly about the room for some sort of weapon to use, if the opportunity should come. However, his experience was vast—other women must have tried that, and he knew what she was thinking.

"There is nothing in the room that you can pick up, except the sofa pillows. And I hardly think they will do much damage."

His laughter was low and menacing as he pulled the cork from a bottle and poured out two drinks. She saw him tip some kind of white powder into one of the stemmed glasses. *"Oh, Lord, no,"* she thought, *"not that!"*

He picked up the two glasses. Moving slowly toward her, he swirled the contents of her drink around and around and held it out to her.

"Here, drink this."

"NO!"

He set his glass on the coffee table in front of her and moved closer. "I said drink it."

"NO! I won't! I'd rather die than drink that or submit to your filthy hands."

She hardly had the words out of her mouth before he moved, and she found herself pushed back into the sofa cushions with his hand prying her mouth open as he began to pour the liquid down her throat. She spit out all she could and his hold tightened until she thought she would suffocate. Finally, her instinct for survival made her swallow, and that was all that was needed to give him success. The drink spilled into her mouth, burning her throat and making her cough.

When the glass was empty, he released her and smiled maliciously. "You'll be relaxed soon." Knowing that she could do nothing to hurt him, he turned his back, picked up his drink, and moved to an easy chair opposite the sofa.

In a few seconds Dorothy began to feel dizzy and fought to keep her senses, blinking her eyes and slamming her hands down on her knees. Her anger at seeing his leering smile from across the room helped to hold off the drug's reaction. She struggled to her feet. If she could just keep walking, perhaps that would help.

"Don't worry, you won't go to sleep. I didn't give you that much." The Colonel got up, moved to the stereo unit, and turned on some music, its loudness pounding into her brain and making her disoriented. It seemed to work in unison with the drug, and she leaned against a wall to get her bearings.

She saw him lower the lights and move lazily toward her, saying things she never wanted to hear; her mind was too relaxed to blot it out.

She tried to summon God's Word to her mind, so that she might not be aware of his words. *"The Lord . . . is . . . my . . . rock . . . and my . . ."* What was the word she wanted! *"Lord, speak to me with your Word."*

Her mind whirled, turning faster and faster until even her thoughts seemed upside-down. Then it unwound like a top, spinning out the Colonel's words into extended motion, until slower and slower . . .

And then, she slid gradually and helplessly to the floor.

Thad had stepped to the window that night, hearing the jeep move off down the street, but had not thought much about it. Then the telephone rang about thirty minutes later, and Grandma Perry asked if Dorothy had stopped by after helping Mrs. Cummins. It took Thad less than one minute to enlist Tom's help, and the men made plans, knowing full well that if Dorothy had been kidnapped by soldiers, they would not find her until dawn.

Tom sent Leigh to stay with the Perrys so that they might encourage each other while they waited, and asked Uncle Paul to stay at home, on the smallest chance someone would call. Then he and Thad left for the army barracks, recruiting two friends from church and an old van from a plumber he knew.

And the long night crept by, agonizingly slow and silent. Leigh walked the floor, talked with Dorothy's invalid grandfather, drank coffee, prayed with Grandma Perry, and cried. She jumped at every sound in the hope that it would be someone returning with Dorothy unharmed; she wrestled with God as Jacob once did, demanding that He show her why such things had to be.

Tom stationed the two friends at the exits where girls were usually left; then he and Thad prowled continually around the high fence that surrounded the military installation. Thad was almost beside himself with anger, threatening to kill the first soldier he saw; Tom knew he dared not leave him alone. "Thad, killing someone will not get Dorothy back," he reminded his cousin.

The last time they called home from a nearby telephone booth, Tom questioned his father. "No news? Nothing from Leigh, either?" He looked at Thad out of the corner of his eye. "It's after 5 A.M. If she's in there, it won't be too long before we find her." Lowering his voice so that Thad could not hear, he said, "Dad, pray that we find her alive!"

They arrived at the second gate just as the eastern sky began to lighten from black to a pale blue, standing in an alley that ran alongside an abandoned warehouse, across the street from the military post.

"Not a thing yet," reported the young man waiting in the shadows where he had an excellent view.

"Look!" Thad urged Tom, pointing to the left.

They watched a jeep pull to a stop. An officer got out, yanked a girl from the front seat and guided her to the gate. As she passed through the lighted exit, Thad moaned, "It's her!"

It took both friends to hold him back, and for a minute Tom thought he might have to knock him out. "She needs help," Thad pleaded. "Look at her—she can hardly walk!"

"Wait until the jeep is gone, Thad! We can't help her if we're all shot by that officer."

Dorothy stood bewildered and vulnerable at the edge of the road. But the Colonel did not care; he had already started the engine and pulled away from the desolate figure under the light. As soon as the jeep was gone, Thad started across the road.

"Thad, don't frighten her. Go slow; tell her who you are. Man, be careful—she's frightened to death!" Tom moved in behind Thad, whispering his warnings as they walked softly toward Dorothy.

Hearing footsteps, she looked up. "No, please no more!" she whispered, holding up a hand to ward off the approaching men and taking a step backward.

Thad stopped just a few feet from her, his hands clenched at his sides, but his voice gentle and calm. "Dorothy, don't be afraid. It's me, Thad. I've come to take you home." And he held out a hand.

"Thad?" she asked, staring at him in confusion. And then, mercifully, fainted.

Thad held her in his arms and all the way home kept whispering, "It's all right, Dorothy. You're safe." But he could not break through the wall of shock that surrounded her, and her dazed silence shook the four men in the van to the core.

Dr. Evans answered Uncle Paul's summons and arrived shortly after 7 o'clock that morning. He checked her carefully and with infinite kindness. He had seen so many cases like this recently and felt a great frustration and sorrow.

"I can't put her in a hospital where she belongs because I'm a Christian," he said to Grandma Perry and Leigh. "I haven't had a patient admitted anywhere in the city for a year now. I'll do what I can."

After giving her a sedative, he returned to talk with the men waiting in the Perrys' front room. "She should sleep through most of the day. I want her in bed at least through tomorrow and away from the nursery for the rest of the week."

Grandma Perry spent most of her time nursing Dorothy, and Leigh stayed during the evenings. They tried to help her feel secure and loved, and talked about her experience only when she wanted.

Thursday night when Leigh arrived, she found her friend in an intense game of chess with her grandfather. She looked up with a big smile and said, "Leigh, I'm going to the nursery tomorrow." And to forestall any objections she added, "I've got to get busy and get my mind off things. Besides, I miss my little ones.''

And for the first time since her ordeal, she wanted to visit with Thad. She wanted to explain to him that she had to believe that God loved His children too much and was too wise not to bring into their lives what He felt was best. She had to leave it at that, for her sanity's sake.

Chapter 7

On Sunday evening Leigh was thinking of her favorite hymn while preparing supper—a vegetable casserole thinly layered with cheese. She had just returned from the afternoon service at church and knew that Uncle Paul and Tom would not be home, but it was one of Thad's favorite dishes. The hymn kept running through her mind:

"He'll keep you through the darkest night,
Son of God, eternal Light,
Even though your faith is dim,
He will keep you close to Him."

The casserole was in the oven and she was setting the table when she heard Thad open the back door and push his bicycle into the hallway where it could be safely kept.

"I'm in the kitchen," she called out with a smile and waited for his usual reply.

Normally he was talking and joking before he was halfway down the hall—it was his method of humoring her, she thought with amusement. But now his steps were dragging and heavy as he walked toward the kitchen. His silence puzzled Leigh, and she turned to look at him as he entered the room.

He stopped by the table, staring at a newspaper he had bought on his way home from visiting a friend. His face was a study of shock and disgust.

"What's the matter—no sports page today?" The city newspaper, always full of government propaganda, had long ago dropped Thad's favorite section, and this question had become a private joke between them. She used it now as a shield against a rising suspicion that he was bringing catastrophic news.

He made no response, but there was a hint of compassion in his eyes as he looked up, thinking that she would have to know sooner or later. Shrugging his shoulders in helpless resignation, he tossed the paper down on the table in front of her.

There on the front page was the picture of a man dressed in the black uniform of the American Peoples Army, and the headlines screamed at Leigh:

MAJOR STEPHEN HOUSTON NEW NIO DIRECTOR. It was Steve!

Leigh gasped in disbelief. A wave of weakness swept over her and she caught hold of the chair to keep from sinking to the floor. The color drained from her face, and Thad, thinking she was about to faint, reached out to help. But she pushed his hand away and stared at the picture, grief knotting the muscles of her stomach.

Her world came crashing down over her head in one single moment. The emotions of disbelief and shock rushed through her like the winds of a tornado, and she gasped for breath.

"How could he!"

As Thad watched, feeling very inadequate, his mind was filled with mounting hatred. It was deep, and it seared his mind. It took control of him in a way he never dreamed possible. First, Dorothy; now, Leigh. And unable to do anything about Dorothy's assailant, he vented his anger on Steve Houston.

"I'll get even with him. No man's going to hurt you like this and live!" He did not realize he had spoken aloud until he heard Leigh speak and felt her restraining hand on his arm.

"Thad, no!" Her voice broke and tears flowed unnoticed from dark eyes. "Leave it with God," she begged.

"With God! Hah, what will He do? What did He do for Dot!" The scorn spilling over his words seemed to slap her in the face.

Silently, she turned and left the kitchen. Supper was forgotten. She was unaware of the need to eat as desperation filled her entire being, and, walking into the living room, she sank down on a chair. The newspaper shook in her hands, and the tears continued to stream down pale cheeks. All the sorrow and grief she had felt for Dorothy was now compounded with this shock, and she simply could not handle it all.

Thad sat in the chair opposite her, watching carefully and waiting to help, while she stared at the picture, letting the information in the accompanying article penetrate her mind, all the while struggling to accept the stark truth.

It was a full ten minutes before she became aware of her brother's presence and looked up with a start. "You haven't had any supper," she said in a rigid voice.

Getting up from her chair, she looked once more at Steve's picture and with sudden disgust, hurled it across the room where it scattered to the floor. So much for budding dreams, she thought bitterly.

"I don't need anything, Leigh."

Ignoring his protests and driven by an unrelenting need for activity, she began moving about the kitchen. From counter top to table, to the stove and back to the cupboard, she picked up plates and set them down, cleared off the table as though they had already eaten, opened the oven to take out the casserole and then left it there. The pots and pans weren't where they should be, and she did not seem capable of setting anything right.

"Sis," Thad interrupted her activity gently, "you've already filled that once; you needn't do it again." He took the coffee pot from her hands and put it back on the stove, realizing that she must start talking before she blew up.

"Judging from your reaction to the news, I'd say you're in love with this guy."

A dish clattered down on the table as she stared at him.

"I said . . ."

"I heard what you said," she murmured and looked down at the plate with unseeing eyes. "I . . ." she paused, searching for the words she wanted. "I thought I cared for him."

Thad shook his head at the bland expression she had used, but chose to ignore it for the moment. "And you feel guilty?" He continued probing. "He seems like a traitor now."

"I . . . I don't think I need to discuss my feelings with you," she retorted stiffly.

"Why not?" He folded his arms and leaned against the counter top. "Because I'm not a Christian and therefore can't possibly understand?" The question was spoken sharply in an attempt to arouse her still more.

Leigh responded as he had hoped; she felt as if she had been slapped, and sat down quickly. "Of course not!" Her voice was full of anger and frustration, and it broke as she tried to explain. "I . . . just can't think."

"Or don't want to?" He goaded her on. "You do feel guilty, because you're not sure what to think of him now. Right?"

She nodded her head, and, determined not to give in to tears, said angrily, "You make me sound so bigoted!"

"You know I'm not trying to do that."

"This is ridiculous! I hardly know the man, so why should I care what he does!" It was a weak attempt to ease the hurt she felt, and Thad knew it.

He knelt down beside her chair, took her hand in his, and admonished gently, "Leigh, admit it; you're attracted to him. There's no shame in that."

"Maybe I was, but it . . ." She took a deep breath. "This is it, as far as I'm concerned. He had his fun at my expense, but that's all. Anyway, I'm not likely to see him, now that he's so important."

"You know very well you haven't seen the last of him."

"I'm not interested. I don't care!"

"Be honest, Leigh." Thad shook his head. "Don't try to solve anything with a lie."

She gritted her teeth in anger. "I said, I don't care what . . ." The sound of the front doorbell interrupted her declaration; she moved out of the kitchen to answer its summons but was stopped by Thad in the dining room.

"You know you're not to answer that door." His warning held her back, and he walked to the window overlooking the front steps. Pulling the curtain aside, he peered out and said sarcastically, "What do you know—it's your blond friend."

In spite of what she had just vowed to Thad, there was unconscious pleasure on her face as she opened the door to face Steve. He saw it, rejoiced in it, and then watched it disappear as she looked down at his uniform. With a sharp intake of breath she backed away as if seeing a poisonous snake on the front doorstep, coiled and ready to strike.

"May I come in?"—the same soft gentleness she had remembered so often, and she was appalled at its power over her. In that instant she had to admit that she did care what he was doing with his life.

She could not respond, for she was immobilized by the shock and disbelief she had felt earlier, and stood staring at him with wary, sad eyes.

"Well, well. Look who is here—the new director of the National Intelligence Organization! Too bad we don't have a drum roll for you!" Thad leaned against the dining room door frame, his arms folded, looking deceptively at ease, but anger dominated his face, his eyes snapping furiously.

Turning to speak to him, Steve felt concern at the wall of hostility in Thad and knew it would surely come to an untimely explosion. It would serve no good purpose to remind them that he could now demand to see Leigh, using his present position of authority to obtain what he wanted. "Thad, I'm sorry to trouble you, but I must talk with Leigh."

The urgency in his voice struck a cord of response in Thad, but he refused to acknowledge it. "Haven't you talked with her enough, Major Houston," he demanded, spitting the words out like water hitting a hot stove. "Why don't you go back to your big, important headquarters. I'm sure you have lots of spying to do. Or is that your purpose here?"

It was his mounting fury that finally shattered Leigh's silence, and in a faltering voice, she pleaded, "Stop it, Thad. Don't do this." The two men had to be separated before Thad lost all control."

Trembling from head to foot, she glanced up into Steve's face and saw the unmistakable look of tenderness in his eyes, but turned sharply away to avoid it. Reluctantly she said, "Come into the living room if you wish." She had caught a glimpse of determination that said he would not be opposed and knew she could not escape this confrontation. "Let's get this over with."

Thad stalked back into the kitchen, muttering to himself that the two women he cared for the most had been hurt by military men, and someday he was going to get his revenge. He spooned some of the casserole onto his plate, sat down, and tried to eat.

In the living room, Leigh stood clutching the back of a chair as though she would fall into a bottomless pit if she were to let go. She heard the door click shut and felt Steve move nearer. Her heart cried out silently that she not be hurt further. Being with him now when her emotions were in wild upheaval and her mind still numb from this latest blow was almost more than she could manage.

His voice was low and close behind her. "It seems ironic that I must always apologize to you." He waited for a comment, and when none came, added, "I'm sorry to have hurt you, Leigh."

"If you came to apologize, then you've done it, and you can go," she responded.

"Please, turn around and look at me."

Reluctantly she obeyed, leaning against the chair for support, and loath to look at him as he had requested, stared down at her tightly clasped hands. "Do you . . ." she asked nervously, "do you want to sit down?"

She moved toward an easy chair, to put as much distance between them as possible, but he caught her hand. "Yes," he said, "but I want you beside me." Ignoring her struggle to get free, he held her hand tightly and led her to the sofa. Then leaning forward so that he might see her face, he began to speak cautiously.

"How are you?"

"Fine, thank you!" It was a stilted, over-bright response.

"Any trouble getting home from the conference grounds last Sunday?"

She shook her head. "No."

"But something has happened to you since then." He saw a sadness in her eyes that had not been there before. "What is it?"

She turned to look at his uniform and then up into his eyes. "An officer, in that same kind of uniform, abducted Dorothy last Monday night." It was an accusation of his alliance with such wicked men. "Can you imagine what I thought when I read the newspaper today?"

Steve shifted his position and sat staring across the room, his hands clasped across his knees. "You can be assured, Leigh, I'll find out who it was and see that he's punished. You have my word."

"Your word?" Leigh asked in astonishment. "What do I know about your word now?"

He took her hand quickly, holding it in his own and said, "Leigh, about that last night at the conference. I told you that I care for you. I meant every word. And, if you remember, I asked for your trust."

Her eyes turned to his as she protested. "Yes, but you didn't tell me about your appointment. You're a . . . a member of the army, part of the New Democracy that is anti-God! What am I supposed to think?"

"I couldn't tell you then and I won't explain now, for your own safety. That's why I asked for your trust."

His free hand rubbed the back of his neck in a frustrated gesture while he waited, watching her face mirror her inner struggle. He disliked being the cause of her distress, but the thought of life without her was unbearable. He had to take this chance.

"I asked if there were someone else in your life."

"No, there isn't anyone," she said, emphasizing the last word.

"I could have followed my predecessor's example and have you imprisoned or forcefully installed in my apartment . . ." His voice was tinted with irony, and his hand crushed hers.

At her startled glance he smiled. "Haven't you asked yourself why I haven't done that?"

At her look of distress, his voice softened. "I'm not as unprincipled as you seem to think."

"Then why did you come?" The question was wrenched from her in anguish. "Why pick on me?"

"Why!" He looked away. "That shouldn't be too difficult to understand, after what I've said. Don't condemn me until you've heard all the facts."

"I'm waiting to hear them."

"No," he said slowly. "Not yet. Put a little faith in my words, Leigh."

He sighed and sat watching her for a long moment, trying to frame his explanation to be at once satisfying and unrevealing, for her safety and for his assignment.

"I shouldn't be here. It's difficult for me to go anywhere now without being followed. I'm jeopardizing your safety. I came . . " He paused and looked down at her small hand in his. "I came because I need your support. I need your trust. Won't you believe me, Leigh?"

"Believe what?" she demanded. "After seeing your picture splashed all over the paper and reading that you're the new NIO director, and, as such, will be jailing my Christian friends, what can I believe?"

Releasing her hand, he stood up and began pacing back and forth. Her eyes followed him, noting the black uniform that fitted him like a second skin and feeling repulsed by all it represented, yet in all honesty recognizing her desire to believe the best of him. But the question uppermost in her mind and upon which everything seemed to be suspended was—did he know Jesus Christ as his Saviour? Was he a believer? But she could not form the words; fear of disappointment held them back.

He passed the scattered newspaper, stopped to move the front page with his toe, and then shot her a quick glance and a wry smile. But he made no remark about seeing it lying in rejection on the floor.

He stopped before her then, and the fierceness in his voice and absolute self-assurance in his manner kept her eyes riveted to his.

"Believe that my feeling for you is pure love. There is nothing corrupt in it." His voice was low but loaded with power. "Believe that there is a good reason for my position as NIO director. And except for that, I must not tell you more."

He leaned toward her slightly as he spoke a solemn warning, "Leigh, if you were ever questioned by the wrong person, it would be to your advantage to know absolutely nothing!"

Before she had time to assimilate that information, he gave her something else to ponder. "I won't be able to see you often, and if we meet in public we must pretend to be strangers."

He sat down again and took her hand; she felt his eyes searching her face. The room was silent, but filled with tense emotion, and Leigh did not dare look at him.

"I have nothing to offer you, Leigh, until this is over, except my love."

The doorbell rang shrilly through the quietness of the house— four short rings, like a signal. Leigh sighed, thankful for its interruption.

"One of my associates, reminding me of my evening duties," Steve said lightly. He stood, pulling her up with him, and, reaching into the pocket of his uniform, said, "I've had something made for you." He slipped a ring on her finger.

"This has special markings on the back. It's a code for a private telephone in my office. I want you to call if you ever need help." He explained the code and made her promise to use it.

"I love you," he whispered, and pulling her close, searched her face intently for a long moment, and then kissed her with a gentleness that took her breath away.

With his arm around her waist, he guided her to the doorway. "Can't you say you care for me? I know you do, Leigh. Don't belittle what we have between us."

Heedless of any consequences, she blurted out without thinking, "How can I speak of my feelings when you wear that uniform, when I don't know if you are a Christian?"

His hand was on the door knob as she spoke, and he turned toward her with a strange and unreadable expression on his face. Clearing his throat, he said slowly, "I never thought you would question that, my dear." She heard a note of victory in his voice when he continued, "You do care for me. I knew it."

Leigh only looked at him silently, feeling uneasy and sad as he said good-bye. "God keep you in His care," she whispered after the door closed behind him.

There was a strange barrenness in the room, for all the life and vibrancy were gone. Her trembling legs were unable to hold her any longer, and sinking down on the nearest chair, she looked at the ring on her hand. It was a small blue stone set in silver carvings. What was she to do? He had put himself on the side of the enemy, and a great gulf stretched between them. No matter what she did, she knew he was not going to let her go.

"That's a pretty ring you have," Thad said quietly. She had not heard him enter the room and jumped at the sound of his voice. He held out a cup of coffee. "Here, you need this," he said gently. "And you had better come and have something to eat."

He did not mention the ring or Steve again, but she knew he was suppressing his emotions, and she was afraid. What might he do with all of that anger and resentment building up inside?

Chapter 8

Leigh arrived at school the next morning showing all the signs of a sleepless night; dark circles underlined her eyes and a white, haggard face contrasted sharply against her dark hair. She had spent most of the night alternately attempting to understand what God wanted in her life and how Steve could possibly be involved in the NIO. How could she ever let herself become involved with someone like that? It was a betrayal of her family and friends and God. Slowly but surely, during those night hours, she built a massive wall of defense against Steve.

There was a reason for her decision to be at work earlier than usual, for she wanted to avoid the staff and children, and especially any discussion with Dot. Uncle Paul had walked with her, and Thad promised to come later with Dorothy. Forcing her mind to the staff reports on her desk, she sought to forget the previous evening.

Several reports from teachers spoke of children whose fathers had either been killed or imprisoned in the last week, and others who had moved away, and still others who had just simply disappeared. She groaned aloud in her despair for the children and wanted to lay all the blame at Steve's feet.

A light tap on the door interrupted her fitful concentration, and with a breezy greeting, Dorothy came in and sat down in the easy chair in front of the desk. "It's a lovely day. Did you notice that the leaves are turning color?''

"Hello, Dot." Leigh's response was void of feeling and her voice slightly strained. "The leaves are nice.''

Her friend frowned and characteristically came quickly to the point of her visit. "Well?''

"Well," Leigh swallowed hard, blinking her eyes quickly to keep back the tears. "Well, I knew you'd be in here the first thing this morning." She toyed with a pencil on her desk. "Last evening's paper told all I know.''

"It's the same man?''

"Unfortunately, yes," Leigh answered. She bitterly reproached herself for crying over someone she hardly knew and blindly reached into a desk drawer for a handkerchief. "I . . . I wish it weren't. I'm a stupid fool to be crying over someone I don't even know.''

"He came to see you, didn't he?'' Dorothy stated matter-of-factly.

"Why, yes. How did you know?''

"I've never seen that ring before, and I just guessed that he'd given it to you. Right?''

"You ought to be working for him in the NIO," Leigh remarked ruefully, trying to keep the bitterness from her voice.

"It was a wild guess. But if he does care for you, wouldn't it make sense for him to see you as soon as possible after the news broke? What happened?'' When Leigh hesitated, Dorothy reminded her of their friendship. "We've shared quite a lot in the last week, Leigh. Don't turn from me now.''

After a moment of silence, she prompted, "Leigh?''

"All right. He came to see me, just after I'd seen the newspaper article." Hesitantly she told of the visit and ended by saying, "Just before he left, I questioned him about his relationship with the Lord.''

Dorothy leaned forward, intent upon Leigh's reply. "What was his answer?''

"He said, 'I never thought you'd question that.' ''

"That's great, Leigh. He's a Christian, then.''

This seemed debatable to Leigh; she put out a hand to stop the thought and shook her head. "I don't know. He had the strangest expression on his face. I can't decide if he were surprised I would question him or if he were lying about it. Besides, you of all people should wonder how a Christian could wear that uniform.''

"Yes, but I've heard there are militia spies in the army.''

Both girls lapsed into silence, thinking about the possibilities the situation presented.

"Why did he give you the ring?''

The blue stone shone on her finger, and Leigh turned it idly as she remembered Steve's warning—the less you know, the better off you are, and she wanted to protect her friend. And so, not revealing the special code, she replied honestly, "I'm not really sure.'' She could not bring herself to admit that he might have given it to her out of love.

Noises from the hallway announced the arrival of the nursery children, and Dorothy stood up to leave. Adjusting the belt of her red shirt, she said thoughtfully, "Leigh, I know something of what you're going through. How long has it been that I've loved Thad—but nothing has happened yet to change our relationship.'' Turning from the doorway, she smiled encouragingly.

"Don't doubt God's love though, no matter what might happen.'' Then she added significantly, "I ought to know.''

Later in the afternoon Leigh went home to get a spaghetti dish she had prepared the previous evening. For several months the staff, the children, and their families had been sharing supper on Monday evenings before the nursery prayer service. Transportation was a problem and prevented many from traveling home for supper and back again for a meeting. And praying together had become a vital part of their lives since the civil war had begun; few felt they could miss that time.

Stepping up to the back door of the house, Leigh noticed it was unlocked and thought that Tom must be home. It was not unusual for him to be there at odd hours since his working schedule on the railroad changed weekly. She walked down the hallway toward the kitchen, expecting to see him or hear him call out.

"Tom, are you home?'' She called up the stairs as she passed by, "You're coming to church for supper, aren't you? I've made enough for all of us.''

The house was silent and still—too still, and an odd awareness crept over her as she walked into the kitchen and opened the refrigerator door. She was not usually uneasy while alone nor did she worry much about the creaks and groans of such an old house, but this time she had a strong sensation that something was not quite right. Just as she turned from the refrigerator with the bowl of spaghetti in her hand, she heard the front door click shut.

Fear sent chilly waves washing over her, and she stiffened with apprehension; but knowing she must find out who opened the door, she determinedly set the bowl down, slipped out of her shoes, and ran silently to the front window in the dining room.

Walking down the street was a strangely familiar figure in black uniform. She had no proof it was he who had left the house, but she continued watching, searching for some clue to the mystery. Seeing him cross the street at the end of the block and turn to look back, Leigh strained forward, trying unsuccessfully to see his face clearly, but he was too far away and his black cap shaded part of his features. He got into an NIO staff car and drove away. Her eyes shifted then to another figure just turning the corner and was greatly relieved to see that it was her cousin.

"Tom, the strangest thing happened," she informed him breathlessly as he entered the front hallway.

"You lost your shoes," he said, looking down at her feet.

"No! This isn't funny," she persisted. She described succinctly what had just occurred, and his face grew serious as his quick mind went over all of the possibilities, beginning first with the fact that he worked for the militia and the government could be checking on him.

"Did you look through the house to see if anything is missing?"

"Missing?" she echoed blankly, her face white and strained.

"Yes, if that soldier were here, he was searching for something. We'd better take a look."

They began first with the living room and her father's study, then went into Thad's room. There seemed to be nothing wrong anywhere, nothing was out of place, nothing had been touched. Then they opened Leigh's bedroom door.

"Tom! What on earth was he looking for?"

Her room was a shambles of clothing tossed out of open dresser drawers and thrown out of the closet, of books and papers scattered everywhere on the floor, and of furniture turned upside down.

Leigh was staggered, but Tom was even more astonished. He had fully expected to see his room in this condition but not Leigh's; he asked if she knew why anyone would do such a thing.

"Didn't Thad tell you about Steve Houston?"

Tom's eyes narrowed slightly and he paused, his hands full of books he had been gathering. "Steve? You don't by any chance mean the Steve Houston of the NIO, do you?" It was incredulous that her answer would be in the affirmative, and his heart sank as he heard her reply.

In a few simple sentences Leigh explained the situation as best she could, while they worked to restore order from the chaos before them. She ended by saying that she just could not believe Steve was responsible for the search. Her eyes pleaded with Tom to agree.

But Tom was not in a position to explain his involvement with the militia or with Steve, and as a result was hardly able to reassure her.

Tom leaned over to pick up the last of the books and set them back on the shelf beside the window, mentally berating himself for being ignorant of what had been happening right under his nose. As a militiaman he ought to have been aware of this long ago. He remembered then how dreamy and preoccupied Leigh had been after returning from vacation. He should have known! "Are you going to ask him about it?"

"No! What if he did order this? What if he's using me for some reason?" Leigh sighed deeply, her scepticism of Steve's integrity mushrooming by the seconds. "It wouldn't do me any good to tell him, would it?" Her words were bitter and revealed her inner feelings about Steve Houston as surely as if she had put it into words, and Tom wished with all his heart it were not so. What good could ever come from this relationship?

Leigh finished bringing order back to the closet and shut the door; then a new thought concerned her. She moved into the middle of the room and watched Tom work. "Please, don't tell Thad! He's so resentful of Steve, and I just don't know what he might do. I'm really worried about him."

Tom agreed that Thad was getting extremely tense and high-strung, but he hesitated before reassuring Leigh. "Well, we won't say anything yet. But we'd better finish cleaning this up; it's almost time for him to be home."

They hurriedly picked up the rest of the papers and soon had all the clothing tucked away in the proper places.

Tom took a quick inventory of the untouched second-floor rooms while Leigh went to get their supper from the kitchen. They were leaving by the back door a few minutes later when

Thad arrived on his bicycle, and they all walked to the church together.

Leigh gave Tom a warning look as they entered the dining room and was relieved by his responding wink. She would have been even more reassured had she known that he would soon instigate a militia investigation on her behalf. However, because he did not know Steve Houston's part in the matter, Tom continued watching for the man Leigh had described. If it proved to be someone from Steve's office, he would eventually discover his identity and reason for ransacking Leigh's room. He could only hope that time would not thwart his success.

Unfortunately, that was not the only incident concerning the intruder. Several weeks later Leigh was completely unnerved again upon finding her office in a similar state as her room had been. Someone had been there during the night and had gone through every book, every file, every desk drawer. Nothing had been left untouched.

She telephoned Tom immediately. He was at home for a few hours' rest, and he came right to the church to help her.

These unsettling experiences made her highly suspicious of the most ordinary events of the day; she soon realized the house was under surveillance and that she was followed away from home. Tom demanded that she not go out alone, and Uncle Paul became her constant companion when she went shopping.

All of these events seemed tied somehow to Steve and brought her only more confusion and distress as she tried to reason it out. It further heightened and fortified the wall she was determined to build between herself and the tall, handsome blond who had invaded her life so forcefully. It was also causing her much loss of sleep and weight, as she lay awake nights listening to the gunfire and wondering about Steve.

Leigh was not the only person questioning Steve Houston's motives and activities; one day Steve was called to the office of the President of the New Democracy.

The telephone call had been a polite summons: "The President requests your presence this afternoon at 2 o'clock," but Steve's mind was keenly aware of the tight rope he walked, and of exactly how he must handle his reports that afternoon.

The conference room at the High Command building was a large, barren room with a long table running down the center area, surrounded by straight-backed chairs. The windows were set high on the walls, their frosted, triple-thickness a deterrent to invaders.

Steve showed his I.D. card to the guard at the door, returned his salute, and walked confidently into the room. The briefcase in his hand was bulging with reports not yet seen by anyone outside his office and written to fortify his arguments.

He saluted sharply. "Mr. President."

The man seated at the far end of the table was not what one would picture to be a strong revolutionary leader. He was small of stature, had a receding hairline, wore wire-rimmed glasses, and was showing his age. But he was a ruthless man, and Steve never took any appointment lightly.

The President grunted, his raspy voice booming in the large room. "Houston." He took out a handkerchief and began wiping his glasses. "Sit down," he ordered, indicating an empty chair at his right.

Steve took his seat and opened his briefcase to lay the reports on the table in front of him. Only then did he acknowledge the presence of four cabinet advisors, doing so with a grim, business-like nod. He smiled inwardly, watching their reactions of barely concealed fear of the man who held their lives in his hands and had almost as much power as the President. Then, he pointedly ignored them and turned to his left, waiting for the game of intimidation to be concluded. His life depended on his bravado, and so he waited, refusing to give in by showing any nervousness.

"Well, Houston, that's done," the small man murmured, shooting Steve a knowing glance and slight smile to acknowledge his calmness. "I've been reading your reports. They are completely different from your predecessor's. His were full of plans to eliminate what he called 'an undesirable element in our society, the Christians.' Your reports are full of plans to eliminate the black market. Will you kindly explain your reasons for this shift?"

Steve picked up his first report and handed it to the President. "Sir, as you will see in this paper, we've cut the black market back dramatically since I've been in office." Tapping the stack of papers in front of him, he continued, "I am proceeding on your orders to trim it down as much as possible, so that the country will be in a stronger economic condition. That in turn, should cut out a lot of the militia's influence."

"And this Christian element?"

"It's not detrimental to the economy of the nation, Sir."

"And what of the militia?" The President's immobile face did not reveal his thoughts. No wonder he scared people so badly.

"We're making good progress with that, too, Sir. These reports will give you up-to-date information on what has been accomplished." Steve laid a thick folder before the President, who looked over at the aides seated before him; only Steve could see his taunting amusement as he asked, "Do any of the men wish to challenge Houston?"

There was coughing and a general stir among the men, until one finally spoke up. "No, Sir, not if you are satisfied."

"Think for yourself, Thorpe," the nation's leader commanded angrily. "I know what I think!"

Suddenly on the hook, Thorpe uncomfortably stretched his neck, darted a look at Steve and then said hesitantly, "We've had reports from the army about an increasing morale problem with enlisted men. They also say they have evidence of spy infiltration."

The man to Steve's left smiled maliciously at him, sat back in his seat, and watched him ruthlessly.

But if he were looking for something specific, he was disappointed. Steve had his arguments so well in hand that he was a step ahead of every point raised. Finally, the President grew tired of being out-maneuvered and said, "That's enough, Houston. We can see by your reports that you have things well in hand. I want a detailed outline next week on your present espionage personnel and techniques, from both the overseas and national departments. You're dismissed." He nodded to everyone, stood up slowly and walked out of the room.

Steve followed shortly afterward, not even glancing at the rest of the men. It was turning a knife a little deeper into their guilty consciences, and Steve enjoyed it tremendously.

But he heaved a sigh of relief when he was alone in his office. He had passed the test once again, but he didn't know how long he would be so fortunate.

Chapter 9

One cold, windy Saturday morning in November, Dorothy sat in the Gordon kitchen planning the nursery Christmas activities with Leigh, but her mind was not on the schedule, and she looked worried.

"Dot, is something bothering you?" Leigh pulled the paper away from her friend and laid it aside. "Is it something with your grandparents? Grandpa Perry isn't worse? Have you been having nightmares again? One of your nursery children having a big problem?" Leigh rested her chin on her hand, wondering what was troubling Dorothy. At every question she had received a negative shake of the head, but she knew it had to be more than the usual difficulties. Dorothy's optimistic temperament made her a cheerful person, who saw each trial as an opportunity to trust the Lord. "He has promised never to leave us," she would say, "I guess we can trust Him for this problem."

Finally, Dorothy spoke. "Leigh, I'm . . . I'm . . ." She faltered, unable to speak and shook her head. Getting up from the table, she walked to the window, and leaning against the wall, stared out at the cold winter scene outside. Puzzled, Leigh moved to put a hand on her arm, trying to imagine what was causing such distress. She waited.

Dorothy turned to look at her, eyes brimming with tears, her face white and strained. "Leigh, I'm pregnant," she whispered miserably.

"Are you sure?"

She nodded her head and her shoulders began to shake with the force of her tears that started silently but were soon hard, wracking sobs. Leigh had heard her cry like this only twice before. The first time they were about five years old, and Dot was a small, lonely little girl missing her dead parents. The other time occurred when they were teens, and Thad had taken another girl to a special Valentine's banquet at church. And Leigh thought, "I'm as grieved over her exposed pain now as I was then."

She reached out to put her arms about Dorothy, feeling her despair and wanting to say something comforting. But words aren't always necessary when you are close friends; Leigh held her tightly and cried with her, the tears a painful knot in her throat. Finally the sobbing stopped and Dorothy took a long, steadying breath.

"What will I do, Leigh?" she asked, turning toward her chair. She sat down at the table, her face in her hands. "What will I do?"

"Does Grandma Perry know?"

"Yes."

"You aren't planning an abortion," Leigh said, knowing her friend's convictions, "so that isn't your question, is it?"

"No," Dorothy replied slowly, her voice low and ragged. "I can't take a life . . . no matter how it happened. But what will I do when Thad finds out, and what will my nursery children think, and . . . and . . . how will I raise a child from such a terrible experience?"

"Slow down, honey. One problem at a time. About Thad, do you want me to tell him?"

"No, I think I'd better do that." Dorothy smiled sadly at Leigh's acknowledgment of that wisdom. "He's going to blow up, but perhaps I can control it a little. He has been getting more uptight every day. I am so concerned that one of these days he will do something we will all regret."

"You are probably the only person who can keep him calm." Leigh squeezed her hand reassuringly. "He has been gentle with you, Dot, more than I've seen him be with anyone in the last year . . . since . . . that night."

"Yes, he has, and I'm grateful."

"And the nursery children - well, they can accept the fact that the baby's father is not here." Leigh shrugged her shoulders in want of a better answer.

Dorothy shuddered at the mention of the father; her eyes went blank as she relived moments of that night. "Leigh, it was terrible. He . . . he . . . how could anyone . . ." She closed her eyes as if that would eliminate the memory, and Leigh saw her shudder.

"Every living person, Dot, whose life is not covered by the saving work of Christ, has that same seed of wickedness within him." Leigh paused, and then added, "I'm not excusing what he did."

Dorothy nodded. "I understand what you are saying. And I'm also aware that I made a stupid mistake that night by going out alone. I can't blame God for what happened.

"What does Grandma Perry say?"

Dorothy sat back in her chair and sighed. "You two are the most understanding, loving people I know. She gave the same answers you have, but sometimes, Leigh . . . it just seems unbearable. I don't know what I would do without such support. I just don't think I could make it without you."

Leigh lowered her head and stared somberly at the table. "I wish . . . I wish with all my heart it had never happened!"

"But it did," Dorothy responded sadly, "and now I will just have to trust God to bring right out of wrong. Above everything else, I want people to thank Him for what comes from this."

They heard Thad's bedroom door open and his footsteps coming down the hallway; Dorothy raised her eyebrows and said reluctantly, "I might as well tell him now." She left the table and went to meet him; Leigh heard her ask Thad if they could talk in the living room for a few minutes.

Leigh sat at the kitchen table, waiting and praying for two people she loved so dearly, asking the Lord to guide what was happening in the other room. *"Thad,"* she thought, *"for goodness sake, be sensitive to Dot right now. Don't get angry!"*

* * * * * *

The first hard winter storm came overnight. It was a wet snow that clung to the trees and rooftops like whipped cream on a cake, and the nursery children accepted its arrival as though it were a birthday present. The boys made a fort and loaded it with snowball ammunition; the girls created a mini-family of snow people. It was difficult to maintain discipline, for a party atmosphere invaded every classroom.

Glancing through one door, Leigh noticed that the children were using up excess energy in exercises. Another class marched to lively music, and the next group sat in a circle suggesting figures they could make in the snow. One of the older groups was memorizing a Bible verse, and Leigh caught a phrase as she walked past the door—"though your sins be as scarlet, they shall be as white as snow."

As she passed the main door on the way back to her office, she glanced through the window and was alarmed to see two soldiers striding briskly up the walk. Mentally bracing herself, she waited, determined not to be afraid.

"Good morning." Her voice was cool and restrained. She did not want even the faintest sign of friendliness to be a mistaken invitation to camaraderie. "Is there something I can do for you?"

The older of the two men spoke with a pretentious attitude, looking down his nose at the young lady before him. "I want to see the nursery director," he answered in a manner which indicated that this girl in brown slacks, white blouse, and beige cardigan could only be a nursery helper.

"I am the director," she said firmly.

"You? Ah, well, I - ah - I had expected an older woman." He lost his train of thought, much to Leigh's satisfaction, but then regaining his composure, went on. "I'm Lt. Palmer from the National Intelligence Office. We've been instructed to have a guard at the school from now on. Sgt. Rogers," he indicated the man next to him with a nod, "will be at the school every day. If there are any problems, he is to be notified immediately."

"A guard! Why do we need a guard? Surely the government doesn't think these children capable of rebellion!"

"I'm not in a position to question my orders, Ma'm. Sgt. Rogers will be here every day." His voice was haughty and showed his irritation at her questions.

"Must he wear that uniform?" Leigh found it impossible to hide her disgust of the outfit as she looked the soldier over. "It will frighten the children."

"While on duty, yes. If you want to challenge it, you may call the NIO office." His tone of voice implied that it would be an unthinkable thing to do. No one questioned the government any more, unless he wanted to lose his freedom, his job, or even his life.

"And just where is he allowed to go in the building?" She suddenly had visions of a guard walking freely into any room whenever he pleased. No teacher would be able to relax undisturbed. It would have been a wise plan, she thought belatedly, to have some of the church men around during the day. Perhaps Uncle Paul could help them even now.

"His orders are to guard the building, and he'll do what he thinks necessary. That means unrestricted entrance into any room," he added spitefully.

Turning to the younger man, he ordered, "Sgt. Rogers, carry on." And then with a gleam in his eye that said he would enjoy guarding such a pretty young woman, he executed a crackling salute to Leigh and left the building.

Leigh nodded with just the slightest move of her head in response, for she was finding it difficult to control her deepening anger. This was surely Steve's order. How dare he send a guard to spy on me, she thought. Staring at the soldier, her eyes flashing, she fumed inwardly. If Major Stephen Houston were in her presence, she would give him a piece of her mind. What did he think he was doing? Why?

Her steps beat an angry staccato sound on the tiled floor as she walked down the hall and opened her office door. She refused to give Sgt. Rogers the satisfaction of even a glance, but she felt him watching her progress. Frowning defiantly she entered the room and shut the door with a firm, disapproving hand. It was provoking to know that she had no control over a situation, which this soldier was going to find highly amusing.

Leigh had barely seated herself when she remembered that all the teachers must be informed immediately. The guard had to be explained to the children before any problems arose. She sat a moment, trying to compose herself, praying for wisdom to deal with this representative of the New Democracy.

Taking a deep breath, she picked up several books from her desk and started toward the door. Perhaps the Sergeant would think she was delivering them and not reporting his presence.

He stood at the dining room door, checking over the room's interior and apparently ignoring her, and she tried to stage a normal routine as she walked from room to room. Presently, however, she caught a knowing smile and realized he knew what she was doing, and perhaps, had even given her time to inform the teachers before he made any entrances.

He waited until she was back in her office to begin his own tour. He stopped to look into each room, and the result satisfied him immensely. While teachers tried to ignore his presence, the children stared at him in wide-eyed wonder. He felt very important, and it bolstered his courage so that, after visiting each classroom, he walked to Leigh's office, opened the door without knocking, and looked in.

Taking his time, he studied the room, his eyes finally resting on her rebellious face, and asked sternly, "Is there another door to this office?"

Leigh's eyes turned dark and stormy. "Do you see one?" she asked. He had been here less than an hour, and look what he was doing. "Is there something you want?"

He peered at her, drawing the moment out to his satisfaction, and then said carelessly, "I'm just checking the rooms, Miss Gordon." He turned, walked out into the corridor, and without a backward glance, shut the door.

Leigh slid down in her chair and grimaced at the closed door. This was unbearable, and she felt helpless. Swiveling her chair around, she stared out of the window at the empty playground. What she had been dreading had finally come. Now what could they do? It will be a strain on all the teachers, and that will in turn influence the children.

It was becoming most difficult to teach Christ's love—in the middle of a revolution of hate. But if the nation were to survive, the children must be taught the true values of life—that God had meant for His creation to live in love, and it was mankind who had polluted everything with selfishness, pride, and hate. They must be taught that Jesus Christ had so much love to offer that He had willingly endured the torture of a cross and separation from God in order to give salvation to those who followed Him. They must be taught that the only true and lasting revolution was one of Christ's love within the heart.

The teachers had all responded as she knew they would, accepting a troublesome situation in faith that it would work out right. But Leigh was worried about Dorothy, for her reaction to the news had not been good. A cloud had passed over her eyes, and her mouth had tightened; Leigh knew she was struggling with her emotions.

Another knock on the office door interrupted her thoughts,

and Leigh tensed in anticipation, but it was only one of the teachers asking for help at lunch time. "The children are so wound up, and I have one little girl who isn't feeling well."

"Of course, I'll be glad to help. Do you want me in the lunchroom?"

"Yes, if you don't mind. I'll take Annamarie into the lounge and see if she has a fever."

Leigh nodded and glanced at her watch. "The city nurse should be here in half an hour for her rounds, unless the government changes its mind again."

Leigh went to the classroom, and it was just as the teacher had indicated. Every child was filled with excitement over the snow and the soldier in the hallway. It was not an easy task to get each lunch to its owner, all hands washed, and each child to the lunchroom. But Leigh was grateful for the noisy activity; it took her mind off this most recent problem.

"Miss Gordon, Miss Gordon." A little voice patiently repeated her name until she responded. It was Mark, and Leigh smiled as she leaned over the table to hear him above the noise.

"Yes, Mark?"

"Miss Gordon, is the soldier going to be here all the time?"

"I have been told he will."

"Do you think he would teach me how to march?"

"Oh, I don't know. I'm afraid he will be much too busy to do that." Leigh did her best to discourage the little boy, for it would hurt her deeply if he were influenced by a soldier of the New Democracy.

"Does he love Jesus?" Mark's eyes were solemn as he watched her carefully for an answer.

She was suddenly ashamed. This little five-year-old boy sitting before her had cut right through her frustration to the clear reason for the soldier's presence. He could be exposed to God's truth here.

"Mark, I don't know. I haven't asked him."

He said no more but went on eating his lunch. A milk spill nearby claimed Leigh's attention, and an argument between two boys about the best snowman in the playground kept her further occupied. After everyone had eaten, an assistant helped her herd the group of laughing, chattering children back down the hall and into the classroom for rest time. Mark gave her a squeeze as she watched the group re-enter the room, but she didn't notice that he had not followed them inside.

"Mith Gordon," squeaked a little girl's high voice. "Mith Gordon, Mark isn't here."

"Oh, where is he then?" Leigh asked placidly as she tried to settle two playful little boys down on their nap rugs.

"In the hall," the little girl told her importantly.

Stepping to the door, Leigh was extremely disturbed to see Mark talking with Sgt. Rogers. There he stood, small and vulnerable, looking up at the soldier with those lovable eyes; she started to call him back when she heard him ask, "Mr. Soldier, do you love Jesus?"

The daily news became more somber and threatening as the weeks went by, and Leigh continued to fight her own battles of fear and confusion, all the while watching Thad grow into an intensely bitter man. He was gentle with those he loved, but that headstrong personality lit an inner, growing rage whenever anyone mentioned the government and national problems. Leigh hated to have the radio on in the evenings, for it was frightening to watch her brother's face grow tense and white and to sense what was happening to him.

One evening the news reported a mother's protest march for food in the downtown area, in front of the capitol building. The march was a quiet, well-organized protest, but some nervous soldier couldn't keep his hand off his gun. In the end, three people were killed, a dozen hospitalized for injuries inflicted by a frightened mob, and no one was able to speak to the authorities to voice his complaint.

"Is that what your God wants—to cause needless deaths and allow people to starve?" Thad's voice hardened in denouncement. "Does that make Him happy?"

"Be honest with yourself," Leigh responded automatically, knowing her words would not impress him. "You can't blame God for the society we've built. If man persists in shoving God from his life, to go his own selfish way—what else can be expected?"

Thad shook his head in disagreement and growlingly observed, "It's a good thing Tom gets food on his runs in the country. We'd find it difficult to scrape by otherwise."

Neither Thad nor Leigh were aware of where much of Tom's edible treasures came from, for he knew they would want an explanation of his connection with Major Steve Houston.

Then one day another log was added to the flame of anger within Thad when he, too, came home unexpectedly and nearly caught an intruder going out the front door. Thinking that Leigh would be terribly frightened if she knew, he tried to straighten up his father's study before she arrived home.

She found him on his knees in the middle of the study with books and sermon notes scattered all over the floor. He was hardly prepared for her response to the scene.

"Again!"

"Again," he repeated in astonishment. "What do you mean, again?"

Knowing she could no longer keep the information from him, she answered as calmly as possible. "It's happened before. About a month ago my room was torn up, and my office was also searched."

"What!"

"Hitting the roof" is an expressive description of anger which hardly measured up to his response, but Leigh continued working quietly beside him. "Why didn't you tell me?" he demanded.

"Because I knew you would react just as you're doing," was her weary response. "Let's just get this mess cleaned up."

They soon had the books gathered and placed in proper order on the shelves that lined two walls of the room, but it was going to be a much longer job getting all their father's sermon notes back into good order, and Leigh sighed, discouraged at the thought. That would take a good day's work. But worse than that was the unnerving thought that someone was getting into their house so easily; she jumped when she heard the front door open.

"It's just us," Uncle Paul called as he and Tom entered the house.

When Thad learned that they both knew about the previous searches, he became angrier. "I'm Leigh's brother, and while her parents are away, I'm responsible for her protection."

Tom glanced at his father with raised eyebrows. "You need to curb that temper then, if you're planning on taking good care of her, Thad."

"Some boyfriend you've got," Thad growled in frustration with a glance at Leigh.

She felt that she had been physically hit, so cruel was his implication, and kneeling on the floor with her hands full of papers, she stared at her brother. In her confused state of mind about Steve, she had no reply to make, but it hurt to hear Thad voice her suspicions. Sighing, she went back to picking up papers and placing them in little piles on her father's desk.

"That was a low blow, cousin," Tom said reprovingly, and added, as Thad cast an apologetic look at Leigh, "Did you see the man? Would you recognize him again?"

"No, all I saw was a medium-sized man in a black uniform."

Uncle Paul went with Leigh to the kitchen, hoping he could comfort her while helping with supper. He could see that she was very upset about the incident, and he was not happy about her association with the director of the NIO, though he knew there was nothing he could do about that.

While Uncle Paul peeled a few potatoes, Tom questioned Thad more thoroughly, but received little satisfaction from the meager information he could give. Tom felt he must find out who the intruder was before something happened to Leigh. For some reason, he felt strongly that all these searches were linked personally to her. Someone might be planning to kidnap her or frame her with anti-government activities. Perhaps he should get a little more protection for her. Since her parents weren't here, he could have a couple of friends move in upstairs; if their schedules worked out right, there could be someone around most of the time.

He wished he could take Thad into his confidence, but he was too angry and volatile to trust.

Chapter 10

Several nights later someone pushed an envelope under Leigh's office door; she discovered it when she went to work the next morning.

It contained four tickets to a symphony concert the following Saturday afternoon. She searched the envelope in vain for a clue to the sender, while an uneasiness crept into her mind as she faced the stark truth that neither her home nor the nursery were immune to someone's key.

She was amazed that such an event would take place now. It was incongruous. But in an effort to bring some semblance of stability to the nation's capital, the New Democracy had embarked on several propaganda programs, one of them being a cultural series during the winter months. In light of the current hostilities, it seemed ridiculous.

There was an incredible amount of publicity to be heard daily about such events, but very few of the average citizens could afford to attend such performances.

The concert was to feature part of the Philadelphia Symphony Orchestra, and Leigh suddenly wanted very much to go. It would be so good to attend.

But she had some difficulty in getting Thad to agree because he felt sure the tickets were from Steve. Since only those who moved in official circles could get in, and because none of their acquaintances had attended other concerts, Leigh had to agree.

He had been adamant at first. "No, I won't go. I don't intend to be obligated to Houston for anything!"

"But, Thad, Dot and I can't go alone."

"Ask Tom or Uncle Paul then."

"Tom has to work, and Uncle Paul has charge of a Bible study at the Johnson's."

"All right, all right! I'll go. But only because you two won't be safe on the streets alone."

On the day of the concert the weather dipped into the sub-zero temperatures, and a strong wind plummeted the windchill factor even further. The girls dressed as warmly as possible to insulate themselves against the cold bus ride and walk, and the concert hall, which would not be warm either.

The old but warm black wool pantsuit and bright red scarf Leigh decided to wear over several layers of thermal clothing turned her hair into shining ebony, and her dark eyes sparkled with anticipation.

Putting on her shoe boots and heavy winter coat, she caught sight of the ring on her hand and wondered if Steve would be at the performance. A sudden longing to see him, even from a distance, swept over her with such strength that she caught her breath. It had been weeks since he had been at the house; in fact, she counted back, it was over two months ago.

She heard a great deal about him, however, for the radio kept the public highly informed of NIO activities. The news broadcasters reported daily on the work and success of the intelligence organization and its director, Major Houston. One week he was overseas with the President at a peace conference; the next he was in Texas organizing intelligence activities there. Not leaving his work to subordinates, he had also been in at least three other countries in the last month to organize American espionage organizations more effectively. And he was leading a successful fight against the local black market and national militia activities.

It was difficult to know what to believe. Was it true that the NIO was cracking down on local black marketeers? Were there really dozens of dishonest businessmen being arrested? Was the NIO actually winning its battle against the civilian militia so that thousands across the country were being jailed? It was rumored that some Christian leaders were also imprisoned. Was that true also? No one she talked with had actually seen any of them in jail. But if it were true, then it cemented her resolve against Steve.

At least, she wished that it did.

Two months ago, she was torn apart every time she heard a report mentioning his name, one moment caring for him, the next wishing she had never met him. Now she had successfully worked herself into a false security, saying that he no longer meant anything to her. But if she were truly honest, she would have to admit that her feelings were as stable as a ferris wheel where Steve Houston was concerned, one moment up and the next down, so that she did not truly know what she felt. But she had tried to harden her heart against him.

They left home after a quick lunch and walked three blocks to catch the bus for the concert hall, arriving just in time to get seated before the curtain rose and the orchestra began its first number. The fourth ticket had not been used, and so the end seat next to Leigh was empty. She hoped no one would sit there and spoil her afternoon by chattering through the performance. She took a deep breath and settled back, determining to forget everything else but the music. It was beautiful and soothing, and she began to relax for the first time in weeks.

Only after the last note of the opening number had died in the applause of the audience did she become aware of her surroundings and feel a curiosity about those nearby. They were seated in the third row from the front, and as she watched uniformed men whispering to fashionable women, she was startled to see a pair of familiar blue eyes staring at her. His face was void of expression, but his eyes fairly blazed with feeling, and Leigh was imprisoned by his gaze. He was seated at the end of the curved front row, an aide on either side, and with one hand rubbing his lips, he watched her unobtrusively. This was, Leigh thought, just what he had planned.

She attempted to keep her emotions suppressed, her face masked, but it was almost impossible to slow the frantic beating of her heart as he continued to stare at her.

As the second number began with the slow, staccato sounds of the violins, she forced her eyes back to the platform where the moving arms of the conductor hypnotized her, and she willed herself not to look back into those eyes again.

Suddenly an army officer sat down in the empty seat next to Leigh, and, deciding she was there for his enjoyment, leaned over to speak to her. As he did so, she saw Steve give a frowning order to one of his aides, who was soon standing beside the officer with a whispered invitation from the Major to join his party. When Leigh braved another cautious glance in Steve's direction, she encountered his stern countenance as he looked from the empty seat back to her again, strongly implying his displeasure over the seating arrangements.

The intermission came, and the stage was emptied of performers. The buzz of conversation filled the air, and people were moving up and down the aisles. Steve talked with the young aide to his left, his eyes moving over the audience to settle often on the place where Leigh sat talking with Dorothy.

"Are you tired, Dot?" Leigh saw Dorothy stretch her back and wondered if she might get uncomfortable before the afternoon was over. "Do you want to leave?"

"Oh, no, Leigh," Dorothy said with a smile, "I wouldn't miss this for anything. I'm fine, really."

"I must admit," Thad said, leaning over to speak to the girls, "That it has been a . . ."

But a loud blast of sound cut off his words, and it roared so loudly in Leigh's ears that she covered them quickly as she watched in unbelief. The back wall of the empty stage exploded as though some giant fist had ripped through it.

"A bomb," someone screamed, and the audience began to panic. But Leigh stood fascinated, not believing what was taking place. It had not been strong enough to hurt anyone, she thought, but the aisles were full of screaming, frantic humans. As she stood transfixed at the scene around her, she felt someone pull her roughly into the aisle.

"Leigh, come with me," Steve ordered. "Thad, hold on to Dorothy and don't let go!"

Without a word of protest, Thad put his arm around Dorothy and followed Steve and Leigh toward a side entrance to safety. They were nearing the door when they were, without warning, swept up the aisle instead, and in the crush of humanity Leigh felt Steve's arm encircle her waist and heard him telling her to hold on tightly.

She saw Thad and Dorothy being pushed ahead and then lost sight of them entirely. The smell of smoke in the air ignited panic in the minds of those rushing madly up the aisles, and they pawed and pushed and shouted and cursed. And Leigh was terrified, but not for herself.

Turning her head she looked up into Steve's face and cried, "I can't see them anymore. Dorothy is pregnant, Steve!"

She heard voices screaming, "Get out, get out!" while others called out calmly that if everyone would just walk slowly no one would be hurt.

Steve held her tightly by one arm and with the other tried to protect her from falling bodies and flashing arms. She could hardly breath and leaned weakly against Steve's body, feeling him push forward determinedly. She felt as though she were being crushed to death, and the smoke made her choke on each breath. At any moment, she was sure she was going to faint; her fingers slipped away from Steve's arm, and her vision blurred.

After what seemed like an eternity, they reached the foyer where a fearful concern for Thad and Dorothy revived Leigh. She searched frantically through the crowd who still fought their way toward the exits.

"There, Steve, on the floor by that mirror."

Steve forced their way over to the still figure lying only inches from the path of an insane mob rushing past into the street. They knelt down, and Leigh put shaking fingers on Dorothy's wrist and sobbed in relief when she felt a faint pulse. There was a nasty head wound pouring blood down over an unconscious face, and Leigh was frightened.

"She's been hit with something. What can we do?"

Steve gathered the still form up into his arms and spoke to Leigh. "Take hold of my belt and hang on for dear life. We've got to get her out of here."

The cold air that hit her face when they finally reached the sidewalk was like a gift from heaven, and Leigh gulped in a deep breath, trying to clear her mind. She needed to think; she needed to help Dorothy.

"Leigh, what happened to Dot?" Thad struggled through the mob of people that continued to spill out of the concert hall until he stood beside Leigh. Even in her own anxiety she could see his concern. "She was jerked right out of my arms! She's all right, isn't she?"

"She's alive, but unconscious," Leigh replied. "I'm afraid for her, in her condition . . ." She did not need to finish the sentence, for he knew exactly what she meant. Dorothy was pregnant, and there was no way of knowing how much she had been hurt. "We must get her to a hospital," she said, turning toward Steve, her eyes imploring his help. She was unaware that in seeking his aid she was revealing her trust in him, but Steve caught its implications.

Still holding Dorothy in his arms, he turned to an NIO staff car in the street and spoke to the driver. "Barnes, we need to get this woman to the nearest hospital."

He motioned Leigh to the back seat where he gently laid Dorothy, and then ordered a lieutenant standing at the curb to evacuate the area and call for ambulances for the injured. "I'll be back as soon as I set up emergency care at the hospital, Lieutenant. See that everyone is out of the theatre; if there is a doctor around, get started on the injured. Get one of our crews down here immediately to check the explosives used."

Thad slid into the back seat beside the two women as Steve moved in beside the driver, who switched on a siren and pulled the car swiftly out into traffic.

Leigh's eyes never left her friend's face as she pleaded silently for God to help them. She was unmindful of the blood seeping onto her coat and suit, but watched intently for signs of consciousness. But Dorothy lay silent and still, and did not hear Thad pleading softly for her to wake up because he needed her.

Numb with disbelief, Leigh watched Thad walk beside the stretcher after their arrival at the hospital. Dot was being taken to the emergency room, and Thad kept urging the orderly to hurry.

Leigh heard calm, efficient orders being given by nurses to their aides, saw white-uniformed men and women moving back and forth down the hallway as they prepared for the first ambulances to arrive. Just ahead, Steve's aide walked with the doctor, evidently describing what had happened, and for the first time she took a good look at the man.

And her hand flew to her mouth to stifle a scream.

She leaned against the hard, cold wall for support as a scene flashed through her mind, that of a man in black uniform strutting away from their home. This was the man who had searched her room! She was sure of it when she saw his unusual walk. There could not be another man on earth with a strut like that.

The hand on her arm brought a gasp from her lips, and she wrenched herself free to stare up with wild eyes into her brother's face. Taking a deep breath she tried to compose herself as he led her down the hall toward a small waiting room. She knew he considered her reaction to be deep concern for Dorothy, and she was not going to enlighten him. He was overwrought as it was; what might he do if he knew what she had just discovered?

He paced nervously around the room, his hands in tight fists as though he were waiting to hit the first person who came through the door. "Why don't they come and tell us something?"

Leigh stood staring out the window. Lights from the hospital cast timid little fingers out over several snow-tipped trees and a single stone bench, but she saw none of this, only jumbled pictures of Dorothy's still form and a man in black uniform.

"It's only been a few minutes, Thad." Closing her eyes and leaning against the window frame for strength, she prayed silently.

In black despair she turned to her only source of shelter and security, to the loving heavenly Father who controlled the events that shaped His children's lives. While her intellect affirmed the certainty of the loving-kindness of God, her trust was as fragile as the icicle hanging from the hospital window. One flick of the finger and it would lay shattered on the ground below.

Thad's voice, halting and anguish-filled, interrupted her prayer. "Leigh, I've always taken Dot for granted. I never realized how much I love her."

She turned slowly from the window and stared, amazed at the admission he had just made. His face was pale and drawn, and she reached out, putting a comforting hand on his shoulder. "All these years and it has finally broken through to you. Oh, Thad, I pray that God will give her back to us. We need her so much."

Sounds of moving carts and soft footsteps could be heard in the busy corridor as the victims of the wild mob of concert goers were brought in. Neither spoke as they waited anxiously for someone to come with information about Dorothy's condition.

"Thad," Leigh spoke suddenly, "we must call her grandparents. They have a right to know what has happened. I'm sure this will be on the radio soon."

"Right. I'll go find a telephone."

"Tell them not to worry. Tell them that we will call just as soon as we have more news."

The door clicked shut behind him, and turning toward the window again, Leigh willed her mind into control, forcing herself into a degree of outward calm, thin though it might be.

Hearing the door open, and thinking it was the doctor, she whirled around to ask about Dorothy's condition. "Oh, it's you," she said flatly.

Steve walked slowly into the room and shut the door behind him. The only indication of his recent experience was a large dark blot on his overcoat, probably blood from the wound in Dorothy's head. He tossed his military cap on a table, and having never taken his eyes from her, moved across the room.

In her present state of mind, she was devastated by his sudden appearance. How could anyone have a nature that was at once so cool and commanding, so vibrant and so forceful. No wonder soldiers gave him their fearful respect.

As he came nearer, he saw the anger in her eyes. "I'm sorry, Leigh," he said with quiet dignity. "I never realized anyone would get hurt when I left the tickets for you. This is the first time the militia has pulled a surprise on me. Forgive me?"

"There is nothing to forgive," she replied stiffly. "Each of us wanted to come, and Dot would be the last person to judge you for that."

She pressed back against the window as he stood before her. Permitting herself a quick glance, she saw a puzzled and watchful look forming in his eyes as he reached for her hand.

"Don't!" She jerked free of his touch, but it caused her great agitation, and shivering uncontrollably, she hugged herself closely.

"What's wrong? What have I done to make you so angry with me?"

There was a long silence as she stared at him. His dynamic presence in the room was unnerving and weakened her resolve. To bolster her dying anger, she demanded accusingly, "Why did you send Barnes to search our house and my office?"

"Barnes!" A storm gathered on his face instantly. His eyes turned ice-blue and hard. He became the professional soldier she knew he was, a mountain of intensity and cool strength.

With his arms folded across his chest and his feet planted firmly apart, he towered over her. "What do you mean; what was searched?" His face was a cold mask of power.

She bit off each word as though it tasted bitter in her mouth. "My room, Dad's study, my office."

"Why didn't you report it to me?" He glanced at his ring on

her finger. "Did you try to call?"

"No." Her answer was low, an admission of her confusion. He did not ask why not; he knew. She was afraid he had ordered the searches.

His blue eyes challenged hers. "Did you see who did it?"

The question was asked quietly, but there was no doubt about the powerful authority waiting to be unleashed. She wondered for a moment at her audacity in speaking to him like this, for he had unquestionable influence, and could, at a mere word, have her imprisoned. Were she able to think this through logically she would understand why she was not afraid, but she pushed on in her distraught anger.

"I saw a man walking away from the house on the day my room was searched, and Thad nearly caught him the day he took Dad's study apart. There was something unusual about the man's walk, and I saw that same strut in the hallway just a few minutes ago." She lifted her head and said defiantly, "It was your aide."

His eyes narrowed and his words were harsh. "And what makes you think it was Barnes?"

"His walk!"

She was sick with the thought that Steve might be linked to those forages, but how could it be otherwise? Barnes would surely have no reason to do it of his own initiative, even though her one brief encounter with him had led her to believe he was a cruel, scheming man. All the time she had been answering Steve's questions, she had resolutely stared at the black tie he wore, afraid to look into the sternness of his face, and now she closed her eyes to shut him entirely out of sight.

His next words cut into her heart like a knife, and her eyes flashed open as she heard them.

"I think . . . I think that I asked too much of you when I asked that you trust me." Never had she heard him speak with such regret or seen him so disappointed and weary.

Her mouth flew open to protest, but the door opened then and the entrance of a doctor and Thad brought an end to their conversation.

The doctor's words, spoken in a kindly tone, were hurried and to the point.

"Miss Gordon, your friend took quite a beating from that mob. She is losing her baby, and she's hemorrhaging. We're taking her to surgery to get it under control, or we'll lose her, too."

Leigh gasped and stared at him with wide eyes, vaguely aware of the anguish on Thad's face and the concerned look Steve flashed at her.

"Do you mean . . ." Hardly able to speak, not even wishing to think of what he might mean, she whispered with a breaking voice, "Do you mean . . . she might not live?"

He nodded his head in acknowledgment. "It's going to be a tough battle. I'm sorry."

There was nothing more he could add, nothing to soften the blow; and his parting words, called over his shoulder as he left for surgery, were that they would be notified of any change in her condition.

The room was thick with Thad's anger. Leigh felt it as she turned to face him and saw his eyes flashing hatred. Abruptly he took a step toward the man beside her. One tightly clenched fist jerked upward.

But the three stood motionless: Leigh horrified of what he was about to do, Steve watchful and prepared to accept the angry blow, and Thad consumed with the desire to make someone else hurt as he was hurting. Then, he dropped his hand and turned savagely toward the door.

"I'm going to call Dot's grandparents."

Leigh jumped as Thad slammed the door behind him, and slumping back against the wall, was immensely relieved that his fist had not followed his desire. She, too, felt a deep concern for Dorothy, and at the same time was aware of an inner voice urging her to accept this test of faith and put her trust in God, but the events of the day had pulled her emotions out like a taut wire, and they snapped.

She felt Steve's hand on her shoulder turning her around to face him, and heard his assurance that the best doctors would be caring for Dorothy. But even that did not seem to be enough to stop what happened next.

Looking up at him, she began to cry great drops of tears, and they rolled, one by one, down her face. She felt his hands on her arms, pulling her close, and as he murmured words of comfort which she did not hear, she tried to get away, her fists beating ineffectively against his chest.

"Why . . . can't you . . . leave me alone," she pleaded. "Why do you . . . hound . . . me so? Go away! Go away from me!''

Forcefully, yet gently, Steve pulled her even nearer, one arm around her waist, and the other holding her head against his chest as she wept convulsively. "It's going to be all right, my love, please believe me."

Gradually her sobbing faded away. Then words began rushing involuntarily from the hidden thoughts of her heart—words she had been unable to speak to anyone, even to her dearest friend who was now near death.

"Why did you have to pick me? If you're using me for some great plan of yours, why don't you just go ahead and tell me now? I've lost my inner peace; I'm torn between my love for you and guilt at betraying Christ."

In the next moment she jerked her head. She had not yet admitted this to herself; she was dazed by what she had just revealed. Now he knew, and this disclosure rendered her completely vulnerable to his commands. She stared at him with dark eyes still shimmering with tears.

"Oh, Leigh, I thought I would never hear you say that."

His face was serious as he studied hers, but the soft brilliancy of his blue eyes revealed his love. "But . . . why guilt?" he asked gently.

She stood silent in the circle of his arms, unable to look at him or speak, defenseless against the thoughts that beat incessantly like sleet against a windowpane. Her thoughts outlined doubts and guilt . . . the uncertainty of Steve's inner life . . . his controversial position at NIO . . . Barnes' ransacking visits . . . Thad's distrust of Steve . . . her inability to sustain an unswerving faith.

As she struggled against the pandemonium within, Steve drew her closer again and whispered, "Can't you trust God with all these doubts?"

The questioning hope that sprang into her eyes was left unanswered, for a voice severed their conversation like a sword.

"Well," Thad snarled as he stepped further into the room, "what a pretty picture."

Before either of them could respond to this outburst, the telephone rang; with one arm still around her, Steve reached out to lift the receiver to his ear. It was one of his staff at the concert hall, and as they talked Leigh moved away to sink down into a chair nearby. She leaned over, buried her face in her hands and heard Steve end his conversation by saying, "I'll be there in fifteen minutes."

He touched her lightly on the shoulder and said he would return as soon as possible. Leigh made no response, but watched him pick up his cap and settle it on his blond hair before turning to leave. At the doorway he paused. "Don't leave the hospital until I return," he commanded quietly, and was gone.

"In case you're interested," Thad said dryly when they were alone, "Dorothy is in the recovery room."

Leigh's head shot up, and seeing the evidence of her recent cry, he apologized. "I'm sorry, Sis; that was cruel."

The next four hours dragged by slowly as they waited for word about Dorothy's condition. Several times Thad went to the recovery room and returned shaking his head—no change. The wound in her head had given her a concussion, and she was still unconscious.

Thad looked so haggard that Leigh's heart went out to him, and she tried to speak encouragingly while they waited, but he would not hear any mention of God. His sharp response made her feel physically ill.

"God! He just takes and takes and takes! Now he wants to take Dot!" He slammed his fist down on the table. "What is He, this selfish Sovereign God of yours?"

"He is a loving God who uses circumstances to bring us to Himself," she answered, trying to impress that fact upon his mind and at the same time admonish her own weak faith.

She finally coaxed him into going home for the rest of the night. She argued that she could more easily get nursery replacements than he could be absent from his teaching position, and he needed rest. What really concerned her was the knowledge that he needed to be away from the hospital where he was becoming more rigid and tense by the moment. She was afraid he might do something wild the next time Steve appeared.

Later that night as she sat alone beside Dorothy's bed, she remembered others who had been in similar circumstances, but those stories had concluded joyously. And this was not a dramatic film complete with soul-stirring background music and a happy ending. This was reality, and she was frightened.

How on earth could her pitiful, weak words be effective enough to reach the God of the universe? She did not know. But His Word was too clear and ingrained in the structure of her life for her not to turn to God and plead for her friend's life. And she did so as she held the still, quiet hand.

Her petitions to God continued through the night, broken only by short spans of sleep and anxious watching whenever a nurse stopped in to check on the patient. She was not encouraged by their stern looks and silence. It only meant that Dot's condition had not improved.

Early in the morning hours she heard the shrill, shrieking sirens as a number of ambulances neared the hospital, and she saw the flashing red lights as they arrived. She lost count of the number that rolled up to the emergency door to deposit a load of suffering, bleeding forms once created in the image of God; the procession seemed endless. One of the nurses, in response to her inquiry, explained that the patients were wounded soldiers from a skirmish with the militia. Leigh shook her head sadly. Only government soldiers were treated at the hospitals; the militiamen were not so fortunate. They cared for each other unless captured; then they would receive dubious treatment in ill-equipped prison hospitals.

All night Leigh had resolutely pushed from her mind any thought of Steve and their most recent encounter but felt totally defeated for her efforts when, hearing a sound, she turned to see him standing in the doorway. His presence had the same effect on her as an ocean wave did on a sand castle.

Despair and wretchedness swept over her as his eyes searched her face. A nurse moved past his still figure into the room, and as she began working over Dorothy, said quietly, "Miss Gordon, go and have some breakfast. I'll stay here until you return."

"Breakfast?" Leigh repeated with surprise, and for the first time looked at her watch, amazed to see that night had passed, and it was nearly seven o'clock. A quick glance at Steve let her know he was not leaving the room until she went with him; reluctantly she stood and followed him through the door and down the hall. He took her to a small lounge at the end of the hallway where a breakfast tray waited.

"I know you won't eat unless someone orders you," he said "so I'm ordering you."

Wearily, she sat down before the tray of food and stared at the fruit, cereal, and coffee. How could she eat anything now. Particularly if he insisted on watching her every move.

Taking his cup, he sat down in a chair opposite her. "Go on," he motioned, "I've already eaten."

"I just can't," she said flatly after trying a peace slice. She laid the spoon back on the tray and pushed her hair from her forehead. "I just can't eat."

"You must, if you want to help Dorothy through today. By the way, I'll have someone stay with her if you wish to be driven to church this morning."

"Oh, it is Sunday, isn't it. I had forgotten." She shook her head, "No, I don't want to leave Dorothy, but thanks." The offer was certainly puzzling to Leigh. Did he realize the importance of fellowship with believers, or was he trying to get her away from the hospital? She didn't pursue the subject; she had something else bothering her.

"Steve . . ." She felt confused and hesitated, but she needed to apologize to him. "About . . . about last night . . ."

He interrupted her with one of those rare smiles that made her light up inside as he said, "We'll talk about last night some other time. Right now, eat."

Obediently she tried, swallowing each bite as though it were a lump of clay, all the while her senses acutely aware of the man who sat like a guard over her breakfast.

Staring down at a now empty cup, she tried once more to broach the subject of the previous evening.

"I'm sorry I made you angry last night."

It was a whispered apology from an uneasy heart that did not know what nest of hornets might now be stirred up. She played restlessly with the white paper napkin, folding and unfolding it as she waited for his response.

He reached over to press her hand to stillness, and as she stared down at that sizeable hand completely covering her own, she marveled that there was not only strength but tenderness in that touch.

"I wasn't angry with you, Leigh." He saw the look of relief and curiosity in her eyes but merely shook his head and changed the subject.

"The doctor feels that by this afternoon she should start responding to us. And if things go well, she won't need any more blood after today."

She looked up, astonishment written plainly on her face. "You've seen him today? Why did you talk to him?"

"I'm concerned, too," he said, a soft reprimand partially hidden in his tone.

"Yes, of course you are. You've been so good to her. I'm sorry."

"If you aren't going to finish that food, Leigh, I'll walk you back to the room. I must get to my office soon."

Steve did not miss the veiled interest of an orderly standing idly at the nurses' station when he left Leigh in Dorothy's room. And he made the correct assumption. Quietly following the man down to the end of the hallway he saw him step up to a telephone and nervously dial a number.

Unwisely standing with his back toward the corridor, the orderly had a short conversation with the recipient of the call, not realizing that Steve stood close behind, listening to every word.

"You told me to report anything. Well, he was just here with her . . . yeah, o.k. . . . but that'll take more money, ya know."

Slamming down the receiver he turned swiftly and grunted as he collided with the solid figure of the very man he had been discussing. He winced as a strong hand gripped his wrist tightly and wrenched it up behind his back.

"I believe we need to have a quiet talk, my friend," Steve said firmly, guiding him into the lounge and pushing him down into a chair.

Leigh watched the still form on the hospital bed. She saw the blood dripping slowly down the tubing and the pale face with a bandage over the head wound. She wished her very desire would bring Dorothy to consciousness, and she willed the faint heartbeat to grow stronger. She had no nursing ability, but was thankful that she was free to be in the room. The hospital staff was so overworked, particularly after battles such as the one last night, that they were not able to give constant care; she had been given instructions on what to do should the situation worsen. It was now nearly noon and to her distress there had been no sign of life aside from the slow, faint breathing.

Then she felt her hand being squeezed slightly.

She sat up straight, holding her breath and staring as eyelids fluttered and opened slowly; Dorothy turned her head slightly to look at Leigh with expressionless eyes.

"Hi, Dot," Leigh said, standing up and leaning closer. "I'm right here. Everything's all right."

Dorothy tried to speak, laboriously forming words with her mouth, but she did not have the strength to utter a sound. Her eyes searched the room.

Leigh took a guess and said soothingly, "Thad will be here soon."

This was evidently a satisfactory answer, for the searching stopped, eyes closed, and there was no more response. There was not even any sort of small acknowledgment when Grandmother Perry arrived in the afternoon, through a small miracle of Tom's doing, for he had made arrangements to bring her in a friend's car.

All day they waited, Grandma Perry and Leigh praying and ministering, and an agonizing, tormented Thad joining them in the late afternoon.

He stood beside the bed holding the limp hand and staring steadily at the motionless face; Leigh could not bear to look at him; it was too pitiful and frightening.

Finally, thirty hours after the accident, about nine o'clock in the evening, the tension had built to such a force that it gripped each person waiting and seemed almost explosive. When Leigh felt she could not stand much more, Thad leaned over to whisper once again into Dorothy's ear, while he gently brushed back her hair.

"Dot, please come back to me. I love you, Dot!"

Heavy eyelids opened and there was a responsive glance in his direction. Leaning nearer he heard her whisper one word, and it crushed him as nothing else could have.

"Jesus."

One word murmured so softly it disappeared quickly on thin air struck so deeply into his heart that he turned white and sank into the chair beside her bed. Not his name, his stricken eyes seemed to say to Leigh, but the only name that meant life and even death to his beloved. He slumped over, holding his head and moaning softly to erase that sound from his mind. But it echoed again and again as a whispered word runs through a darkened cave.

"Jesus, Jesus, Jesus."

Only Grandma Perry was able to give Dorothy constant care, and Leigh brought her supper in the evenings when she and Thad came to visit.

There was no medical reason, the doctor told them, for the lack of improvement. Everything was under control, but they needed to remember that she was suffering from shock. His prognosis was a sad one, and he implied that a miracle, "if you believed in them," was needed.

Chapter 11

By Saturday morning, six days after the accident, Thad was a physical and emotional wreck but insisted on going shopping with Leigh and Uncle Paul "to buy something for Dorothy," he said in a strange voice. Leigh thought his manner was cold, but dismissed it from her mind as the fruit of anxious days.

The wailing sirens and gunfire were daily penetrating reminders of the civil war. The city was saturated with military forces—a convoy of trucks filled with black-uniformed soldiers passed by. Groups of soldiers moved along every street, guarded almost every business, rode every bus and train. and they were aware of them as they walked to the mall.

Leigh was thankful to have two men with her. As they stopped at a corner to wait for the signal to change, she glanced behind them.

There it was—the unmarked black car following half a block away. She said nothing, fearing Thad's present mood, but linked arms more closely with her companions. Whoever was spying on them did a continuous, if somewhat obvious, job of it, and she forcefully put it from her thoughts.

Thad left them as soon as they entered the shopping center, saying he had someone to see. Leigh watched him stride quickly away and then turned questioningly to her uncle. He merely shrugged his shoulders and said, "I don't know what's going on in his head, Leigh."

Walking through the mall was depressing, for its former beauty had faded. The lush green plants were gone; the brass fountain, focal point of the center, was dry, tarnished, and broken; most light fixtures were shattered, and the atmosphere was dim and dreary; walls were peeling and in need of paint; some stores were boarded up, while others were only half full of merchandise. Rows of men, sitting in helpless despair down one end of the mall, saddened Leigh. They were out of work, had no money, and had nothing to do.

"I don't really have anything to get," Uncle Paul said as they neared a bench area. I'll just sit here and wait for you. Perhaps I can talk to some of those men about the Lord."

Leigh indicated a nearby store and said, "I'm just going to the drug store for my list of things. I won't be long."

"No hurry, dear. Just be careful."

Leigh concentrated on the purchases she wanted to make: aspirin for the school medical kit, powdered milk that was now a scarce commodity, and any available vitamins and food supplements for the children. She also wanted to find some body powder for Dorothy and found two bars of cheap-smelling but welcome soap for herself. She felt fortunate to find all her items without waiting in line for hours, even though the prices were almost more than she could manage.

As she stood in the check-out line listening to the idle chatter of others, she became aware of an abrupt, uncomfortable silence settling down on those about her. Customers and employees were silent and tense, and she could see them glancing out into the mall corridor. She strained to catch any sounds that might reveal the cause of the uneasiness about her.

"Soldiers."

The whispered explanation ran through the waiting line and spurred her on to pay for her things hurriedly. Uncle Paul was the nearest refuge if there were trouble, and she wanted to get to him. Turning quickly, and with a heart pounding against her ribs, she started out the door, catching up her package as she walked away. Intent on retrieving a slipping bottle, she did not see the tall man standing in her pathway.

"Pardon me, Miss."

The impersonal but familiar-sounding voice was startling, and looking up, she found herself standing just inches away from a black-uniformed Steve Houston, who now held her by the shoulders to prevent a seemingly inevitable collision.

His whole manner was so stern that it was difficult for her to comprehend, and the pressure of his hands painfully gripping her was hardly reassuring. Taking a deep breath, she tried to recover her balance.

"I'm s-sorry, St. . . . ah . . . Major," she stuttered. "I didn't see you."

"No need to apologize," he said in a clipped voice. His hands dropped slowly from her shoulders, and he added for the benefit of listening soldiers, "Perhaps you'd better stand clear."

With great effort she tore her eyes from his uncompromising expression and looked around. There were soldiers everywhere. "Is something wrong?" Her purchases began to slip again, and she re-adjusted the package with shaking hands.

"Only some black market trouble." Turning impatiently to the group of soldiers, he motioned them to proceed. One flick of his hand sent a dozen men into instant action.

As they moved quickly into another store and Leigh and Steve were left alone, she looked into his eyes and caught only a quick gleam of inner warmth before they grew cold and remote again.

"You make it very difficult for me to continue this charade," he said quietly through stiff lips. "I should order you out of the mall." He frowned down at her from his greater height and questioned sharply, "You didn't come alone, did you?" He glanced around them, concerned that their conversation would be overheard, and lowered his voice. "It's dangerous for you to be alone, even in here."

Her face was white with anxiety and concern, the perfect foil for those who were watching. Barnes stood a little distance away, unable to hear their conversation, but seeing clearly Major Houston's stern expression. He smiled cruelly. How satisfying it was to see someone else be the recipient of the Major's sharp tongue. That man could reprimand his victims in fewer words than anyone Barnes had ever heard, and he felt sure the girl was experiencing it just now. However, he had no wish to receive the same kind of verbal attack, and it was very possible he could if he were caught standing here. Reluctantly he gave up watching his superior and turned into a clothing store on his left where he ordered the soldiers to find the owner and stop wasting his time.

The emotions he had seen in Leigh were not the result of any harsh condemnation from Steve but were actually coming from a sudden uneasiness in her mind.

Staring up over his shoulder, a movement in the shadows caught her attention and Leigh realized what was wrong. With fascinated horror she saw a man's hand come out from the shadows of one of the side corridors on the second floor—and in that hand was a gun pointed straight at Steve's back.

She saw the gun, the shadow of the man leaning slightly out of the hallway, and Steve a perfect target. She could hear the conversation of people nearby, the shuffling feet of unsuspecting shoppers, and the soldiers talking with the merchant just brought from one of the stores. But the loudest sound was the roaring one within, the screaming desperation that sought to deny the danger and the fact that she recognized the assailant.

Leigh shook her head in disbelief, and whispered, "No." This must be a nightmare from which she would soon awake. Her eyes were wide with terror, and she tried to scream a warning.

But there was no need, for Steve saw her expression and was instantly aware of danger. Years of military and espionage experience had honed his senses for just such moments, and in one quick move he spun around, pushing Leigh out of the way as he looked up to the second floor. But he could do no more; there was no time.

A shot rang out and Leigh watched Steve slump slowly to the floor. She tried to get to him, but struggled unsuccessfully to be free of the one against whom she had been pushed.

"Please, let me go to him," she whispered, not realizing what she was doing, only aware that she wanted to help Steve.

"No, Leigh, you can't." It was Uncle Paul who held her and who realized she must not be identified with the Major. She was still clutching her packages as she stared at the blood seeping through Steve's shirt and spreading over his jacket.

"Dad, take her packages. We've got to get her out of here now!"

She relinquished her things to her uncle and looked up, wondering how Tom could be standing there beside them when he was supposed to be at work.

They had to forcefully guide her around groups of gawking customers and stunned soldiers and down to the end of the shopping mall. At the door her knees buckled, refusing to function any longer, and Tom caught her before she fell to the floor.

"She can't walk home like this, Tom. Now what?"

Before Tom could answer his father, for he, too, was wondering what they would do, help came. A heavily whiskered old man, carrying a battered carpenter's box, shuffled by and motioned with a faint nod of his head that they were to follow him.

"I've got a van outside. I'll get you away."

An ambulance was heralding its arrival at the mall as they drove out of the parking lot, and Tom gave directions to their home. Within five minutes they were stopping at the back door of the Gordon home. Uncle Paul helped Leigh down from the van and into the house while Tom turned to question the driver, who smilingly offered an explanation.

"I've seen you several times at militia meetings. Knew you needed help." He shrugged his shoulders in a dismissal of his kindness.

"Glad to do it. Say, what happened at the mall?" The carpenter gunned the motor as though he did not expect a detailed reply.

"Major Houston was shot."

"Yeah? Well, guess I'd better go check that out, eh?"

Without another word, he waved a careless hand at Tom, threw the gear into position, and drove away.

Tom soon had a blazing fire in the living room fireplace where Leigh sat in shock, shivering and frightened, but vainly trying to be calm. And each time the shooting flashed through her mind like an instant replay on television, she came nearer to losing the small amount of self-control that was left. Sheer panic tied her stomach in knots. She stood up and began pacing the floor, unable to sit still and unable to tell the men all she knew.

"Leigh, come and sit near the fire. You need to get warm." Her uncle's concern was comforting but served to bring the tears nearer the surface.

"How . . ." She stopped and swallowed hard, but the lump in her throat refused to be dissolved. "H-how can we find out about Major Houston's condition?"

Tom gave the deceptive appearance of being totally relaxed in his chair by the roaring fire, but he was watching her carefully.

"Well," he answered, "as soon as Thad gets home we'll go over to the hospital and see Dorothy. I can probably find out then." He knew several hospital employees who were militia members and would get the information he wanted.

Leigh stopped pacing and stood looking down at him. Her slim hands betrayed her emotions, for they shook uncontrollably when she raised them to her mouth and pressed hard. When she spoke, her voice was tremulous.

"I . . . I don't think Thad will be coming home."

"Was he going straight to the hospital?"

Unable to speak and with eyes full of tears, Leigh stared helplessly at her cousin who frowned and asked, "Leigh are you trying to tell us something? I'm getting the feeling that you know something we don't."

Uncle Paul looked at the trembling girl with her face as pale and colorless as a winter moon, and although Tom had informed him of the Major's interest in her, he could not understand why she was so upset. "I'm sure Major Houston wasn't hurt too badly, dear."

"Leigh, what about Thad?" Tom was beginning to suspect Leigh's worry involved her brother in some way, and he prodded her again. "Leigh?"

When the answer finally came, he sat straight up in his chair, momentarily losing his normal self-control. "What did you say?" he demanded.

Leigh shook her head and sighed, halting her uncle's next comment with an outstretched hand. She hated to repeat her words, for they shattered the pretense of composure she was attempting to build.

"I said," came the choked reply, "that it was . . . Thad . . . who shot Steve."

Both men spoke at once. "How do you know? Did you see him?"

She sank down into a chair, slightly relieved that she could share this burden, but still engulfed in fearful concern for Thad and Steve.

"Yes, I happened to look up and saw Thad standing in an upstairs hallway, pointing a gun at Steve. I couldn't say a word, but Steve realized something was wrong, and pushed me out of the way."

"But how can you be so sure it was Thad?"

"I saw him, and I heard Steve whisper his name just before the shot was fired."

The words were out. Though spoken softly, the result was

electrifying. Uncle Paul's face turned grey, and he slumped forward in his chair. Tom sprang up and started out of the room, his mind clicking off every possible course of action like a computer.

"Dad, turn on the radio. See if you can get any news."

He moved quickly to the hallway closet where he grabbed his coat and scarf. Carrying his boots in his hand, he returned to the room in time to hear a radio report of the mall incident.

". . . and the hospital reports that Major Houston is in serious condition, awaiting surgery for removal of a bullet just inches from his heart. The National Intelligence Office representative informed our correspondent that the assailant has been caught, but no other information is available at this time. . . . And now, for the National news. . . ."

Tom leaned over and snapped off the radio, glancing at the pathetic figure huddled in the chair beside the fire. His first concern was for her safety, but he also needed information about his cousin as quickly as possible. This was imperative if they were to help him, for he could be shot before morning if some unbalanced, fiery officer had his way.

"I'm going to see what I can learn. Leigh, don't leave this house for any reason. I'll be back as soon as possible."

Motioning his father to follow, he walked to the front door, pausing there to pull on his boots. "Don't let her out of your sight, Dad. I'm not sure what she might try."

But Leigh sat immobile, drained of every ounce of physical and emotional strength. Wave upon wave of panic and despair washed over her, threatening to drown her completely. With a great effort she concentrated on her uncle's voice.

"I . . . I'm sorry, Uncle. What did you say?"

"I asked if you knew why Thad shot Houston?"

"He's never liked Steve . . . the Major . . . from the beginning, and his dislike just grew stronger after he was appointed NIO director. Thad blames him for everything that goes wrong, even the bread riots."

Her uncle nodded his head understandingly and added, "and Dorothy's condition was the last straw."

"Yes, I'm afraid it was. He refused to see God's hand in any of this. Oh, Uncle Paul, what will happen to him?"

For the first time since the shot was fired, the severity of Thad's position came to her, and she cried out, "What is it going to take to bring him to God?"

Chapter 12

One . . . two . . . three . . . four . . . five, five steps to the glazed window that gave light but no view.

"Oh, God! What have I done?"

One . . . two . . . three . . . four . . . five, five steps back to stand before the steel door with its small guard window.

"Hah! Why am I calling on God?"

Stark reality dressed in prison grey mocked Thad, when after a night of endless pacing, he finally became aware of his surroundings. Looking around the narrow cell he saw that it was grim and bleak but not filthy dirty as he had expected. Major Houston probably demanded clean cells for all of his unwilling guests, he thought, and turned to walk again, taking the five steps back to the window, staring at it helplessly.

How many times in the hours since entering this cell had he reviewed the events that brought him here. Over and over, like a broken gate swinging in the wind, the scenes had repeatedly slapped at his consciousness. He saw a madman holding a gun and squeezing the trigger—had that really been he? Then the dash down the darkened corridor to a small storage room where his escape waited. But the drop to safety had never come, for two soldiers burst into the room before he was halfway out of the window.

He stood again before the wounded Major, and, astounded,

heard him say, "Barnes, keep him under guard but leave his interrogation to me. That's an order!" The strange expression on his face puzzled Thad yet, for it was neither hate nor revenge, but instead a sympathetic sadness.

It came to him once more and he beat his fist against the wall and cried softly, "What have I done! What have I done!"

It seemed that he walked miles inside the small cell while the battle raged in his heart and mind, and through the storm of conflicting emotions came a quiet thought. It was so strong it could have been spoken aloud.

"You've been running from Me."

"NO!"

A rap on the door and a guard's admonition to keep quiet told Thad that he had shouted aloud, and he began pacing again.

But the struggle went steadily on.

"Why don't you stop running?"

"I don't want God controlling my life," he muttered.

"You would rather be in the mess you're in now? That's what your strong will has done."

"No. It's because of what Houston has done!"

"Your will, your own stubbornness . . ."

No matter how much he tried blocking it out, the words kept returning again and again.

He contended that a supreme God could not allow suffering. Oh, he had often built quite a case with that argument. Only the simple-minded accepted this as being "God's will."

But then, he had to admit that his father was a discerning man whose faith was an intelligent one. In fact, he was compelled to concede that many members of his father's church were extremely articulate and knowledgeable about their faith. And he remembered what Leigh's answer had been, "If man persists in shoving God from his life, what else can be expected?" It was not as though he had never heard the answers to this problem, but it was a convenient post behind which he tried to hide from God.

The eternal Spirit of God is, however, a persistent follower through the twisted and darkened paths of a needy soul. He alone knows every murky hiding place, every empty hypocrisy, and every unbroken link in the chain that binds the soul to eternal darkness.

Thad tried to convince himself that God was a selfish old man who only wanted to take the good things of life from mankind and was sadistically delighted to see people suffer. Why else would He have allowed man to spend all of his earthly years, from earliest civilization until the present, in endless fighting, murdering, and war.

But that voice continued.

"Is it I who have been selfish?"

Thad would not give up, but looked for other excuses to build up his crumbling defenses. He would not, he thought, he could not follow a God who was unable to keep such a wonderful person as Dorothy from physical assault or death.

"But My ways are far above yours, and My thoughts out-distance your small ones. One day you will know why I have allowed all this. Why don't you stop running? I have loved you with an everlasting love, and I have so much to give to you, My son."

All afternoon, all that night, and on into the following morning Thad fought with himself as he paced the floor. He fought God's loving Spirit with every emotion he had. It is not an easy thing for pride to bend its knee before God; it is indeed soul shattering, but there is no other way for peace to come. And, oh, how his battered heart wanted peace, was starved for peace.

Finally, after all those hours of struggle, he handed over to God, one by one, the arguments he had held so tightly—his pride in being a self-sufficient man—his intellectualism which had sought for false answers outside the spiritual realm—his strong will—his desires—and finally, his love for Dorothy. And having handed these previous items over to the One who had given His life upon a cross, Thad was emptied of self and filled with the peace of God. He became a new man—in Christ!

He was totally unprepared for the flood of love and joy that came over him, but his excitement grew as snatches of Bible verses and conversations began to fit together in proper place. One Scripture in particular seemed to come so strongly to mind: "Behold, what kind of love has the Father bestowed upon us, that we should be called the sons of God." He marvelled that he had fought so long and been so blind. Even his bitter remorse for attempting to kill Steve Houston had been tempered with his confession and God's forgiveness. He amended that thought as he wondered if Major Houston were still alive.

For the remainder of the day he was left alone, except when a guard brought his meals; he prayed as he never had before. This was a new thing, talking with the God of heaven as a son and realizing that He was here in this small cell, listening to every word and meeting every need in his life. Thad spoke to the Lord of all that had troubled his mind about the destruction of the country, the revolution and civil war, his corroding hatred, his family's needs, and Dorothy's present condition. There grew within him a conviction that everything would be all right, even if he were never to leave the cell alive. And, strangely enough, he was willing to leave that in God's hands and feel no concern.

And the heavenly Father began answering Thad's prayers. For just as He had transformed him spiritually, so on that very afternoon He began a slow transformation in Dorothy's health. The doctor had no answer for the way in which she began to improve. And when Leigh smilingly asked, "Is this your miracle, Doctor?" he merely grunted and left the room.

Later that afternoon when Dorothy and Leigh talked about the explosion at the auditorium, Thad's name was mentioned for the first time.

Dorothy smiled and patted her friend's hand. "He's all right, Leigh. I know something has happened that you're not telling me, but Thad is all right. I just know it."

Five days later, the metal window slid open to allow a face to peer in, then closed as a key turned the lock; the cell door opened. A soldier stepped in and gestured impatiently.

"On your feet, prisoner!"

Thad stood up cautiously and waited while the belligerent man, smartly dressed in his black uniform, looked him over with disdain; it only increased his discomfort, for he knew what the lack of a bath or shave or clean clothes for days did to his appearance.

"Follow me!"

The soldier started out the door as Thad stared after him.

"Hurry up! Major Houston hasn't got all day."

A wave of intense relief washed over Thad, and he blinked away his tears as he followed the soldier from the room. He had not killed the Major; God had not allowed him to do so. With an increasing sense of peace, he became aware of his escort of two soldiers with drawn guns, and he watched the route they took through the building.

From the cell block they walked down a hallway crowded with soldiers to an elevator and rode silently up to the second floor where they went straight into a large waiting room.

The soldier motioned for Thad to sit on one of the wooden benches along the right wall while he spoke to a secretary who was also in uniform.

The room was filled with waiting people, and all seemed to be staring at him. Thad guessed that those seated with him were prisoners, but he was certainly the dirtiest. Each one had the same shuttered, blank expression as Thad was sure he himself now wore. He did not recognize anyone along the line, and for that he was thankful.

Turning his attention to those seated facing him, across an invisible line that created two worlds in the room, he assessed what he saw. A few women were there, tense and anxious, obviously waiting to plead for the freedom of husband or son. Many of the men looked with bored amusement at the prisoners and were probably waiting to share some helpful information that would produce a few extra dollars for their greedy pockets.

The strange silence of so many people in one room was worse than being alone in a cell, and it began to play on Thad's nerves. He was even relieved when Lt. Barnes came through a door on his right to motion to him, saying, "Prisoner Gordon, in here."

Obeying that command, Thad slowly entered the room and came face to face with the man he had attempted to kill.

Chapter 13

Leigh approached the Christmas celebrations with a heavy heart. She tried to get excited with the children as they prepared a program for their parents. She listened as they recited original poems and Scripture passages and sang the beautiful old carols. She watched their rehearsals, smiling at their anticipation of parental approval. She helped teachers fit costumes on wiggling, squirming shepherds and kings and angels. And she wanted to cry when she heard one chubby little angel intone in a loud voice, "Fear not, for behold, I . . . I . . ."—a deep breath, then a rush of words, "I bring you good tidings of great joy!"

Mark was the only child who seemed subdued the day they rehearsed the entire program in the church sanctuary, and Leigh watched him with growing concern.

"Mark," she called softly as he passed her, walking slowly down the aisle in a purple robe with a foil crown tilted precariously on his blond hair. "Come sit with me for a minute." She watched him hitch up the robe and climb up on the bench beside her. He looked up at her with utmost patience. "Do you like being a king, Mark?"

"Yes, a lot," he smiled.

She reached over to brush his hair back, moving her hand slowly over his forehead to see if he had a temperature. That seemed normal, but she asked, "How are you feeling today?"

"I'm o.k.," he said, ducking his head.

"Mark," she probed quietly, taking his hand, "is something troubling you?"

He did not answer, but a little tear escaped to create a streaked line over a cheek that had gotten a bit dusty in play. Everyone else had gone from the sanctuary, and they sat alone in the quietness. Leigh held out her hands, offering him a haven in her arms if he wished. He took the crown from his head and laid it carefully on the bench, then with a quivering chin, leaned close to her, trying so hard not to cry.

"Daddy told me I should be a big boy and not cry while he is gone," he said, his little voice full of misery.

"Daddies sometimes cry, too, Mark."

"They do?" He looked up with surprise in his face.

"Yes, I'm sure your father won't be angry with you if you feel like doing that now."

With that, the tears filled his eyes. "I want my Daddy to see me be a king," he said. "I want to see him for Christmas, and Mommy wants him to come home, and she doesn't feel good, and . . . and . . ." He was too small a boy to have such big problems bottled up inside, Leigh thought, as the worries spilled out between little sobs; she held him tightly.

"Could the Lord bring Daddy home this Christmas?" His face was hidden in her shoulder; he looked up for her response, then asked in surprise, "Oh, Miss Gordon, are you crying, too?" He reached out to touch her cheek.

She nodded and smiled. "I do when I see you cry, Mark."

"Why?" he asked, his face full of wonder.

"Because I love you," she replied, giving him a quick hug. "Let's pray about all this, Mark. We don't know what the Lord will want to do, but He always gives us what is best, even if it doesn't seem that way."

Before she could say more, he slid from her lap and knelt down beside the bench; with his hands folded and his eyes on hers, he waited for her to join him. As she knelt, he began to pray.

"Dear Lord, I want to see my Daddy so much, and Mommy isn't feeling good. Could you help us, please? I want to be a nice king in the play, so help me to be a good boy. And I thank you that Miss Gordon loves me. I love her, too, Lord. Thank you. Amen."

Leigh had a difficult time keeping her voice under control as she added her prayer to Mark's. Nothing she could say would make his petitions any more effective than they were, for he was full of faith and trust. But she silently pleaded for the Lord to be gracious to this little boy who had such a special place in her heart.

The next day the children had a wonderful time in their own celebration. They had worked diligently making gifts for friends, teachers, and parents. Leigh had enjoyed helping some of the children work on these items, amazed at their creativity. The ladies of the church had worked for months to have a gift for each child, and no amount of warnings from the teachers could control the classes as they waited for the afternoon hour when they would begin their party in the nursery dining hall. Leigh watched as they sat around the tree and sang a carol, their faces so earnest, their hearts so full of love toward the Savior who had come as a tiny baby in a faraway country, so that He could be their Friend.

There was a package for every child, and as they were handed out the room seemed ready to burst with excitement. It was pleasing to see how grateful they were for a new shirt, warm slacks, a sweater or coat, or hat and mittens. Each item was desperately needed and fully appreciated.

When the excitement had nearly died down, and the children were admiring the gifts their friends had received, Mark came up to Leigh with a small box in his hand. His face was shining with love, and she thought that gift was all she really needed, but he held out his hand.

"Miss Gordon, this is for you," he whispered. "Hurry up, open it. I made it for you, and Mommy helped me." His flow of words revealed his excitement, and she opened the box to find a small silk flower pin. It was a little out of shape, and there was a small smudge of glue on the tip of one petal, but he had worked so hard and was so proud.

"It's beautiful, Mark! Thank you. May I wear it now?"

"Oh, would you," he breathed in awe.

"Of course." She pinned the flower on the lapel of her jacket. "Is your mother coming today?"

"No," his face clouded a little. "No, but I promised to tell her all about it. Will you come sometime and sing the carols with me?"

"Yes, I promise."

Soon the parents were there, and the sanctuary was filled with tiny people singing and talking about the wonderful news that God had sent a Gift to mankind; as one little boy said, "That was the bestest gift of all!"

After the program Leigh walked through the crowd, greeting parents and admiring the gifts their children had given to them. She kept looking for Mark, wondering suddenly about his prayer and where he was at the moment. Perhaps he had gone to the back room to remove his costume, but it was over an hour later before she was able to look for him. "Have you seen Mark?"

Dorothy looked up as she pulled a white robe over the head of a little girl. "I think I heard Marian say that she was taking him home. Why?"

"Oh, nothing. I just wanted to talk with him for a minute."

She went to her office, picked up a gift she had planned to give the little boy, a little toy truck that once belonged to Thad, started out of the room and saw Marian's husband, Jed, coming down the hallway. His worried look stirred an uneasiness in her.

"Leigh, I've been looking for you."

"What is it, Jed?"

"Soldiers broke into the Kelly's apartment trying to find Mark's father, and they forced his mother to go down to NIO headquarters."

"Why?" Leigh asked angrily.

"They said she knew where her husband was, and they wanted to question her."

"And?" Leigh's growing anger zeroed in on Steve Houston, for she felt he was to blame.

"We just got a telephone call saying that she had collapsed on the way downtown and was rushed to the hospital." He stopped and searched Leigh's face, and then added, "She's dead, Leigh."

"No!" Leigh turned quickly to grab her coat and hat from a hook on her office door. "Where is Mark?"

"In our apartment with Marian, and he's asking for you."

Leigh struggled into her coat as she started to run down the hallway, calling over her shoulder to one of the teachers, "Tell Dorothy I've gone after Mark."

She did not wait for Jed, but ran out of the door and down the steps, not caring or even thinking about the danger of being alone on the streets. She heard footsteps behind her and assumed it was Jed, but did not take time to look back. Down the slippery, snowpacked sidewalk, darting between cars to cross the street, and on two blocks further she ran toward the apartment building, praying silently for the Lord's help.

Panting hard, she struggled up the flight of steps just as Jed arrived to unlock the front door to the building entrance and the door of the first apartment where they lived. She pushed the door open, her eyes only on the frightened little boy sitting on Marian's lap. She took a deep, steadying breath, walked softly across the room and knelt down beside Mark.

"I've come to take you home," she said in a low voice.

His blue eyes were full of fear and confusion, and he fell into her arms, not crying, but holding onto her as though he would never let go.

They went to Mark's home, packed a suitcase for him, left a note to his father, which he insisted should be written, and then walked back to the Gordon home. And all that while, he had not shed a tear.

Uncle Paul helped Leigh prepare a bed in Thad's room where he was now staying, and later that evening as Mark got ready for bed, Leigh tried to answer all the questions he was suddenly asking about his mother.

"Will she be cold in the ground?"

"No, Mark, she is safe with Jesus. When we go to be with Him, He gives us a new body, and we don't need our old one again."

"Will she get enough medicine in heaven?"

"She won't be sick, ever again. She is very happy now with Jesus."

"Will she miss me?" His voice broke. "I miss her."

"She loves you very much, dear, and prayed that God would take care of you if she went to be with Him."

"Why did God take her?"

"I don't know." Leigh stopped for a moment, trying to find some explanation he would understand; before she did, he was speaking.

"I think God needed Mommy in heaven, and He didn't want her to be unhappy any more."

"Yes, I'm sure that's it."

"Will you love me now, like Mommy did?" His eyes filled with the tears he had suppressed all evening.

Leigh held him close and cried with him. "I love you very much, Mark. You can be my little boy as long as you want." And that was the only night he cried himself to sleep in her arms.

Three days after he had moved into the Gordon home, they attended his mother's funeral. Mark held Leigh's hand throughout the entire service, and only when they were ready to leave the graveside did he express any emotion. Everyone had left them alone, and he stood looking at the grave and the coffin holding his mother's body. Then he turned and looked slowly around the cemetery, making a complete circle before he whispered to her in a disappointed voice, "Daddy didn't come."

In the days that followed, he often asked for his father, worried that he might not see the note left at the apartment, and Leigh promised they would do all they could to contact him. She talked with Tom one night, asking if he could get any information on Mr. Kelly.

"I'll see what I can do, Leigh," Tom said and then changed the subject. "Have you heard from his grandparents?"

"Yes, and they have no way to get Mark to the farm until summer. They've asked us to keep him until then."

Tom smiled sympathetically. "How will you let him go, Leigh?"

She shook her head. "I don't know, Tom. It will be like tearing my arm off."

On Christmas Day Mark received a letter from his father. It was hand delivered by Marian and Jed, who said they had found it in their mailbox that morning. It was the best gift the little boy could have received.

Tom and Uncle Paul spent the day with Leigh and Mark, playing games and singing carols, doing all they could to make it a happy experience for the little boy. But several times, Leigh caught him staring at nothing, looking sad and lonely, and she knew it would be a long, long time before the pain and hurt would be healed.

When Dorothy came in the late afternoon, they took some food to several older neighbors, and Mark enjoyed reciting his Christmas poem to them.

He carried his father's letter with him everywhere, and Leigh had to search his pockets before washing any of his clothes for fear she might accidentally destroy that precious item.

She wondered if Tom knew Mr. Kelly, or if the letter had come through some other channel. But it was useless to ask, for he would only laugh and tease her about being an inquisitive female. She did, however, thank him one day.

"Thanks, Tom, for getting in contact with Mr. Kelly. His letter has made Mark a much happier little boy."

"What makes you think I did anything?" Tom asked, rattling the newspaper he was reading.

"I don't," she said with a smile, "but I just thought I'd thank you anyway. Mark is very important to me, Tom, and you were able to help him. Thanks."

Tom grinned and shook his head. "You're welcome," he said.

Chapter 14

Leigh shivered as she stared out the front window. It was a strange winter night. The sky was a charcoal grey, the white winter moon cast a bizarre metallic shade on all it touched, and the bare tree limbs stretched up like pleading arms beside black buildings. It was a depressing black and grey sketch.

"Would you like some music?" Uncle Paul spent as much time as he could with Leigh and Mark now, and often caught her standing before the window staring out with unseeing eyes.

"Yes, thanks." She turned, sighed deeply, and picked up a study book as she moved nearer the fire, thankful for that extra warmth in the cold house. She hoped the winter would not be a hard one and tax the dwindling fuel supplies of the nation. She expected the church board to close the nursery by the end of the month; there was not enough money for more fuel. What would she do for an income? Perhaps, if Thad were home . . . She sighed again, unable to find a solution.

Her uncle took a quick glance her way and turned on the stereo. A beautiful hymn, one of her favorites, that sang of the loveliness of Christ, filled the room.

"Thinking of Thad?"

"Yes. I wish I knew what prison he is in. It would be nice to let him know Dorothy has recovered."

"What would you do if you knew where he was? We would

never let you visit him. It would be too dangerous.''

"I know, I know." Her voice betrayed her frustration. "Uncle Paul, tell me something. Why is it that Tom gets any information he wants? He learned about Thad so quickly.'' She stared at the open pages of her book, pretending an interest in them she did not feel.

"He just likes to be on top of things and has a number of friends in the right places.''

"Are you sure that's all? Is he a member of the Citizens Militia?''

"Leigh, I wouldn't answer that question if I could.''

Propping her chin in her hand, she frowned at him. "I know, the less I know, the better off I am.''

He smiled at her mocking tone. "Exactly.''

"And, of course, you won't tell me why he moved those two young men into his old room upstairs.''

"It brings in extra ration tickets for coal and food, and cash for you.'' He laughed at her grimace and added, "Give up, dear child; I'm not the one to answer your questions.''

"But Tom won't tell me anything!'' Leigh bit her lip in annoyance, and then admitted, "I am thankful you two moved downstairs after the . . . arrest.'' It was still difficult to speak of her brother's trouble, and she hesitated. "With you in Thad's room, Tom in the study, and the two men upstairs, Mark and I feel well protected.''

"Speaking of being well protected, why don't we read together.'' He reached for his Bible, opening it to the Psalm which she suggested, and began reading of the protection and refuge of God.

He had just finished the verse that suggested the folly of trusting in horses and chariots rather than trusting in the name of the Lord God when the sharp sound of the front door bell arrested his next words, and they both looked up.

It was rather late for callers, but his placid attitude never left room for jumping to bad conclusions, and Leigh was too weary to wonder who it might be.

She settled back into the cushions of her chair while he went to the front door. None of the men allowed her to answer any such summons if they were around, and besides, she had to admit that tonight she really did not want to move an inch from her chair.

But move she did!

In one swift reaction she was on her feet, feeling as shattered as a delicate piece of glass thrown to the floor. There was no mistaking that deep voice in conversation with her uncle, and she looked around wildly for an escape as they neared the room. She snapped off the only light, a lamp near her chair, and ran toward the study door.

There was only one thought uppermost in her mind, and it bore her along as she quietly closed the study door and turned to the one leading out into the hall and thus to her room. Escape was an absolute necessity! Her hands shook as she reached the door, and her legs were weak with the dismay she felt.

With a feeling of great relief that she was near her goal, she turned the handle, pulled open the door and ran into the hallway—straight into the strong, unyielding body of Steve Houston.

"Oh, no!"

Her involuntary cry spoke volumes to the man who stood holding her tightly by the arms. In a storm of anger and frustration she fought to get away, but the struggle to be free was useless. She was no match for his strength, and the more she battled with him the tighter his grasp became. Finally, she stood quiet, panting like a runner, her anger only slightly controlled.

"You've refused to see me twice now, Leigh, but no more!" His voice was low but unyielding, and with one hand still grasping her arm tightly, he led her back into the living room where he closed the door and guided her over to a chair.

"Let me go!"

By the firelight the ruggedness and determination in his face were even more pronounced, and she refused to return his long look. He pushed her firmly but not unkindly down into the chair with a look of frustration in his eyes at the sad picture she made. In her long, blue-quilted robe and with no make-up on her face, she looked more like a little girl undergoing punishment as she stared down at her tightly clasped hands.

"Will you stay there while I stir up the fire, or must I continue to hold you?"

Afraid that he would do just that, she shook her head, and when he turned away, lifted her eyes to watch him work with the wood, hating herself for allowing his presence to wreck her composure.

"I see you're not in uniform tonight," she said sarcastically, and then repented immediately when he turned, still kneeling before the fire, and looked her calmly in the eyes.

"I thought you'd like it better if I weren't."

Leigh said nothing as he took the chair opposite hers and leaned back. His long legs stretched out the distance between them until they nearly touched the hem of her robe. He made a steeple of his fingers and studied her over the top of them.

Finally, unable to endure the silence or his presence, or that steady gaze, she blurted out, "Why am I so honored with your presence?"

"Do you find sarcasm an adequate shield when you are upset? It really doesn't become you." The softness of his reply did not hide the hurt she had inflicted, and she squirmed uncomfortably.

She was startled by his question, because there was truth in it, and anger flared in her eyes. There was no reason to stay here with him and be insulted, she thought. But her quick move to leave brought an equally sudden one from him. Raised eyebrows and a tensing of muscles in the arm that shot out were undeniable reminders that he meant to detain her until he was finished; with an audible sigh she sank down in the chair and frowned at the floor.

"You've built up quite a case against me again, haven't you?"

"I don't know what you mean."

It was unthinkable that this man could cut her defenses to shreds so easily and turn her feelings upside down with his quiet remarks.

"Yes you do. Look at me."

He repeated the command when she refused to comply, then made a move toward her which brought instant obedience. He sat back against the cushions.

"That's better. Now, I said that you've built up quite a case against me." He smiled slightly as he saw the admission in her eyes and began numbering his offenses.

"First, I was on the hike when your group ran into trouble. There was also this sly-looking man at camp to see me. And then I became the NIO director. Am I right so far?"

Her eyes blazed, and he nodded.

"Right. Then, I was the one who sent the concert tickets—the concert where Dorothy was hurt by a mob of frightened people. Oh, I almost forgot; I'm also responsible for the armed patrol at the nursery. Now, what else? We might throw in several bread riots, the street fighting downtown, your home being ransacked, and the bombings last week of downtown bridges and banks. And, my soldiers caused Mrs. Kelly's untimely death.''

He paused again, watching her mobile face intently as it betrayed her thoughts. Never before, in this society where deceit and treachery were the rules by which men played, had he seen one so guileless. For one moment, he felt hesitant, realizing that at all costs she must remain ignorant of his plans. Someone like Barnes would find it extremely easy to get any information he wanted from her, no matter how reluctant she might be. He knew he walked a tightrope, balancing his love for her in one hand with the plans of his compatriots in the other. Then, his hesitancy was gone, for the determination not to fail surged through his very soul. He must not, he would not fail!

She stared down at the floor, thinking of the recitation of his misdeeds, but the tiny frown now wrinkling her forehead revealed her thoughts. He went on, deliberately creating the impression of detachment with an impersonal note in his voice.

"But, I believe my worst offense is in being shot by Thad and having him imprisoned.''

As he had expected, he touched a raw nerve with this, and she sat up straight.

"He's my brother! What did you expect me to feel? You put him in prison; am I supposed to be thankful for that? Have you hurt him? Have you . . . have you tortured him? Oh, how could you!''

Now that he had brought out into the open the reason for her present antagonism, he had to treat the matter carefully.

"Leigh, listen to me. Thad is all right. He is in no physical danger, believe me.''

"Where is he? I want to see him.''

Steve hesitated. He wanted to reassure her, and for selfish reasons, absolve himself in her eyes, all without allowing her to guess the arrangements he had made. Should Barnes ever get to Leigh, her best defense would be complete ignorance.

"I can't tell you, for your own good. But I can say that he isn't suffering, and you needn't worry.''

Leigh brought her fist down on the arm of her chair. "Stop saying, 'for your own good.' '' Her eyes were fired with protest. "I want to do something for Thad's good.''

"Then stop worrying about him. You can't do anything. It's impossible. I would never allow you near a prison!" The cold finality of his statement made her wince, but her protest was silenced by a lifted hand and a look which plainly said the discussion was closed.

"When are you going to start trusting me?"

His question stunned her into silence, while waves of doubt, uncertainty, and chagrin washed over her face. She sat back in relief when he did not press the issue and changed the subject.

"You look exhausted, Leigh. Haven't you gotten much sleep lately?"

"It's been difficult. We were at the hospital every night until Dorothy was released, but the problems at the nursery are worrying me. The children aren't getting enough food at home, and it's almost impossible to get enough for school lunches. Almost half of the fathers are missing, and that is emotionally hard on the children. They grow more fearful and unsettled by the day. And the additional guards you sent along don't help." She shrugged her shoulders helplessly and rested her head against the back of the chair. "You know all that already, don't you?"

"And just what do you think would happen if those soldiers weren't there and some of my more rowdy (there was a strong emphasis on the word) men would decide to invade the school for a little entertainment?"

A shiver went through her as the unsavory implications of his question swarmed into her mind, and she admitted to herself, reluctantly but painfully, that his action had been justifiable. His next words were so unexpected as he whispered, "Look at me," that she obeyed without protest, knowing it was useless to resist.

He held her gaze for what seemed like an eternity. The stereo clicked off, and there was no sound in the room except that of the crackling fire. She was sure he could hear her heart hammering against her ribs as he looked across the space separating them.

"Your defenses are crumbling," he murmured. Her eyes widened in surprise as she wondered how he knew. "I told you," he smiled tenderly, "Your heart is often in your eyes."

She longed for an explanation of the list of grievances he had mentioned earlier, and her eyes clouded over. Why would he not defend himself when he obviously knew how she felt?

He left his chair to stir up the dying embers in the fireplace until sparks flew, added another log, and sat down again. "Waiting for me to answer your questions?"

"Can you read my mind?" She frowned at the fire and moved uneasily in her chair. "I don't like it."

"Why not?" She heard the amusement in his voice and knew without looking that laughter had softened his blue eyes and was pulling at the corners of his mouth. He knew very well what her reason was, she thought in frustration.

Trying to phrase an answer that would not be self-revealing, she stood up, meaning to move into the shadows away from the fire where he could not see her face, but he caught her hand as she moved away.

"Come and sit beside me." He pointed to the footstool beside his chair and only released her hand when she sat down. "Well?"

She sat facing the fire, and her response was barely audible. "It makes me too vulnerable."

"And why are you afraid of being vulnerable with me?" His hands reached out to turn her toward him; he was intensely interested in her answer.

"I - I don't know," came the mumbled reply. She hesitated, then plunged impulsively into an explanation. "I don't know who you really are—the man I hear about on the radio who leads the Peoples Army on into glorious victory, who investigates and arrests anyone he wishes, whose uniform and insignia brandish that defiant, atheistic fist?"

She reached out to touch his arm and searched his face for understanding. "Or this man beside me who asks for trust and love? How am I to reconcile the two?"

There was one other problem she had not mentioned, but it was the most important. What was his relationship to Christ? She knew there could never be anything lasting between them if he were not a Christian, for she could not be without the peace of God in her life. This continual warfare in her heart was almost unbearable, and she longed for release so desperately that she felt she would be grateful for any solution.

"Hey, where did you go?" He ran his finger lightly over her cheek to bring her back to the present. "I'm not answering any of your questions, Leigh, until you're safe from men like Barnes. Then I'll tell you everything you want to know. In the meantime, will you just trust instead of worrying?"

"If I knew I weren't disobeying the Lord, I could."

He made no comment, least of all one that would be satisfying, but reached into his shirt pocket and pulled out a small box which he put in her lap. "I almost forgot your Christmas present. I'm sorry I didn't see you then. Did you miss me?"

Unconsciously she nodded, unaware of what she had just admitted as she stared at the gift in her hand.

"Aren't you going to open it?"

She lifted the lid with fumbling fingers and caught her breath at the beauty of the piece of jewelry inside, an old-fashioned gold cross with a small diamond at the center, hung on a delicate chain.

"It's beautiful, but, Steve, it . . . it looks so expensive!"

"It was my mother's; will you wear it?" The appealing tone of his voice was hard to miss.

Staring at the cross she fought hard to hold back tears, unwilling to give in to the desire to trust him completely, and trying to remember he was employed by the enemy, she asked in a small, tight voice, "Is this a bribe?"

Whatever she had expected as a reaction, she was unprepared to hear his indrawn breath and to feel his hands gripping her shoulders to swing her around toward him.

"Is that what you think? Anger whipped through his voice and flamed in his eyes as they stared at one another. She had, she realized, perversely goaded him into this reaction; the knowledge set off a desire to cry, and she was unable to answer.

He gave her a little shake, even though his anger was dying. "Is it? Answer me, Leigh."

A tear spilled over as she shook her head and formed the word "No" with her mouth, and his self-control, held in such tight check all evening, finally broke. His hands tightened, and he pulled her close into his arms. She heard the jewelry box fall to the floor, felt the tiny cross dig into her hands as she clutched it tightly, and saw his eyes bright with something she was afraid to define.

"Oh, Leigh," he whispered, and slowly lowered his head until their lips met, and Leigh was kissed with a tenderness and strength that made her feel loved and cherished. It brought an awareness of security that she did not want to lose.

"You've been given to me, Leigh, and I'm not letting you go—ever!" The finality of his statement sent a trembling shock through her bemused senses and tears to her eyes again.

He held her close for a long moment and then released her to take the necklace still clutched in her hand and put it around her neck. As he fastened the clasp, he glanced at his watch.

"It's late. Do you want me to go now?"

She responded automatically. "No." Sitting on the footstool, she hugged her knees in an effort to stop trembling.

"You don't have to be anywhere tonight?" Her voice was shaky, and she turned to glance at him quickly before looking back into the fire.

"At one o'clock I have an appointment." He reached out to lay a hand on her shoulder, and she knew he could feel her trembling. "You don't mind if I stay here until then?"

"No. I just thought the militia would take advantage of all the bad weather, and you would be extremely busy."

"We do expect trouble. Most of my men are on duty, and I'll be working the rest of the night."

"You weren't invited to any parties?" As soon as the question was out, she wanted to bite her tongue. He knew what she was thinking of. She had remembered the resentment she felt upon seeing a news article reporting his attendance at some holiday celebration. He was pictured in a local restaurant, The Concord, and among the guests at his table was an attractive woman looking extremely seductive.

"I was, but declined to attend."

"The beautiful ladies will be disappointed."

"You saw the newspaper article. The owner of that restaurant is a . . . a business associate, and I can only talk freely with him there. Were you jealous of the lady at my table?"

Leigh ignored his question and decided it would be better to steer the conversation to a safer topic.

"This was the first time in years the church did not have a New Year's Eve service. It was impossible with curfew."

"What did you do Christmas Day?"

Uncle Paul and Tom entertained Mark most of the day, and in the afternoon we visited some of the older couples in the neighborhood."

"Were you lonely?" he asked tenderly.

Her answer was slow in coming for she knew she was on dangerous ground again. "Yes, I missed Mom and Dad . . ."

"And Thad?"

"Yes." Fearful that he was going to ask if she had been lonely for him, for she would not admit that even to herself, she said the first thing that came into her mind, turning as she spoke and frowning a little at the knowing smile in his eyes.

"Your wound, Steve, is it . . ."

"It's fine. Nothing there but a small scar. Did you miss me, Leigh?"

She ignored his question and went on hurriedly. "I'm sorry it happened." She deeply regretted the incident; not only had it nearly taken his life, but it had also involved two people close to her heart, pitting them against each other and placing her in the middle.

His eyes were closed and sympathetically she reached out to touch his face. He looked utterly exhausted. Knowing how he must have pushed himself after the operation, she was afraid he had not regained his strength.

He smiled and reached up to take her hand. "Never mind. It's over now. You didn't answer my question." He sighed and kissed her hand before murmuring, "I'm sorry you can't meet my parents; they would have loved you dearly."

"Would have?"

He did not respond, and she thought perhaps he had fallen asleep, but he broke the silence.

"They are both dead."

"I'm sorry. Can you tell me about it?"

His words had sharp edges of anger and hurt. "They were killed in . . . an accident . . . several years ago."

She waited for him to continue, but when he added nothing more she realized that was all he was going to tell her.

He gave in then to the weariness he had been fighting for many days and fell asleep, not even stirring when Leigh pulled her hand gently from his and got up to tend the fire. She returned to her own chair and sat watching him while a hundred thoughts scampered through her mind. Questions about his life, doubts about her feelings, worries about their future. Why? Why had God allowed him to come into her life? Was it a test of her faith, or was he truly meant for her? And why could she not find God's answer, when she had prayed so desperately, for so long, to know His will? Her mother had told her many times that she must learn to wait for the Lord to work out His plans, but her impulsive nature always wanted an immediate resolution to a problem.

And this problem needed an immediate answer, she thought.

At almost one o'clock a light tap on the door brought Steve to his feet before she had barely moved. Even straight out of sleep he was unruffled, calm, and in control. She shook her head and wondered at the man before her. He reached over to trail his finger across her cheek as he walked by.

At the door he talked with someone she could not see, but she caught words like "all clear . . . new plans . . . set." The other voice was barely audible, but she wondered if it might be Tom, and it only served to make her more confused about the two men and their activities.

She knew he was standing behind her before his hands came down on her shoulders. "Leigh, don't turn on any lights after I've gone. We don't want to give anything away to Barnes."

He had made the comment with humor in his voice, but she immediately sat up in her chair, concern spilling out in her voice. "Does he know you are here?"

"No, I sent him on a long errand today. But I've been keeping one of his boys busy tagging along behind me all day." He grinned at the thought and added, "I lost him before getting near this part of town, but I'm sure he is outside now waiting to see if I am here. Barnes is determined to get every scrap of information he can to build a good case against me, so he can take my job." He pulled her to her feet and kept her hand in his as they walked to the door.

"What will you do, Steve?"

"I have a helper who is going to lead our friend on a wild chase so I can get back to my office unseen. Stop frowning. This is nothing new to me."

He gave her a quick hug and kissed her once more before she could protest. "Now, get that ring back on your finger and don't take it off again!"

"I didn't think you had noticed."

He smiled as his eyes searched her face once more, as though he were memorizing every inch. "There's not much I miss concerning you."

Just as he left the front room, Tom slipped out the back door and walked hurriedly down the alley. In a coat and cap similar to Steve's he caught the attention of a shadow that began following him away from the house. Tom guided the unsuspecting man through dimly lit streets and dark alleys until he was sure Steve was back at his office. Then he turned down a wide street, cut across the parking lot of a shopping mall, and sauntered through the front entrance of the local hospital. Taking his cap off, he leaned against the reception desk and began talking leisurely with one of his friends who worked the night shift. His eyes wandered over the waiting room as they talked and he watched with great satisfaction as his stalker entered the doorway and stopped dead in his tracks, staring in dismay at Tom. Frustration and disgust flooded his face as he turned and stalked angrily out into the night, and Tom grinned as he thought of the useless report Barnes would receive hours later.

Leigh went to her room after looking in on Mark and saying goodnight to her uncle who was still up reading. She was grateful that it was Friday and she would not have to get up early for work, for she felt too keyed up to sleep. As she slipped into bed she thought of the familiar black car that haunted their block and wondered if it had hindered or helped Steve's silent departure.

She felt as though she had just been through a violent hurricane where the winds of fear, anger, frustration, and love had beaten her to the ground. Suddenly too weary, too spent for logical thought, she silently lifted all her troubles up before the Lord, whispering, "Take them all, Father. I do want your will." When she finally fell into fitful sleep she dreamed that she was wearing a long black dress while being held prisoner in a cage by a wild and sinister Barnes.

Chapter 15

Difficult days erupted into desperate ones, each one intensifying suppression and terror, each night whispering promises of greater afflictions to come.

From the radio reports one could easily speculate on the increasing national hostilities. Trains were plundered, trucks were hijacked, and there was scarcely a warehouse that had not been looted. Stolen goods either ended up on the black market or were distributed to that ever-growing mass of the destitute.

Leigh never questioned the mysterious appearances of food packages in the nursery kitchen, but was, instead, grateful for additions to the dwindling nursery school supplies. They had been without a cook for two weeks, for she had been ordered to work in one of the public schools, and that job was added to the growing list of duties for which Leigh was responsible. Water rationing was now in effect, adding to her problems.

As the attendance at school declined sharply, Leigh's concern increased over the government reports that she filled out daily—in ways which she hoped would not implicate anyone. And she worried about the children. She was only too aware that some families had stolen away in the night to search for safety, and others suffered greatly because fathers had been killed or imprisoned.

She tried not to brood, realizing that Christians should "be anxious for nothing," letting their requests be made known unto God, but the troubles continued to mount; the latest one causing her much anxiety came just when she felt she could not take one more.

Tom's work schedule as a train engineer had taken him through the small town where the Bible conference grounds were situated, and Mrs. Gordon had met the train in hopes of seeing him.

He broke the news to Leigh as gently as possible, but even that could not ease the pain in her heart as she learned that her father had suffered another heart attack and was in serious condition. Unless God gave them a miracle, he would not live through the winter.

"Your Mom also said that the conference grounds are scheduled to be turned into a prison camp, and she has been ordered to take charge of the cooking. The cottage will become the camp commander's home, so your parents have been moved into one of the rooms behind the dining hall. She asked me to remind you not to worry; they were confident of God's protection."

"But, Tom, can't Rev. Miles help them in this situation?"

"Rev. Miles has disappeared." He hurried on to explain when he saw her shocked expression. "He's gone underground, Leigh." He shrugged his shoulders and amended his statement. "At least, that's the rumor I hear."

"Do you think this business with Thad precipitated Dad's attack?"

"It's possible. But knowing your father as I do, I'm sure he has put Thad into God's hands."

It was now a Friday evening, three weeks since Leigh had last seen Steve. She and Dorothy were preparing a meager supper as they discussed the present fuel problems. Mark sat at the kitchen table, arduously printing his name all over a sheet of paper.

"I can hardly stand it, Dot! In most of our families both parents work or else the father is not in the home; what will the children do when . . ." She switched on the stove to heat the soup, so filled with anger and worry that she could not finish her sentence.

"Now, Leigh, calm down. Perhaps the finances will come in. The church board hasn't given up yet."

"I know," Leigh sighed. Do you think we could keep some of them here at the house? It's terrible not knowing what to do!"

"Well, I suggest that we pray about it and wait." Dorothy

smiled understandingly at her friend's impatience and reminded her of her natural inclination to instant pessimism. "We'll work out some plan with the other teachers."

Hearing the front door bell ring, they both tiptoed quickly to the dining room window to peek out cautiously through the curtain. Startled, they watched a man ring the bell once more and then prop an envelope on the edge of the mailbox before turning to hurry down the steps and away from the house.

"Open it, and see what it says," Mark said excitedly. "Is it from my Daddy?"

Leigh sat down at the kitchen table and with trembling hands opened the envelope, spreading the plain white piece of paper out so that Dorothy could see and read the short paragraph aloud.

"If you will meet one of our militiamen in front of the John Harris statue at 6:00 p.m. today we will take you to your brother Thad, who has escaped from prison and needs your help."

"We've got to go, Dot! It's ten after five now, and that leaves us only fifty minutes. If the buses aren't running on their regular schedule we may not make it. Quick, finish eating and let's go!"

Dorothy hesitated, unsure of what they really ought to do, but the feeling of impending calamity was so strong that she trembled. "Don't you think we ought to ask Uncle Paul or Tom or somebody, Leigh, before we go dashing off like this?"

"We can't. Uncle Paul got a pass to go see Mom and Dad, Tom won't be home until at least seven, and I don't know where the other two men are. We can't wait; it will be too late!"

"Well, how about Steve?"

Leigh stopped eating her slice of bread and gave Dorothy a quizzical look. "Steve? The radio said he is in Atlanta for some meetings. I don't know if I would tell him anyway. I'm going if I have to go alone!"

"No, no. I'll go with you, but what about Mark?"

At the mention of his name, the little boy looked up. "I'm going, too," he said. "Tom said I'm to protect you when he isn't here."

Leigh hesitated, knowing there was not enough time to find someone to stay with him and afraid that he would get extremely upset if she suggested he could not go. "You can go, Mark," she said, shaking her head at Dorothy's questioning glance.

"At least leave a note where Tom will find it when he gets

home," Dorothy suggested.

"O.K. We always leave them here," Leigh said as she opened a cupboard and scribbled a line on the notepad tacked to the door. "Come on—if we hurry we can get a bus in five minutes."

The four men seated in the black car across the street saw the three rush out of the house and down the street. They followed, keeping a half-block's distance between them, and reported on the CB radio that the two women, obviously excited, had just boarded a downtown bus.

They continued to follow as the winding route led them toward the center of town. The street lights were turned on, the winter sun neared the horizon, and dusk came. Each time the bus stopped, the men searched the groups of silent workers who descended the steps to shuffle wearily home.

Leigh's excitement grew, her impulsiveness blocking out good judgment as they neared their destination, and her heart seemed to be racing faster than the motor of the bus they were riding. But Dorothy was deeply alarmed, so strong was the feeling that they were making a terrible mistake. She tried once to change Leigh's mind.

"I don't think we are doing the right thing, Leigh. Suppose this is a trap?"

Leigh smiled and whispered, "A trap?" She glanced at Mark as he watched the passing scenery with interest. "Oh, Dot, your imagination is overworked. Who would want us, for goodness sakes!"

In her desperate desire to see Thad, she had barricaded from her mind any warnings from her family and had stifled her own common sense. She hardly even noticed the soldier standing beside them as he snapped his fingers impatiently for their citizens' passes to be presented, and Dorothy sighed inaudibly with relief when the expected reprimand for their tardiness did not take place. She could think of several people who would want to set a trap for them, but refrained from saying any more. God alone could take control of these bizarre circumstances and bring good from what seemed to be impending disaster. As she sat beside her friend, she prayed for help, and there came such a calmness of mind that she was assured of God's overshadowing presence.

"Dot, here is our stop. Quick!" Leigh grabbed Mark's hand and swept down the aisle and off the bus.

It was five minutes until the appointed hour, and there was nothing to do but stand beside the statue and wait. The car that had been following them pulled over to the curb a short distance away, and one of its occupants made a call from the telephone booth on the corner.

At precisely six o'clock a blue civilian car pulled up to the curb, and a short, middle-aged man stepped out to greet them.

"Leigh Gordon?"

At her nod he said, "I'm glad we can take you to your brother." Motioning them to the waiting car, he smilingly added, "If you will all get in, we'll go there immediately."

Eagerly Leigh stepped over to the curb and started to enter the opened door when she caught sight of a familiar figure in the back seat.

"No!" She gasped in sudden fear and backed away, fighting the rough hands that now held her firmly and pushed her into the car.

"Come, come, Miss Gordon. Don't be reluctant," a harsh voice grated. "You, too," he motioned toward Dorothy and Mark. "Get in."

The door slammed shut behind them, and the car shot out into the flow of traffic. Leigh sat as closely to Dorothy as possible, holding Mark on her lap and shrinking from the man in the corner, for the first time becoming acutely aware of the consequences of her rash act. Their lives were in jeopardy, and it was her fault. How could she have been so stupid?

Staring straight ahead, she accused the man beside her, "You don't have my brother, do you?"

His laugh was raucous and jarred her nerves. "No, but we will, I'm sure, when the militia learns that we have you!"

"What do you mean?"

Leigh could feel the amusement in his voice as he replied, "Hasn't your boyfriend told you? The militia kidnapped your brother when he was being transferred to another prison."

He let that sink in and then added maliciously, "You needn't act so surprised, Miss Gordon. You've got a lot of information that you're gonna give me. Yes, you three will be very useful in my plans, very useful, indeed."

They must have driven for nearly fifteen minutes through the downtown area, up one street and down another, crossing through a number of alleys and backtracking over the route they had previously taken. The driver wanted to either confuse the women or be certain no one was following them. All the while, the man in the back seat hissed spiteful, insidious remarks that were meant to further frighten the three prisoners.

Suddenly the car swerved onto the main highway, stopped at the gate for the usual search by the military guard, and then headed out toward the country. Dorothy's attempt to keep a mental note of their directions, in case they could escape, had only minor success—she only knew they were in the south side of town.

Leigh's mind was a seething turmoil of self-incrimination and abject fear, and she was not at all aware of the direction they traveled. If this were to be the hour of conflict she had so dreaded, no one could feel less prepared. She had a sinking feeling that she was now to discover answers to those shattering questions about physical persecution, debilitating fear, and God's enabling power. Somehow she must find peace of mind, must be rid of this rising panic that turned her blood ice cold, or else her very soul would be ripped apart by the evil one.

The car left the highway, bounced along a narrow lane, pulled over a slight rise, and moved down into the driveway of an old farm house. Evergreen trees successfully hid it from the main road. Pulling up at the side door, the driver cut the motor and turned toward the man in the back seat.

"I don't think anyone followed us, Lt. Barnes."

"Good. Now, shall we take our guests inside."

Leigh's heart sank as they moved toward the front entrance. It was completely secluded and might as well have been at the end of the world; the air was heavy with a lifeless silence which meant there was no one there to help. In other circumstances she would have enjoyed visiting the house, for it was an old building with decor and furnishings of another era. But now her only thought was of their grim situation. Holding Mark's hand in hers as they walked inside, she knew her nerves were stretched almost to the breaking point, and that if Barnes so much as touched her, she would collapse into screaming hysterics. Where was God and His promised peace? Had she been forsaken? Her heart cried out for His presence and release from this terrible experience.

They were directed into the darkened living room by the beam of a flashlight, and one of the soldiers began building a fire to dispel the cold. Barnes lit several candles that stood on a small bookcase on one side of the room. Even in the shadowy light it was evident that the room had not been used for quite a long time. There was a thin layer of dust on each piece of furniture, the sofa felt sooty to the touch, and a newspaper, yellowed with age, lay open on the end table.

"Is there no one living here now?" Dorothy's quiet question shattered the unnerving silence.

"No," Barnes laughed. "The former occupants . . . left. There's no one here to help you, so forget it." He pulled a small table over in front of the sofa where the women sat, with Mark sitting close to Leigh and watching Barnes with wide eyes. He sank down on a straight chair provided by one of his men, his eyes never leaving Leigh's face as he pulled a gun from his coat pocket and placed it on the table, pointed toward the women on the sofa.

"Please," Leigh pleaded, "you're frightening Mark."

Barnes' eyes shifted to the little blond seated between the two women and motioned to one of the soldiers. "Take him into the other room."

"Don't hurt him!" Leigh cried as Mark was pulled from her arms and taken from the room, his arms and legs slashing the air in resistance. "Let me go," he commanded in a tiny voice.

"Now, my dear ladies," Barnes said in mocking tones, "shall we begin our discussion?" His eyes narrowed into slits, his mouth twisted cruelly. He ordered a candle placed on the mantle and barked, "Miss Gordon, tell me all you know about Maj. Steve Houston."

"What are you planning to do to him?"

"I'm gonna set him up for treason and the firing squad. And you, as my - mistress," he paused, letting his meaning sink in as he leered at her, "as my mistress, you will sit beside me and watch it all happen. I'm gonna take his job as NIO director, and there is nothing you can do to stop me."

Staring at him, Leigh's face drained white, and she shuddered with a repulsion she could not conceal. She was aware of the other men watching her reaction with interest and felt Dorothy's comforting hand on hers; from the depths of her innermost being she spoke and was startled at the strength of her words.

"Never! I'll die first!"

As she spoke there flashed into her mind one answer to her

panic, and it came with such clarity she thought surely it must have been uttered aloud for all to hear: "I sought the Lord . . . and He delivered me from all my fears."

What had plagued her for so long seemed to have an explanation. To find God's peace she must first trust, putting the unknown, the terrifying imaginations of the future into God's hands and leaving it all there. The Psalmist had once written, "I will trust and not be afraid." Perhaps the way to peace was in accepting the circumstances—no matter how terrifying they might be. When she took that step of faith, God would take control. He had promised that nothing—not even persecution or death—could separate Him from those who loved Him.

Angered at her open repugnance of him, Barnes lashed out, "Answer me—what do you know about Houston?"

"Nothing, except that he is the NIO director."

"What about his background?"

"He has never told me anything. Only that his parents were killed in some kind of accident."

Barnes laughed cruelly and said smugly, "Yes, I've found out his parents were killed, accidently of course, when they resisted a New Democracy patrol taking over their business. Very unwise of them." He paused and took a file from his briefcase. "Not many people in the NIO know Houston's background. If they did, they might wonder how he could be the leader of an organization that caused, accidently you remember, his parents' death."

"What kind of business did they have?" Leigh sat forward, unconsciously desiring any information about Steve.

"A very lucrative one—they had plenty of money."

As the interrogation progressed, Leigh began to understand why Steve had not told her much about himself. It was not for selfish, evil reasons, but rather that he had meant to give her some protection for just such an occasion as she was now in. No matter what Barnes might do, she had nothing to tell. With a glad heart that she could not be used to harm Steve, she sat back against the sofa and watched the anger mounting dangerously in the man in front of her.

He tried several angles and then threatened, "Would you rather we take you immediately to the army barracks?"

Leigh felt Dorothy stiffen and reached out for her hand. "No, but if you do, God will go with us." And strangely, astoundingly, she felt as assured as her words sounded.

"God? You're a religious nut just like Houston and your brother. I have a recording of his interrogation with Houston, and he said he'd become a Christian!" His disgust was completely lost on the two women.

"My brother—a Christian? Oh, thank God!"

Barnes was thunderstruck at the joy he saw on their faces and felt he had somehow lost control of the situation. He patted his briefcase and snarled, "I've got enough information on Houston to make him the first Christian martyr in the New America."

"The first?"

"Yes. He's avoided a government directive for you Christians by attacking the black market and keeping a lid on the Citizens Militia, but I'm gonna see that it's properly taken care of. And he's gonna be the first one!" His voice was so full of hate that Leigh did not doubt for one second that he would do exactly what he said if given the opportunity.

She was conscious then, not only of the peace so newly acquired, but that God was also answering some of her nagging questions. In this strange way He had let her know that Steve was a Christian and that there was a reason why he had behaved as he had. He was in a special place of God's choosing, and she had failed him. She glanced down at the ring on her hand and touched it gently, wishing for just one moment to see Steve and tell him she now understood.

Barnes broke into her thoughts. "Where did you get that ring? Give it here!"

Her resistance was stopped abruptly as one of the men leaned over the back of the sofa and snatched it from her finger.

"Just as I thought," Barnes said as he pried the stone off. "Houston had it bugged." He turned and threw it into the fire. "Won't do him any good now."

Leigh felt bereft of something precious, just as though Steve himself had been thrown into the fire, but her mind was jerked back into the present with Barnes' next question.

"Where is your brother now?"

A long sigh escaped her lips, and she silently asked God to help her bear this sudden agonizing loneliness for Steve. "I don't know."

Just then the soldier returned from the other room, interrupting Barnes. "What did you do with the boy?" he questioned sharply.

"He went to sleep. He won't bother us," the man replied.

"Where is your brother?" Barnes repeated, turning back to Leigh.

"I don't know," she answered quietly.

"I'm getting sick of your pretended ignorance!" Barnes leaned over to draw something out of his briefcase; and as he laid it on the table, Leigh took a deep breath and tightened her grasp of Dorothy's hand.

The needle and syringe glittered threateningly in the firelight, and the panic rose again, only to be suppressed in the next moment by the words, "I will trust, I will trust."

"What militiamen do you know?"

"None." It was true, for though she might have her suspicions, she had no absolute knowledge.

"There's a religious leader who is up to his eyes in espionage against the government and I suspect is working closely with Houston. Who is he?"

Immediately Rev. Miles came to her mind, and Barnes saw her eyes cloud over in a revealing action. He grunted in satisfaction, intending on getting that name before the night was over.

He scraped back his chair and stood with his hands spread out on the table. "I'll use this serum," he snarled, "and get all the information I want. You might as well talk. I'm sure you wouldn't want me to use too much on you; it might do a little damage!"

Leigh shrugged her shoulders. "It won't do you any good. I don't know anything." Silently she thanked God that she could feel His calming presence.

Infuriated now beyond reason, he grabbed the gun and pushed his chair away, sending it crashing to the floor while he rushed around the table to stand in front of Dorothy. He raised the gun to her head and sputtered, "If you don't want her killed on the spot, talk!"

His eyes glittered as though he were possessed of an evil spirit, and Leigh knew she was looking at a man controlled by Satan himself.

"No!" Her protest was a strangled whisper, her eyes beseeching him to stop.

The other two men stood staring at him intently, surprised at his fury, wondering if he really meant to pull the trigger. They were unaware of any other movement than the drama being played out before them.

Dorothy sat white and immobile as stone; only the pressure of her hand in Leigh's revealed her anguish. Her eyes were closed; she waited for the click of the gun and the explosive bullet ripping into her brain.

Leigh glanced wildly from her friend's face to the maniac in front of them. "No, please, don't . . ."

His finger moved on the gun, getting a better grip, and he growled, "If you don't want her killed, then you'd better . . ."

He never finished the sentence.

Chapter 16

Months afterward Barnes was to relive what happened next and berate himself for his lack of foresight; but he took his revenge out on the two men who were with him.

The front door crashed open and four soldiers burst into the room, their guns trained on the startled interrogators.

"Drop that gun!" one of them ordered.

Leigh, disoriented by this dramatic change of events, thought the man spoke in a strong western accent, and she wondered what a cowboy was doing in Pennsylvania and why he was not wearing boots and a ten-gallon hat.

"Drop that gun. You'll die the moment you kill her. Drop it!"

Staring at Barnes, Leigh saw him hesitate, saw first rebellion and then defeat in his eyes, and watched as he slowly lowered his arm to let the gun be snatched from his hand. She sensed someone standing behind her and turned slightly to see three more soldiers, each one poised and impassive, yet exuding the vigilance of a seasoned warrior. They must have entered the room from the interior of the house.

Three befuddled men stood with hands raised in the air, shocked to see themselves outnumbered without warning, and as they were relieved of their weapons Barnes ranted, "I thought you said we weren't followed!"

He began cursing and shouting that he would kill them both.

The veins on his forehead were rigid, his face crimson. He spun around then to the man who had so neatly sliced into his plans and growled, "What do you want here?"

"Well," the man drawled with a heavy accent, slowly emphasizing each word with a flick of humor dancing in his tone, "we run a little side business down in Texas, to provide female companions for troop entertainment." Motioning toward the women with his gun he said in a lamentable, mocking tone, "It's downright wasteful to kill these two beauties as you were settin' out to do."

"And what do you plan to do with them?"

"Suh, we can get five thousand dollars for each of them. We do things up big in Texas. Now why should we pay for ladies when you're right willin' to give them to us?" The smile spreading slowly over the Texan's face was one of complete enjoyment, the cat baiting the mouse, the lion cornering its prey.

"You take them and you'll have the entire intelligence organization on your back!" Barnes was bluffing, unwilling to concede defeat.

"And you're the NIO director, I suppose." The leader's voice was full of irony as he needled Barnes further.

"No, but that," he answered, pointing toward Leigh, "is his girlfriend. He'll have you torn apart, inch by inch if you harm her."

"I don't know of anyone in this room who plans on telling him what took place here tonight, do you? Can you imagine, Suh, what he'll do to you when he finds out about this little ol' meetin'?"

Barnes changed his strategy. "He's not gonna be NIO director for very long, anyway. I am. And when I take over you're the first man I'm going after!"

"Texas is a mighty big state, Suh." The soldier chuckled at the man's frustration and ordered his companions to tie up the three men.

"Would you rather sleep sitting up or lying on the sofa?" His question was directed to Barnes.

"I'm not sleeping anywhere!"

"You're wrong there, Suh. We've brought along a little something to give you about eight hours of sound sleep. You look so tired," he mocked. "After all, we do need a little time ourselves. It's a long way to Texas."

Leigh was shocked into numbness at this grotesque turn of events. It was unbelievable that in a matter of minutes they were subjected not only to threats against their lives, but to the prospect of surviving in the devilish pit into which they were now to be taken.

She put her arm around Dorothy's trembling shoulders and laid a comforting hand over her clenched fist. There were unshed tears and the same numbness in her friend's eyes. Dorothy knew by experience exactly what they could expect in Texas. All at once Leigh turned to her friend in concern, "Mark, what will happen to Mark?"

The Texan turned sharply toward her and asked with narrowed eyes, "Mark? What are you talking about?"

Reluctantly she answered, "The little boy in the other room," and was startled to see him open the door and leave them without a word. In a few minutes he returned and whispered some instructions to two of his men.

"You aren't going to hurt him, are you?" Leigh asked as the men went toward the room where Mark slept. "Please bring him to me."

"No," the leader answered, a strange expression on his face as he turned to Barnes who was now tied securely to the sofa where the women had been seated.

Leigh drew Dorothy close and whispered, "I will trust and not be afraid," and they watched silently as the two aides yielded quietly to the needle puncturing their arms. Barnes struggled and swore until the medicine began to take effect. As they waited for the men to fall asleep, the Texan outlined his plans.

He was obviously enjoying himself as he walked slowly around Dorothy and Leigh as they stood together near the fire, looking them over as one would check a new piece of merchandise. His manner was relentless, and his eyes glittered. He stopped and with a firm hand tipped Leigh's face toward the light. He commented appreciatively on her beauty and innocence, and told Barnes he really ought to start a business of his own; it was much more profitable than even being NIO director. Pretty faces and innocent women like these brought in a lot of money, since every captain and colonel liked that kind of "lady friend."

When Barnes could no longer struggle against the drug working in his body, his railings against the Texan became slurred mumblings; finally his eyes closed unwillingly, and he was asleep.

Leigh and Dorothy were each given a neat pile of army clothes and led into separate rooms to change. Wisely keeping them apart, the soldiers knew neither would attempt an escape, leaving the other to face the future alone. Leigh was amazed that the clothes fit, but shuddered to see her reflection in the mirror, dressed in that black uniform she had always hated so.

"Pin your hair up and keep that army cap on. In the dark you'll both pass as army personnel."

Their own clothes were packed in a box and taken to the car. After checking the sleeping men once more, the soldiers carefully went over the room, removing any possible trace of their presence, and then banked the fire so that Barnes "wouldn't get too cold while he rested."

Just before motioning the women from the room, the Texan gathered up everything he felt might be useful, the weapons, wallets, and ID cards of the sleeping men, stuffed it all into the briefcase that held the folder of information on Maj. Steve Houston, and handed it to one of his men.

"Put this in the trunk of your car before you do anything else. We don't want to leave it here."

The women were silently ushered into the back seat of one of the two military vehicles waiting in the lane, the leader sliding into the front seat beside the driver. The parking lights cast a yellowish tint on the one man working quickly on Barnes' car, making it totally inoperable in a matter of seconds. They saw another soldier exit the back door of the house, carrying a bundle in his arms. It had to be Mark, and Leigh wanted to cry when she saw them get into the second car. "Please, don't harm the little boy," she said to the man in the front seat.

His only response was a shake of his head and an order to the driver to move out. Leigh watched the headlights cast a bright light over the house and barn as they made a turn in the driveway, and then they were out on the highway, leaving Harrisburg far behind.

The Texan turned and laid his arm over the back of his seat so that he could observe the women, the dashboard lights shining on his face as he spoke. Leigh was puzzled to see no trace of the harshness he had displayed at the farmhouse, and his voice was gentle.

"There's no way you can open the back doors, so there's no need trying to escape that way." Then he smiled warmly and added, "I'd be pleased if you'd call me Tex." He spread out his hands and shrugged his shoulders. "Might as well be friends."

Neither of the women responded, and he went on, ignoring their pointed silence. "I hope you won't mind being jostled a bit. The highways are mighty messy in spots, but we've got a long way to go before dawn, and more than likely we'll be stopped by patrols."

Leigh was too weary to watch their direction, and it really did not matter, for there was nothing she could do to change their situation. It was a slow, painful process, this lesson of faith, and she wondered why she had stubbornly refused to learn, thus forcing God to box her inside an impossible situation before she would stop struggling against His will.

They were stopped a number of times by army patrols making routine checks, and they passed several tanks on the way to some conflict. Each time they were halted, they produced ID cards identifying them as NIO personnel, and each time they were waved through without any problems.

Twice during the night they made a rest stop, and Leigh noticed that one of the men would make a quick telephone call. Though they were carefully watched against an attempted escape, there was a touch of kindness in the soldiers' manner that seemed totally out of place with their declared interest in women. Leigh could not put her finger on what it was, but something puzzled her about the entire situation.

She saw the other car following them the entire way, but they were never allowed to get near Mark, nor even see him, and she was desperately afraid for the little boy. She alone was responsible for getting him into this predicament, and she asked the Lord to forgive her for being so impulsive.

It was a long night. Though she tried, she could not sleep. Nor was it entirely possible for her to remain calm. Physical exhaustion and the dark, fearful hours of the night weighed heavily upon her senses, making it difficult to keep things in proper perspective. She tried to force her mind away from the insane Barnes and what he had planned for her, tried to ignore the fact that they were traveling further away from all that had once meant security, sought to forget the experiences into which they were being taken. Over and over she repeated snatches of Scripture that came into her mind, hanging onto them as a dying man does to life.

Leigh lost count of the number of times they had to maneuver the car around bombed-out sections of the highway, inching their way through the debris or across the gullies that bordered the road, but finally they skirted a city. Was it Philadelphia or Baltimore, or some city to the west of Harrisburg? Leigh could not tell, nor did she bother to ask. One could not expect a guided tour from men who were only interested in making a financial profit on her. She shivered and forced her thoughts elsewhere.

With eyes closed to shut out the present circumstances, she searched her memory for a picture of Steve's face, remembering the commanding features, the warm, tender smile, and the clear blue eyes. She recalled his inner power and vibrant temperament, which she now realized could only come from a true Christian experience. How could she have blindly refused to acknowledge it? This kind of strength was the outgrowth of a life totally committed to God. Oh, for just one minute to tell him how wrong she had been. Whatever his reason for his present position in the government, she knew it was right, knew it just as surely as she was aware of being kidnapped.

The car finally slid to a halt in a narrow, dirty alley just before the blackness of night gave way to grey morning skies. Noiselessly, they were helped from the car and guided hastily under a sign that read "Concord Wholesale, Inc.," into the back door of the building, now silent in the early hours before the first inundation of employees.

They walked through a maze of cartons and crates, up a narrow flight of stairs, and into a large, cluttered office. Tex pulled a full-length bookcase forward to reveal a doorway through which they entered a smaller room that appeared to be a completely furnished, though somewhat shabby, lounge area. Soft thick carpet blunted the sound of footsteps, and easy chairs and sofas looked inviting to the weary group. A small kitchen area filled one corner, and soft lighting cast a restful appearance over the room.

But Leigh stiffened, and her heart fluttered erratically, as she waited for their first encounter with some army officer interested in making a purchase. A visible shudder of horror swept over her, and with eyes wide with fear she turned to face Tex, one of the two men entering the room, and thought frantically, "Trust, Leigh, trust!"

With restraint bordering on gentleness she could scarcely

believe, he drawled softly, "Relax. Nothin's happenin' now."

She did not have the will to move or speak, for her thoughts were hinged on his last sentence. It was like a warning bell clanging in her brain, signaling the unrelenting promise of the future. She watched enviously while Dorothy sank down into an easy chair and closed heavy eyelids as though already asleep. How she longed to be so full of confidence in God that she too could rest. She jumped at the sound of Tex's voice close by and shrank away from him.

"Here, drink this." He smiled at her hesitation, his brown eyes crinkling slightly at the corners. "It's only coffee."

Baffled by his manner, she sipped the drink and watched him move around the room. He closed the bottom half of the shuttered windows and pulled the drapes shut, turned on a small electric heater, then took two blankets from a cupboard that stood along the outer wall.

"You'll stay here today. The two of us will be with you, but try to get some rest. We'll be taking you . . .," he paused a moment to consider his next words and then added, "out again after dark."

He spread a blanket over Dorothy, relieved Leigh of the black army coat she wore, and hung it on an old-fashioned brass hook beside the door, afterward indicating with a nod that she should sit down on one of the sofas.

Leigh moved mechanically toward the place he had chosen, sat down stiffly and finished her coffee, but it failed to warm or strengthen her. Beyond the point of sleep, she stared at Tex, watching him move toward her. The empty cup was removed from tightly clasped hands and a blanket unfolded over her lap while she was given an admonition to rest.

"Your kindness is out of character." She spoke with cold bitterness, not caring about the seemingly inevitable reprisal, for even a slap across the face would be no more than fitting for someone in her position.

She slowly lifted wary eyes to his face, fully expecting to see the contemptuous disregard he had displayed at the farmhouse, and was quite unprepared for the sympathetic concern that flickered for a brief moment in his eyes. Just as quickly a smooth enigmatic look hid whatever mystery, whatever deliberation he had very nearly shared. He left her then, without a word, to hold a quiet discussion with his aide who had taken up his post beside the window.

As the day wore on, Leigh would one moment feel grateful that the minutes dragged slowly by, thankful for the measure of safety in the room, and the next tense with an apprehensive dread that longed for this nightmare to be finished. Preparing meals helped fill some of the hours, and a local radio station brought the outside world into the small room over an intercom system. There were magazines to read, but every article dealt with such themes as increased crime, inflation, economic struggle, the New Peoples Democracy, or worse, the blatant debauchery which so pervaded the society. She could not bear to allow those subjects into a mind already struggling with the horror of her immediate future, and left the magazines on the table.

Grieved beyond reason that Dorothy had been trapped in this maze from which there seemed no escape, Leigh tried to apologize.

"Dot, I wish with all my heart that you weren't caught in this. Barnes only wanted me."

"You know I would never have let you go alone." Dorothy gave her arm a quick squeeze, and her reassuring smile tore at Leigh's heart.

Tears filled her eyes and choked off her words. "I . . . I know, but . . . I'm sorry." She swallowed hard and then confessed in a whisper, "If I had listened to you, we wouldn't be here."

Dorothy's response was unbelievably calm and confident. "We're in the Father's hand where no one can touch us without His permission. Wait, Leigh, and see what good thing the Lord will do through all this."

Leigh nodded, unable to speak. Always of a temperament that tended to fretful, impetuous worry, she was learning some difficult lessons. She had finally surrendered a lot of things, not because she wanted to do so, or knew it was best, but simply because there was no alternative. Like a tiny baby who is completely helpless and dependent upon others, so she was now cast upon God. There was nothing she could do to alter the direction of her life, nothing she could do to ever see her family again, nothing she could do to see the fulfillment of Steve's love. Nothing! Absolutely nothing!

Nearing complete exhaustion, her groggy mind refused to function properly, and she paced the floor until her legs had no more strength. But still sleep would not come. She was aware that Dorothy had a long discussion with the aide but could not focus on their words.

It was apparent that the radio was used as a signaling device. Each time it cut off for an instant Tex would signal for quiet, and both of the soldiers were instantly ready with their weapons. Then the radio program would continue, and the moment of possible discovery was gone. It came to Leigh's mind once to question where they were, but the next moment she could not remember what it was she wanted to know.

Realizing that she was nearly ready to collapse, Tex was very attentive. From his chair near the door, standing by the window, or prowling around the room, he seemed to watch her constantly. Several times he tried to encourage her to sleep, but Leigh could not reconcile his concern with his previously stated plans for them.

The noise of the day's activity in the warehouse faded away and signalled nightfall. Tex began removing any trace of their presence as he put blankets and food away. Leigh stopped her pacing and automatically began to help. Walking behind the bar in the kitchen area, she picked up a glass and tipped its contents into the sink just as the evening news came on the radio. She heard the call letters of a local station and a national newscaster begin his evening report.

Reaching up to put an unused glass on a shelf above the sink, she heard Steve's name mentioned. It penetrated the hazy fog that had enveloped her, and her hand was held suspended in midair as she listened.

"Maj. Steve Houston, Director of the National Intelligence Organization, has apparently been involved in an airplane accident while on a solo flight from Atlanta to Harrisburg. He radioed engine trouble, and it is believed he went down in coastal waters after only the one signal. The Coast Guard has sighted parts of a plane floating off the coast, but the Major has not been found, and it is believed he went down in the crash. A government spokesman has indicated a full-scale search will be launched at daybreak, but there seems little hope of finding Maj. Houston alive."

The glass slipped from Leigh's hand and fell into the sink, splintering into a thousand pieces. She stood motionless, staring at the window and thinking that the worn, faded drapes must be ancient.

Tex reached her just in time to catch her before she collapsed to the floor, and she was aware of being carried to the sofa where he laid her on the cushions and began rubbing her hands vigorously.

"Get some smelling salts from the bathroom," he ordered sharply to Dorothy who stood anxiously waiting to help. "You'll find several small vials on the cabinet shelf."

The pain that shot through Leigh was a sharp, physical one, and she wanted to scream that it was not true, wanted to strike out at those who now ministered to her. But she had heard the sharp order for the smelling salts, and she stared at the man before her, her dark eyes wide and vacant.

"You've lost your accent, Tex," she said accusingly.

"Only for a minute, Ma'm," he drawled heavily, waving the salts under her nose.

Chapter 17

There was a growing sense of desperate urgency in Leigh's mind now, but she could not focus on the reason. It had something to do with Thad and Mark and Steve. If she could only talk to Tom, perhaps he could help. Aware of Dorothy's arm around her waist, encouraging her to move forward, Leigh saw crates and cartons looming up around them like giant building blocks. The confusion of the room matched the confusion in her mind, and it frightened her.

Tex cautiously opened the metal door that led into the alley, glanced both ways, and motioned for them to follow. Dorothy guided Leigh out into the darkness where a merciless wind slapped sleet and snow over her face and pushed it down into the tops of her boots. Helping them up into the back of a warehouse truck, Tex mounted the high steps, closed the door behind him, and then called out to the driver that they were ready to leave.

It seemed strange, Leigh thought, to see street lights illuminating the interior of the truck like some flickering, old-fashioned movie. She waited for each corner, wondering what scene would be flashed before her eyes. Perhaps if she looked carefully she might see Steve!

But the light only revealed Tex sitting across from her, and she heard him instructing Dorothy. "If we have any trouble, get her back behind that small partition out of sight. From the doorway it doesn't appear to be large enough to hide anyone. Let's hope it works.''

No sooner had the words been spoken, than the truck slowed its speed and one of the men in front called back tersely, ''Barricade ahead!''

From behind the partition where they knelt, Leigh and Dorothy felt the truck come to a stop and heard Tex open the door to question the guard, his voice casual and full of indifference. ''What's the trouble, Sgt.?'' His western accent was missing again.

''The NIO is looking for two women, Sir, who were kidnapped in Harrisburg last night.''

''Interesting. Must be someone important to have all this commotion. Who did it?''

''Army men from the west, looking for some good buys, I hear. I'm sorry, Sir, but we'll have to search the truck.''

The voice moved nearer, and Leigh felt Dorothy's hand tighten on her arm in warning.

''That's quite all right, Sgt., but I'd appreciate your doing it quickly.'' He spoke in friendly, confidential tones as he opened the door for the sergeant. ''We've got orders,'' he touched his pocket significantly, ''about some special cargo for the NIO head office, and you know they don't like to be kept waiting.''

''Of course,'' the guard replied, impressed with the importance of their mission.

The beam of a flashlight played over the interior of an empty truck as the soldier apologized for the delay. It moved to the corner and stopped, then worked its way over the ceiling and back down the other side. All the while Tex kept up a steady stream of distracting conversation.

Leigh grew restless. She was aware of all that was taking place, but felt no part of it. It was another world, a tense drama, and she was merely an observer. Reality for her was the insistent demand within that she solve a nagging problem, and she stirred as though to stand. Immediately, Dorothy's hand tightened like a vise on her arm, but still Leigh tried to free herself. It was imperative that she get out of here. Thad was waiting, or Mark, or was it Steve?

The flashlight played over the partition, and Dorothy's fear seeped through her hand and flowed into Leigh's arm. One of the men in the front seat saw the light and heard Leigh moving;

he coughed loudly and shifted his position to cover her noise. Dorothy prayed for a miracle.

The door slammed shut, and there was an almost audible sigh of relief among those seated in the truck. Whatever their destination with Tex, Dorothy somehow had the assurance that it would not be as disastrous as being dragged back to Harrisburg to face an angry, revengeful Barnes.

They heard Tex say something to the soldier, who laughed loudly and wished him luck in getting his cargo on time; then he opened the door and jumped into the truck, returned the soldier's salute and ordered the driver to move on. No one spoke as they drove quickly away from the barricade. Tex continued watching through the back window until he was sure they were not being followed, then grunted with relief and helped the women from their hiding place.

He sat next to Leigh as they moved on, weighing the rationale of revealing what he knew. It would penetrate the shock she was in, perhaps bring her out of it, but he shook his head regretfully and frowned. No, it was not in his power, for he had given his pledge of silence lest the well-laid plans go awry. Looking at her now, he acknowledged the wisdom of that extracted promise, for without it he would gladly give her information that might reduce her suffering.

She was pale and trembling slightly, staring at him with eyes that revealed an almost childish bewilderment, and he wondered if she would collapse before they reached their destination.

The truck left the highway and moved around the curved road which led to the wharves. They passed darkened warehouses, export and import businesses, and a number of empty boarded-up buildings until they came to the end of the street where the driver maneuvered the truck around and backed up to the loading door of the last warehouse. They waited in tense silence for several long minutes, and when it seemed they had not attracted any attention, Tex flicked on a small flashlight to glance at his watch.

"Right on time. Let's hope the army isn't prowling the docks off schedule." He nodded toward the door. "Let's go."

From where they stood against the building, only one street light was faintly visible, about a block away. Nearby, part of a pier could be seen; the rest was hidden under a blanket of heavy sleet and darkness. The snow had stopped, but the wind, stronger now in the bay area, seemed to drive the sleet right through to the bone. Leigh began to shiver, and no matter how much she clenched her teeth or hugged herself, she could not stop shaking.

Shadowy forms moved close by, and she listened with grave detachment as Tex instructed his men to scout the dock area and the streets for any trouble. As they moved away, their grey forms disappearing into the driving sleet, Leigh could barely make out other larger shapes; perhaps they were ships, but it was difficult to tell.

Tex moved them cautiously nearer the pier, and the two women huddled together under a cement ledge, slightly protected from the weather. He threw a thin rain cape over Leigh and handed one to Dorothy. Neither of them questioned him about what was taking place; Dorothy did not because she dreaded the answer, and Leigh could not because she was too exhausted and numb to care.

A shadow came out of the sleet, and Leigh whispered involuntarily, "Thad? Steve?"

"No, dear," came Dorothy's sad reply. "It's just one of the guards."

Leigh slumped wearily against her friend and took no more notice of her surroundings.

The guard reported quietly to Tex, "The pier is empty, and I left B.J. to keep watch. I think everything is clear."

Tex nodded in agreement and motioned the group forward. The guard went first, holding Dorothy by the arm to guide her. Tex followed, leading an uncaring and dazed Leigh. The sounds of their footsteps were muffled by the wind whipping around them, but all were startled when Leigh stumbled blindly over a loose board and fell to her knees.

"I've got her," Tex whispered as he scooped her up into his arms. They stood motionless, waiting to see if the noise had attracted anyone.

But there was only the wind and falling sleet and silence. Dorothy was sure they would never reach the end of the pier—each step seemed to take an hour, and she waited for a patrol to come out of the darkness and surround them. She nearly cried aloud when the other guard suddenly loomed up in front of them, and her heart beat wildly in her temples as they moved nearer to talk.

"Did the others get here?" Tex asked; at a nod from the guard, he said, "You two had better get back to the truck and out of here before the patrol comes by. I don't want you getting caught."

The man seemed reluctant to leave, and Tex said, "Good-bye, B.J., thanks for everything." Watching the two men leave, Dorothy wondered if that were a final farewell, and she was puzzled. Why weren't they leaving also? Weren't they going to profit from the sale they had talked about?

"Come on," Tex instructed, and still carrying Leigh he moved to the edge of the pier and began climbing a short ladder. As she followed, Dorothy saw that it was a pilot boat and wondered where they were going next. This journey will never end, she thought, and wearily followed the dark form before her.

Tex set Leigh on her feet and steered her to a seat. "Sit down, both of you. It's going to be rough."

He waved to the man at the wheel, and the motor sprang to life, loud enough, it seemed, to attract every soldier within ten miles. He could only hope that the wind would kill the sound, whipping it back out to sea, smothering it under the choppy waves.

And he was right—the bay was rough. They had to cling to their seats to stay upright while each stomach churned in revolt against the reeling, lurching world it was now in.

Dorothy looked questioningly at Tex, for she wanted to know where they were being taken. Were they going further out into the harbor, or to another hiding place along the coast? But his full attention was upon Leigh, and it was too noisy for conversation.

The small boat jerked, pounced, and dropped like a rock all at one time as it moved slowly through the stormy waters. It seemed as eager as Dorothy to be at the end of their destination. Fearful of discovery, she tried to listen for other boats, to hear some indication of potential pursuers, but it was impossible to hear anything other than their own rebellious, thumping motor.

Then it was cut off, and silently the pilot boat bumped against something hard. It jolted Leigh, reaching through her preoccupation for a moment, but she had no opportunity to voice any questions.

Tex put a restraining hand on her wrist and spoke to Dorothy. "You first, up the ladder."

She nodded, but looked doubtfully at the ladder as it disappeared, only to reappear in motion with the boat rocking up and down. She looked at Leigh with a worried frown, wondering how she would ever negotiate that.

"I'll help her," Tex said understandingly, "but you have to manage by yourself."

Wordlessly, Dorothy looked at the rolling boat and the ladder hanging as though it were anchored somewhere above on air alone, and in the darkness and sleet she could only assume it was attached to a ship. She reached out for it just as the floor beneath her seemed to sink a foot and felt Tex clutch her arm to pull her back into the boat.

"Wait! Wait until the boat levels off, then grab it and go!" He stood beside her, his arm around Leigh's waist to support her. "Now!"

Dorothy caught the ladder and began to climb. Behind her, Tex's voice floated upward in encouragement. With each wave the ladder sank down into the sea and then slapped hard against the ship's side. She had all she could do to keep from falling into the water. Just as she neared the top, she felt an additional weight below her but dared not look, for her heart was already in her throat, and she was afraid of losing her balance.

It was Leigh who followed, not really caring where the ladder was taking them, but blindly obeying the voice of the man behind her as he instructed her to hold on tightly and climb.

Halfway up, her mind cleared, and she remembered vividly the radio announcement that indicated Steve was dead: "Maj. Steve Houston . . . not found alive." She sobbed aloud, her hands slipped from the ladder, and she began to slide downward.

But Tex had anticipated she might have difficulties and was close behind. His arm shot out around her waist to keep her from plunging in the sea below, and his voice, low and encouraging in her ear, finally penetrated her senses, and she did as he commanded.

"Take one more step . . . that's it . . . now another . . . Good . . . good . . . we're almost there . . . just one more."

Hands reached down and she felt herself being lifted over the top of a railing and onto the deck of the ship.

"Leigh, thank God you're safe!"

Startled, she looked up to see who had spoken, for the voice was so familiar, and then gasped questioningly, "Thad?"

The shock of seeing him standing before her was more than she could take, and slipping through his relaxed grasp, she crumpled to the ship's deck in a dead faint.

Chapter 18

Strong arms held her as she came back to consciousness and realized it was no longer sleeting. They seemed to be moving down a corridor inside the ship, and she heard Tex saying regretfully, "I'm sorry, but she heard about the plane crash on the radio."

Whoever held her tightened his grip, and an exclamation of disapproval rushed from his lips. There seemed to be heavy weights on her eyelids preventing her from seeing who it was, though she tried several times to look. It was Thad, she thought, remembering that he had been on deck. Then the reminder of the crash and of Steve's death gripped her savagely, and she gladly gave herself over to the blessed relief of complete blackness.

The room was warm and dry, the bed so soft, the violent winds and punishing sleet no longer reaching her; it was good to sink into sleep, for there she could run away from the reality of the past two days.

But it was not to be that easy, for in sleep horrible dreams tormented her. She thrashed about, unmindful of ministering hands which tried to keep her still, and not hearing the ship's doctor in broken English reassure those concerned for her.

"It iss not uncommon. Total exhaustion, dose traumatic events." He nodded and smiled. "Tomorrow she vill be much better. Now she must rest, eh.''

Leigh felt something sting her arm and gratefully succumbed to the drug which took her past the terrifying dreams to deep sleep. But the nightmares returned all too soon. She saw again the deserted house and the wild eyes of Satan himself as he threatened Dorothy with a gun.

"No, no," she cried out in fear. Someone took her hand and a voice spoke in soothing tones, but she could not understand what was said. It was a strong hand, a man's hand—it must be Thad.

The dreams came again, filled with visions of black cars following her everywhere, an airplane crashing into the sea, men bursting into the farmhouse to take them away; it was all so mixed up that she was unable to sort anything out, and it caused her to panic.

She awakened and willed heavy eyes open. Dorothy was sitting beside the bed with her hand on Leigh's wrist, and there was reassurance in that capable gesture; but Leigh was bewildered at the joyous expression on her friend's face. Peace she could understand, for in spite of everything she felt God's peace, but happiness was something else. How could Dorothy have joy when Steve was dead!

Before she could move to let Dorothy know she was awake, she fell asleep again. And the dreams persisted. It was like being drawn into a dark tunnel where horrible demons screamed and lunged at her at every turn.

Then she thought that Thad and Dorothy talked with her, encouraging her to rest and saying that everything was all right. And she heard Steve's voice, so comforting and full of love, and it was this part of the dream that finally brought her into a complete rest, away from the terrors threatening her in sleep.

Once more she awoke, this time to see Thad sitting where Dorothy had been. Searching his face as he stared down at the floor, she saw that it was peaceful and knew that in this case Barnes had at least spoken the truth—her brother had given his life to God. Tears filled her eyes, but she just could not keep them open long enough to tell him how happy she was about his decision.

The next time wakefulness came, sunshine filled the room. Moving her eyes slowly around the cabin, she saw it was decorated in shades of her favorite colors, blue and yellow. Next to the bed was a small table with a Bible lying beside a water glass. There were metal chairs, a dresser, a sofa along one wall, and another low table. This was a room with first-class accommodations, she thought anxiously. How could she ever pay for this? But then, she wondered, had some officer bought her from Tex and supplied these lovely quarters? No, that could not have happened, for Thad was there with them.

She stirred fretfully, and Dorothy, who had been sitting on the sofa, moved quickly to the bed and smilingly reached down to smooth Leigh's hair away from her forehead.

"How are you feeling, Leigh?"

"Much better—not so tired."

"Do you want something to eat or drink?"

Leigh wrinkled her nose and shook her head slowly, but tried to drink a little of the milk Dorothy held in her hand.

"Where is Thad?"

A smile lit up her friend's face in a way Leigh had never seen before as she answered, "Asleep. He will be here after awhile."

"He's become a Christian, hasn't he, Dot?"

"Yes, he told me about it last night." The joy on her face was painful to Leigh, for it reminded her sharply of all she had given up. She had lost something precious through lack of trust and did not deserve a second chance.

Dorothy was aware of her train of thought and inquired anxiously, "Thinking of Steve?"

Leigh closed her eyes and said sadly, "It . . . it's hard to take. I don't remember much after hearing the radio news. Did . . . did I go numb, Dot?"

"Yes, but Tex was wonderful. He watched you constantly and was very gentle with you."

Leigh grinned slightly and remarked, "The only thing I do remember clearly is that he kept losing his accent."

Dorothy was encouraged at this evidence of recovery and laughed lightly. "He was so upset with himself about that, and you kept reminding him." She paused and then added carefully, "We owe our lives to him. He and his men are members of the Citizens Militia and this was . . . was all planned." Her voice trailed away as she finished the sentence, and she searched Leigh's face for any adverse reaction.

Leigh traced a yellow flower pattern on the bed cover with meticulous care and then looked up. "You mean that . . . that

Steve planned it all?''

This was a dangerous conversation for someone barely recovered from shock, but the question could not be avoided. "Yes, he knew Barnes would make an attempt to kidnap you and had this scheme ready for weeks. Tex told us about it last night."

"I wish I could have just one chance to tell Steve how wrong I've been . . . about a lot of things." Leigh bit her lower lip in an effort not to cry.

Dorothy gave her a guarded look, opened her mouth to speak, then changed her mind and sat silently looking out at the blue sky and rolling ocean. It was better to let things take their natural course.

The doctor came again in the afternoon and gave Leigh permission to be up all she wanted, and a long visit with her brother was just the tonic she needed.

Thad entered the room just as the doctor was leaving, and sitting down on the bed, gave Leigh a long hug while she let the tears flow again. "I'm sorry, Thad. I guess I'm going to cry at everything for awhile."

He held her hand firmly in his and quite happily answered her questions about his conversion experience in prison, the manner of his escape from the NIO, and what he had been doing since then. He did not mention Steve's name any more than necessary and felt deeply moved each time a look of sharp pain crossed her face.

He and Dorothy did not share their marriage plans until she asked, knowing it would give her distressing thoughts about Steve. And it was difficult to hide the tearing agony within as she watched the love growing between them. Deep in her heart was the conviction that this kind of love for her had gone down in an airplane crash.

"Leigh," Dorothy spoke, interrupting her thoughts suddenly. "We have a surprise for you." She smiled, excused herself from the room, saying "I'll be back in a minute."

"What is it, Thad? Where has she gone?"

Thad grinned happily at her. "Be patient, Sis," he said, his eyes on the door. "You're going to like this, I think."

Leigh turned to see the door open, and coming into the room was a sight she could not believe, for there holding onto Dorothy's hand was a small, blond-headed boy with a smile of joy lighting up his face.

"Mark!" She exclaimed and sat up in surprise as the little boy rushed quickly across the room to fling himself into her open arms. "What are you . . . how did this . . . what on earth!" And she began to cry, tears this time of happiness because she was holding someone she never expected to see again. "Thad? How did this happen?"

Mark raised his head, kissed her shyly on the cheek, and began talking rapidly, his voice full of excitement. "Tex is my Daddy, and he followed us to the farmhouse, and . . . and now we're safe. Do you feel better now?"

"Yes, I feel marvelous, now that I see you." Leigh smiled down at the little boy sitting impatiently on the edge of her bed. He was so full of all that had happened and so thrilled at being with his father, that he found it hard to sit still. While he investigated the room, seeming to bounce from one place to another, Thad filled in the story for Leigh.

"Tex is one of those brave souls who played the part of a double agent for the militia. He worked closely with Steve's office and many times was one of the men in the car that seemed to be stuck to our neighborhood lately."

Leigh nodded. "I've had nightmares about that black car. It was militiamen, then, who kept us under surveillance?"

"Tex was the only militiaman in the group that had been assigned to our house. Steve knew he could trust him. The rest thought they were acting on behalf of the government."

"And he isn't from Texas," Dorothy added with a smile.

"I thought not," Leigh said dryly, remembering the time he had dropped his accent.

"Daddy says we are going to live where we will be safe," Mark said, coming to lean against the bed.

Leigh nodded, but wondered how many more trips Tex would make back into the country to continue his work; she rather expected Mark would be living with her for a long while. The thought was reassuring. Perhaps she could keep busy enough to be able to ignore, for a little while, the pain of loneliness that held her like a vise.

Thad stood up from his chair and held out a hand toward Mark. "Young man, it is almost supper time. Why don't we go have something to eat. We can come back later. O.K.?"

Mark turned questioningly toward Leigh, silently asking her

permission, and when she nodded agreement, he said "O.K.," put his hand in Thad's, and left the room.

"Dot," Leigh said when they were alone, "I can't stay in this bed another minute. I've got to get up."

"Great. The shower room is right across the hall, and there are some clothes for you in here." She opened a narrow closet door to point to the clothes hanging there.

"Dot, look at these clothes. Where did they come from?" Leigh chose a pretty sky-blue lounging dress and looked questioningly at her friend.

Dorothy only smiled and stooped to straighten out the bed covers. "I'll be here if you need me," she said as Leigh left the room for a quick shower.

Later, when Leigh had returned and was hanging up a towel in in the closet area, she stopped, looked over at Dorothy sitting on the sofa, and said, "I've learned a little through all of this."

"Yes, I have as well."

"I used to worry so about persecution, afraid I would be a coward and deny my faith. I tried to create that strength myself. But I've discovered that it isn't something you can produce. It comes only from God, and He doesn't give it until the moment it is needed. I've never known such peace as in those minutes I thought Barnes was going to kill us both. Trying to explain it is impossible, but you understand, don't you?"

"Yes," Dorothy nodded her head at Leigh's reflection in the mirror. "It was the same for me. It isn't trite to say that God's strength is more than enough for every experience. Sit down, and I'll brush your hair for you."

Leigh followed her suggestion and handed the brush to her, but her mind was still on their experiences. "I will never forget as long as I live the peace I had then. I only hope I remember it the next time I face a similar situation."

"What do you think the key is, Leigh?"

"I'm not sure, for it is probably a bit different for each person. But perhaps God's peace comes when you totally submit to Him, accepting whatever is happening and trusting Him for whatever might come."

She was silent for a moment and then added, "You know what I mean. There was just nothing I could do, so I had to submit instead of fighting it all. It was—Here I am, Lord, you take charge."

"Umm, it's a tough lesson."

"It certainly is. Dot, I've been wondering about Steve's job. What do you suppose he was able to accomplish before he was . . ." Her voice trailed off, and she stared at her reflection in the mirror. Propping her chin on her hand, she fought down the sick longing she felt, and prayed for God to fill the emptiness with His presence.

"Are you still trusting, Leigh?" Dorothy's question was full of affectionate concern, and Leigh understood her meaning.

"Yes," she answered slowly, "I'm trusting, but I can't say I have joy yet."

"It will come." Dorothy searched Leigh's face and then seemed to make a decision. "If you feel up to it, I think I'll leave you for a little while. I'd like to take a quick bath and change. My room is just across the corridor if you need anything."

"That's fine, Dot. Go ahead. I'll just enjoy the scenery." She motioned toward the porthole and stood up. "I'm not really hungry yet. Maybe we can have something together later on."

As the door snapped shut, Leigh took a deep breath and let it out slowly, realizing this was the first time she had been alone since Friday before they left the house to go downtown, and today must be . . . Sunday. She adjusted her walk to the slight roll of the ship and walked over to look out at the sun.

It was beginning to set, and the sky turned a brilliant rose color, then changed to shades of deep orange. It was as beautiful a sunset as the one she had shared with Steve on their first meeting.

"Well, Lord," she whispered, "you took my fears away when I needed you; you will have to take away my sorrow too. Give me joy as well as peace, for I can't manufacture it on my own."

Suddenly she felt a knot in her throat, and the tears building up within began to stream down her face. She wanted to cry as she had never cried before, but that would not alter the fact that she would never see Steve until they were in that eternal life that had been promised them; she had to face it squarely and deal with it before joy would come.

"Oh, Steve, Steve," she whispered, and in her heart there was a desperate cry for peace.

Chapter 19

Three light taps on the cabin door halted her prayer, and after hastily wiping away tears with the back of her hand, she called out with false cheerfulness, "Come in."

Thinking that Dorothy had changed her mind about leaving her alone, Leigh continued to stare straight ahead, unmindful of the riot of colors in the sky and ocean. There was no reason to cause her friend more worry, and that would happen should Dorothy see the evidences of her recent cry.

"Is that you, Dot? I just love this view. Isn't the sky beautiful?" She frowned at the tremor in her voice and tried to steady it with a deep breath.

"Yes, it is," replied a familiar deep voice. "More beautiful than the first one we shared together."

Leigh's stunned gasp seemed to fill the room as she spun around quickly, eyes dark with disbelief, and caught hold of the back of a chair for support. The room began to spin slowly against the easy roll of the ocean waves, and for one moment there seemed to be no doubt that she was going to pitch forward into the black pit of unconsciousness.

"Steve?" The word was no more than a whispered question forced through quivering lips.

He gave the door a quick push, and it went shut with a slam as he strode purposefully across the room with a face grim in concern over her reaction to his sudden unexpected appearance. The last thing he wanted was to cause her more pain.

Leigh stared open-mouthed as he drew closer, not fully comprehending his presence, not believing he was real. Perhaps she had not recovered as completely as she thought and was going into shock again, or worse still, nearing an emotional breakdown. Why else would she see that tall figure, so superb in its physical strength, or the handsome features and the striking blue eyes now searching her face? Why else would he be in civilian clothes here in her room on a ship sailing further and further away from her past, every moment bearing her nearer a future without him?

With a helpless shake of the head she closed tear-filled eyes against this heart-breaking illusion, then felt herself being pulled away from the chair and into strong arms that held her close while she stood as passive and unresponsive as a statue, trying to convince herself that she was not hallucinating.

"Leigh, are you all right?" Uneasy with her forboding stillness, he tipped her chin upward and searched her face intently, noting the tears still clinging to dark lashes and the doubt lingering in confused eyes.

Her voice returned at the sound of his words, and she whispered, "I thought . . . I thought you were . . . the radio said you were . . . dead!" Color came flooding back into her pale face as she realized the truth. He was alive, and she stood within the strong, secure circle of his arms.

"No, I'm very much alive, and terribly sorry for what I've put you through."

He felt her trembling, and thinking that perhaps this had been too much for her after all, led her quickly to the sofa. She was unaware of his urging her to sit down and scarcely felt the padded cushions against her back; the questions began racing from dry lips, and in one breath she asked, "But what about the radio report? What happened? How long have you been on board ship? Were you really in a plane crash? How did you know where Barnes had taken us . . ."

A long, slim finger laid over her mouth stilled the rush of words.

"Hush. I'll answer all your questions now, one at a time. But try to relax, or I'll be forced to call the doctor."

It was a mild threat and one he did not want to keep, but he was satisfied when she took a deep breath and reached up to touch his cheek fleetingly as though to reassure herself that he was truly there.

"You aren't dreaming," he said with a smile. "I'll prove it to you." And without another word, he pulled her close and kissed her for one long, satisfying moment. It was difficult to reverse her feelings and thoughts so suddenly from death to life, but his embrace left her trembling and breathless, and very much aware of his presence.

"The plane crash was a fake to get Barnes and the NIO off my back. He has to believe that I am dead."

"But how did you do it?"

"Oh," he said with a dismissing shrug of broad shoulders, "I just flew low enough to escape radar detection, cut the motor, and bailed out. By pre-arrangement, a motorboat was waiting to pick me up and bring me out to the ship."

Leigh frowned, knowing that he was making an extremely difficult and dangerous act sound simple and routine. "Were you on board when Dot and I arrived?"

"Yes, I carried you in here." His hand tightened on hers as he remembered the searing anguish that had gripped him as he had lifted her unconscious form from the cold, wet deck.

She smiled faintly and said, "I thought it was Thad. I remember hearing Tex talking about the plane crash, and I didn't want to think about it. Were you in the room last night? I dreamed you talked to me, and then I slept without the wild nightmares."

"Yes, I was here and talked to you."

She frowned and glanced up quickly, wondering why he had waited all day to come to her. "Why didn't you stay?"

"The doctor refused. He said you weren't ready for another shock. I've been pestering him all day to let me in here."

The thought of his waiting for permission from a mere doctor brought a smile to her face, but she did not fully comprehend the profound love that sparked such submission and went on to her next question.

"Steve, did you really plan . . . all of that to . . ." She hesitated, not knowing how to phrase her next words, feeling the question was rather self-centered, but she had to know. "Did you do all that to . . . to save me from Barnes?"

"Yes. I'm sorry it was so hard for you, but I had to have a believable plan. He knew there were men procuring women for military personnel, and he will probably turn Texas inside out looking for you. Tex and his men were to kidnap you from Barnes, get you to the warehouse and then out to the ship. We couldn't tell you a thing in case you were caught, but Tex admits he was sorely tempted after you heard the radio news."

She nodded her understanding and replied, "That night at the farmhouse I realized why you hadn't told me a lot of things. Barnes threatened us with everything he could think of, but I didn't have any information to reveal." She paused and shivered slightly, adding in a low voice, "He even said that I was going to be his mistress and . . ."

"He what?" Steve's face flushed with anger, and his hand tightened on hers. Through clenched teeth he pleaded, "Will you ever forgive me for all you've gone through?"

"You got me away from Barnes, didn't you? I'm grateful for what you've done." Confused and apprehensive about the unfamiliar restraint in his manner, she could not bring herself to reveal all that was in her heart, that she had benefited, not only in spiritual exercise but also in being with him once more. How could she say those things when nagging doubts about his feelings were beginning to tease her mind.

"You'll never know how much I prayed for the success of our plans. It was all I could do not to leave my meetings in Atlanta and come for you myself. I'd like to give Barnes the beating of his life!"

"Steve, if you knew what he was doing, why didn't you just get rid of him, have him transferred somewhere else?"

His short, quick laugh was a reply in itself, "Hah, he was a bumbling, inept spy; it was easy to keep tabs on what he was doing. If I had gotten a smarter aide, I would have had a more difficult time keeping up with his activities. And no matter who it was, I knew he would be after you. So, I just had to make plans and wait." And, as an important afterthought, he added, "and pray like crazy."

Her next question was distasteful and unpleasant, and she withdrew her hands quickly from his, clasping them tightly in her lap. From her expression, he knew what the problem was and prodded, "You want to ask why I became the NIO director?"

She looked up, startled once again at his unfailing ability to read her thoughts. "I hated to see you in that black uniform!"

"I didn't care for it either, but several of the nation's Christian leaders knew the government was forming plans to attack the church, and I was in a position to qualify for the job. They felt I could stem the tide for awhile, give them time to prepare believers, get an underground system started, and perhaps, get a few Christians in places of leadership.''

"And Rev. Miles was in on this, wasn't he?''

"Yes, he has been in charge of preparations for quite a few months. I was at the conference grounds that weekend you and I met to confer with him before taking the job.''

Leigh laid her hand on his, wanting to relay her understanding. "You were fighting a terrific battle at the cliff that afternoon.''

"And you were perceptive enough to see it,'' he replied gratefully as he stood to answer a knock at the door.

It was the doctor stopping by to see how this latest surprise was affecting his patient. He searched Leigh's face for signs of tension or fatigue, and holding her wrist lightly as they talked, checked her pulse.

Steve remained near the door, leaning over the back of a chair, his hands loosely clasped together and looking deceptively calm. He watched the physician's actions with more than a little interest. He was not ready to end his visit with Leigh and didn't wish to have that prescribed now.

The doctor seemed pleased with her progress but felt the undercurrent of restraint and tension in the room. He turned to search the young man's face. Evidently what he saw there satisfied him so that he patted Leigh's hand and instructed her to be in bed early.

"If you cannot sleep, I will bring some medication, yes?'' Nodding to Steve and wishing them a goodnight, he left the room.

Steve did not return to sit next to Leigh as she thought he would, but remained where he was, leaning against the chair and staring steadily across the room. Not satisfied with the growing darkness, he reached out to snap on a small wall lamp.

It was impossible to return his penetrating look; puzzled by the enigmatic expression and now knowing his thoughts, she said timidly, "I want to thank you for what you did for Thad.''

He shook his head, dismissing his role in aiding her brother. But still he did not speak.

She tried again. "And I think . . . I must owe you my thanks for saving my life, for this room,'' she motioned with her hand,

"and probably the clothes, and . . . and . . . for everything."
Her voice faded away, an uneasy fear creeping into her heart.
Why wasn't he responding?

His eyes had not left her face as she faltered through her expression of gratitude. "The clothes aren't new; I didn't have time to do much. But that blue dress—no one else could do it justice." His voice was almost cold and formal, and it startled her.

A terrifying thought triggered her heart into wild and erratic behavior. Suppose this reticence she sensed were a growing lack of interest. He had once said he would never let her go. But perhaps he now felt differently. Perhaps she had disappointed and hurt him too deeply by her lack of trust, and now his love had been smothered completely. She had made a miserable show of her Christian faith. He would want, and need, someone better than she.

His usual confident manner was gone. He was too restrained and she too frightened, to touch the subject of the future. But she did want to know what was to happen. Where were they going, and what was he planning to do; what would his life be now? She could not ask, for fear of pushing him into a position he no longer wished to maintain.

He stood silently watching the struggle within her, and for the first time wondered what her thoughts were. She was becoming more reserved and distant by the minute. He saw the bewilderment, pain, and confusion in her dark eyes. He watched her questioning expression, but did not speak. Was she even now unsure of their relationship and of his Christian commitment? He had to know.

"You said you had learned some things, Leigh. What are they?"

It was difficult to put her jumbled thoughts into words; her mind was so tired, his continuing gaze so disturbing, but she tried to remember what she had shared with Dorothy.

"Well," she began, averting her eyes to stare at the wall, "I learned that I don't need to worry about persecution, or weakness, or fears." Her words were slow in coming, as though she were picking them with great care. "The Lord gave me a deep peace when Barnes threatened us. I learned that when God said, 'Be not afraid, for I am with thee,' He meant exactly that. And I learned that peace can only come when we stop rebelling against circumstances."

He waited for her to continue, and then prodded, "Is there more?"

Her voice was shaky as she responded. "I learned that . . . that I did you a great injustice by not trusting you when you needed it. When I thought you were dead," a sudden lump in her throat stopped her words. She looked down at her hands and waited until she could speak. "When I thought you were dead, I wished for just one moment to apologize for not being the person you needed. Now God has given me that time, and I am satisfied."

"Satisfied? With what? Is that all you want of me now?" His questions were explosive and sharp, and he moved quickly across the room to sit with her again. His strong hands held hers tightly, and she winced at the pain inflicted by those fingers crushing hers.

"Well, Leigh, is it?" At her hesitation he added, "Don't play games with me now. We've been through too much not to be honest with each other."

In her agitation, Leigh pulled her hands away and unconsciously began rubbing the finger where his ring had been. "Barnes took your ring from me and threw it in the fire."

"Never mind; I'll give you another one."

She did not catch his meaning, and shook her head, not wanting him to feel any more obligations toward her. How was she to repay him now for all he had done?

Reaching into his pocket, he extracted a small box, opened it, and put it into her hands. Instead of a ring similar to what had been lost in the fire, Leigh saw a set of rings. Through her tears the delicate patterns and simple styling seemed to glitter like a multitude of stars.

"They once belonged to my grandmother," Steve informed her quietly. "Her wedding rings. The only thing of her possessions I have now."

"Steve," she blurted out, "you don't have to marry me if you don't want me any more. I failed you so and . . . and never realized how much I loved you until I thought you were gone."

She stared at the rings, tears falling from pale cheeks down onto her hands.

He turned her face toward him and almost exploded with surprise. "Not want you! Is that what you think? Leigh, if you won't marry me, I might as well throw these rings into the ocean."

His voice grew quiet though unsteady. "I told you once I'd never let you go. I won't, unless . . ."

Having been so sure of her up to this point, he could not voice the terrible possibility of rejection. Reaching into his pocket he found a handkerchief and gently began wiping her face dry of tears.

"Now, look at me. If you aren't going to tell me what you want, I'll just have to resort to reading your eyes."

What he saw there seemed to satisfy him greatly, for he began to laugh softly, and Leigh felt his confidence and sureness return. The reason for that cold restraint had not been a lack of love, but a lack of certainty about her commitment to him.

He tipped her chin up so that he might see her better. "You know it isn't going to be easy."

She nodded and waited for him to continue.

"We're going to face more difficulties, and we have to be very positive that the Lord comes first in our lives, always." The response he saw in her eyes again satisfied him.

Taking one of the rings, he slipped it on her finger and said prayerfully, "May the Lord truly make us one in Him." Then he pulled her close, and his kiss was one of ardor and strength, and left her with no doubt about his heart's desire for her.

It was a long time before he would let her talk again. "Just let me hold you, Leigh. Sometimes, in the middle of all that mess, I would wonder if we would live long enough to be together." He sighed deeply and tightened his hold. "The future was too uncertain."

"The future, Steve. What are we going to do?"

"What we're going to do," he said with a smile, "is to be married as soon as possible."

"That would be wonderful."

The look that passed between them was deep and revealing, and left them both a bit breathless, as they thought of their life together.

"And what else?" Leigh prodded.

"When we leave the ship in Canada, we . . ."

Leigh interrupted, "Canada? Why did we have to take a ship to Canada? Isn't that a little out of the way?"

He laughed and replied, "Absolutely, but Barnes would have the borders carefully guarded. He might not think of a ship."

"When we leave the ship?" she asked.

"We'll have a lot of work to do. There are thousands of refugees trying to get into other countries. We may be able to help them. Or we may be able to help those still in America. There are many things we can do; God has something planned for us."

She closed her eyes and leaned her head against his shoulder. "Those still in America like Mom and Dad and the nursery children . . ."

"Yes, nursery children. And teachers who go running off into the night to rescue them."

Her head came up in surprise, and she stared at him. "How did you know about that?"

"Oh," he grinned teasingly, "I had ways." Then seeing the warning glint in her eyes, he kissed her quickly and changed the subject.

"I went to see your parents one night."

The ship tipped into a long, deep wave just as she sat up, utterly amazed at his statement, and it threw her closer to him.

"Why did you do that?" She struggled in his arms, trying to see his face.

"I wanted their blessing for us, and I wanted to reassure them about you and Thad. And," he paused, "and I have a letter for you."

She looked at him mutely, marveling at the depth of compassion and gentleness she was discovering.

"How could I have been so blind not to see what you were truly like!"

"Hey, no more tears. I'll leave if you keep that up. Doctor's orders." He caught his breath at the look of love on her face and pulled her close again.

And from the vicinity of his shoulder he heard her whisper, "Thank you, Lord, for bringing us together and for answering my prayers."

His quiet "Amen" was all she needed in reassurance that he understood her spiritual quest, her cry for peace.